LAMPEDUSA

LAMPEDUSA

STEVEN PRICE

FARRAR, STRAUS AND GIROUX

NEW YORK

Farrar, Straus and Giroux
120 Broadway, New York 10271

Printed in the United States of America
Originally published in 2019 by McClelland & Stewart, a division of
Penguin Random House Canada Limited, Canada
Published in the United States by Farrar, Straus and Giroux
First American edition, 2019

Library of Congress Cataloging-in-Publication Data
Names: Price, Steven, 1976– author.
Title: Lampedusa / Steven Price.
Description: First American edition. | New York : Farrar, Straus
and Giroux, 2019.
Identifiers: LCCN 2019020216 | ISBN 9780374212247 (hardcover)
Classification: LCC PR9199.4.P768 L36 2019 | DDC 813/.6—dc23
LC record available at https://lccn.loc.gov/2019020216

Our books may be purchased in bulk for promotional, educational,
or business use. Please contact your local bookseller or the Macmillan
Corporate and Premium Sales Department at 1-800-221-7945, extension
5442, or by e-mail at MacmillanSpecialMarkets@macmillan.com.

www.fsgbooks.com
www.twitter.com/fsgbooks • www.facebook.com/fsgbooks

1   3   5   7   9   10   8   6   4   2

For Lorna Crozier;
and in memory of Patrick Lane

And sleep grows within sleep
like a sinister second body.

VALERIO MAGRELLI

APPROACHING
THE MONSTER

═══

JANUARY 1955

In his smaller library he kept a broken white rock, like a twist of coral, taken by a sugar merchant from the natural harbour at Lampedusa. In the afternoons he would hold that rock to the sunlight feeling the sharp heavy truth of it. He was that island's prince but like all its princes had never seen its shores nor set foot upon it. To visitors he would say, wryly: It is an island of fire, at the edge of the world; who could live there? He would not add: A great family's bitterness is always lived in. He would not hold that rock out and say: This is a dead thing and yet it will outlive me. He was the last of his line and after him came only extinction.

As a boy he had listened to his governess tell him the dust of Sicily came from the Sahara and this he had repeated all his life though he did not know if it was true. He imagined it blown across the sea in shimmering red curtains of heat, the hot winds of the sirocco billowing it north, raking the island of Lampedusa in its path. Each morning he would rise and walk his terrace at Via Butera, his steps traced in the sand blown in overnight, leading to the low stone wall over the Foro Itàlico and there ceasing, like the footprints of a ghost, and he would stand peering out at the rising day with his back to Sicily and the southern sea beyond it and beyond that the fiery island of his blood.

He did not love Palermo, its dusty stone streets, its wreckage from the last war. Though he knew he would die in this city of his birth what he felt for it was not love but a fierce desolation that took the place of love. There were greater passions than love. Love was petty, brief, impossibly human. He had loved England, loved Paris, had loved in a doomed way his suffering in the Austrian prisoner camps during the first war, had journeyed by railway and coach north to Latvia loving the vast dark northern forests that scrolled past. Yet he returned always here, to an unloved city, to his mother the dowager princess when she was alive, to the ancient streets of his family name after she was dead. Even as a child in his father's palazzo the city had seemed to him demonic, low-lying and red-hot. Its dust would boil up out of the sea while the ferries from Naples cut sluggishly near, the souls on board drugged by the heat. That alone had not changed. Now, already old, finding himself in the middle of a new century, living in a decrepit palazzo at the edge of the sea, he would stand high above the harbour and scan their white decks in the offloading as if seeking someone he had lost.

And in this way, still in his slippers and morning robe, brushing crumbs of sand from the top of the wall and rubbing his fingers absently together, he would try to banish the night's unhappiness and find his way into the day.

In the years since the Americans had swept the island, he had lived with his wife Alessandra in one half of a small palazzo in the medieval quarter of Palermo, on the narrow Via Butera, their windows glazed and facing the sea. If asked he would admit it was his house, but not his home. His true home stood behind thick walls several streets away, in a slump of cracked stone and wind-rotted masonry from a bomb borne across the Atlantic, a bomb whose sole purpose was the obliteration of the world as it had been. That bomb fell in April 1943 and his wife's estate at Stomersee far to the north in Latvia had been overrun by the Russians in the same month. They had found themselves homeless and orphaned as one. He walked now the streets of his city a different man, a man burdened by his losses, not freed by them. For he had been born on a mahogany table in that lost palazzo on Via di Lampedusa and had slept alone in a small bed in the very room of his birth all throughout his childhood and into his adulthood and for ten years even after he was married and he did not know who he might be without that room to return to.

The war had taken everything. There was no running water in their half of the palazzo and the ceiling of its ballroom had collapsed in the bombing twelve years earlier. He had filled what was left of that with the furniture salvaged from his destroyed palace. And each morning he would wash using a bowl of scummy water left out from the night before in a bathroom that leaked when it rained. A most extraordinary room, he would joke bitterly; no water in the taps, and yet water running all the same.

He thought of that often now, in the early light, when he would rise alone and wrap a blanket around his shoulders and tread softly past his wife's bedchamber. His dying mother had returned to the Lampedusa palazzo after the armistice and lived out her last year in its ruins. His wife held no such attachments to the old world of Palermo. Alessandra Wolff entered a room like a door closing, blocking out the light. She was a linguist and reader of literature and the only female psychoanalyst in Italy and she worked into the night with her patients in their historical library and he loved her for her mind and for the solitude they shared. She was the daughter of the singer Alice Barbi, last muse of the composer Brahms, and when her mother remarried she became stepdaughter to his uncle Pietro in London. Upon meeting her he had been, he recalled, unable to speak. You will call me Licy, she had said from the first. He had liked her black hair and blacker eyes and her broad strong shoulders with the power of a stage soprano in them. From his first glimpse of her in London, thirty years ago, when she was still married to her first husband, he had thought her handsome and remote. It amazed him that so much time had passed. He saw in her now the same woman he had seen then, a woman older than he, more worldly, a woman who strode always some feet ahead of him in the street and spoke to him over one shoulder, without turning, and whose stern grace could be mistaken for arrogance. But there was such tenderness in her. And because she was intelligent and not classically beautiful her opinions had often made her company unbearable to men, and he liked that about her too.

It was on a morning in late January that he was called back to his doctor's offices, for the results of a spirometer test. He had risen in pain and twisted his bedsheets into a knot and swung his soft white feet out onto the floor, startled by a new dizziness, a shortness of breath, as if his body had decided at last to begin its betrayal.

That sensation had passed; but then, at the turn of the high marble staircase on his way out to breakfast, the pain had struck him again and he had gripped the banister white-knuckled, the paintings of his ancestors above hanging in the gloom, and had gasped and wrestled at the knot of his tie. He did not know if he was being fanciful. He had pressed two fingers to his heart and breathed. It was true that a newfound anxiety was in him which he did not recognize. At dinner the night before he had not mentioned his medical appointment to his wife but only smiled calmly and asked Licy when he had gotten so old.

Trees are old, she had said, stone-faced. Princes are ancient.

At the little table in the foyer he adjusted his hat, peering at his face in the mirror, puzzled. A pain rose in his chest, receded.

Ah, he thought.

And he smoothed the wrinkles at his eyes with a rueful finger.

He was a man who had left middle age the way other men will exit a room, without a thought, as if he might go back at any moment. He was fifty-eight years old. He had smoked every hour of his waking life since the armistice of the first war. A sadness crinkled his eyes, a shyness, evident even in boyhood photographs. He had felt foolish in the company of adults then, he remembered, and that feeling had not left him. Soft-spoken, ironic, he had been mistaken for a good listener all his life though the quality of the light had always interested him more than any confided disgrace. He was a man of solitude and appetites and had got fat since his return from England in the 1930s and then fatter still on sweet pastries in Palermo. He did not like motorcars and walked through his neighbourhood with a cane, heavy, stooped, in the ailing body of a man two decades his senior, always a book or two folded under an elbow. He wore a small dapper moustache as he had since his youth and oiled his grey hair straight back and he dressed each morning in a fine blue suit long out of fashion. He read voraciously, in Italian, French, English, and had done so for more than half a century. Il Mostro, his cousins called him, for the way he could devour a book. The Monster.

He arrived promptly at ten o'clock for his appointment and Dr. Coniglio saw him at once. There was something odd in the doctor's manner, stiff, which worried him and alerted him to the seriousness of the news. He had known Coniglio for years. They were of an age. A graceful man, with athletic shoulders, a clean stiff collar and shirtsleeves invariably rolled. He liked him, the cordiality in his speech, the clarity in his face like sunlight on flagstones. Coniglio had treated his mother at the end of her life, when she was dying in the ruins of Casa Lampedusa, had made the long drive from Capo d'Orlando to Palermo each week. Until the war, he had been the family physician for his cousins, the Piccolos, attending them at Vina, their villa, and it was only in the last five years that the doctor had opened an office in Palermo. He remembered now, seeing the man's new consulting rooms, how his mother had used to look at Coniglio, the narrow cold assessment in her eyes. She too had thought him a fine gentleman. She too had not wanted to observe him standing next to her son.

He did not think of himself as shy but a certain shyness took hold in him when he found himself in the company of men such as this, men with a deference for his own station in life, men who had set out and achieved success, men of purpose, men of the world. Their easy manners left him uneasy, their confidence made him falter. He felt himself slow down, grow watchful, hesitant, until he had lost the moment for the quick retort or dry joke that came always to mind. Instead he would blink his lugubrious eyelids, and smile faintly, and meet the other's gaze helpless.

He waited for the doctor to gesture to a chair before he unbuttoned his winter coat and sat. He took off his hat and folded his gloves in its upended crown and rested his walking stick across his knees. He set his leather bag carefully to one side, half unbuckled, the little frosted cakes in their paper wrappers from his breakfast at the Massimo visible, the spine of the book he had brought for later, *The Pickwick Papers*, shining up at him. He reached at once for the cigarettes in his pocket but caught the doctor's eye.

No?

Ah, Don Giuseppe—Coniglio smiled, tsking—not all that is pleasurable in life is forbidden. But some things are, or should be. You look tired, my friend.

Giuseppe withdrew his hand and crossed his legs, the bulleted purple upholstery crackling. The other had settled himself at the edge of his desk, one leg hitched up, his hands folded lightly over his thigh, those hands which turned and weighed and cut into the skin of other beings and sought out the secrets in their flesh. Calmly he met the doctor's gaze.

Well? he said.

It is as I feared. The doctor's voice was slow now, deliberate. Emphysema. It can be checked perhaps, but not stopped. I am sorry.

Giuseppe smiled faintly. He could not think what to say.

The spirometer is not always conclusive, of course. We could examine you again.

Would you advise it?

Coniglio held his eye a moment. I would not, he said at last, gently. Are you here alone? I had hoped the princess would accompany you.

He shook his head, calm.

You should not be alone, the doctor said. He rose and went behind his desk and opened a drawer and unscrewed the lid of a fountain pen. I shall write you out a prescription to help with the pain. But the only true medicine, you understand, is for you to cut out tobacco.

The winter morning was grey and diffuse in the curtains. Giuseppe closed his eyes, opened them.

And will that reverse the effects? he asked.

It is a chronic disease, Don Giuseppe—there is no reversing its effects. It will progress regardless. But it can be managed. You must change the way you have been living. You must exercise regularly. Walk. Eat rather less. Avoid stress and worry as you can.

There is no other treatment?

Well. Let us try this first.

But the disease will kill me? he pressed.

Coniglio regarded him quietly from behind his desk. Any number of things could kill you first, he said.

Giuseppe, despite himself, smiled.

I will give you this for the pain, and to help you sleep. The doctor took some minutes to write out the prescription. He then untied a red folder and withdrew two typed pages and perused them and then slipped them back into the folder. We are getting old, Don Giuseppe, he said. That is the substance of it. We may not feel it, but it is so.

Yes.

Our bodies will not let us forget it.

Indeed.

Coniglio steepled his fingers before him. It was clear he was struggling with what to say next. After a moment, to Giuseppe's surprise, he began to speak, in a casual way, of his wife. He had a French wife who was known to treat him badly. He said: Jeanette has returned to Marseilles. Her sister is ill. She wishes to be with her family. She has written me to tell me she would like me to join her. Permanently.

Ah.

You and the princess lived apart a long while, did you not?

Yes. In the thirties.

I remember your mother spoke of it. Princess Alessandra was in Latvia?

Giuseppe nodded. He did not like to think what his mother might have said about it.

Coniglio was tapping his fountain pen against his wedding ring, click, click. Otherwise his face was calm, his hair smooth, his coral shirt unwrinkled and immaculate. Yes, he said, yes yours was an arrangement that succeeded. So I tell myself, it is the modern world, Coniglio. Be strong. You have telephones, aeroplanes.

Giuseppe did not enlighten the man. Licy had always gone where she chose to go, as she chose it. She had fled to Sicily only when the Soviets neared her estate in Latvia, burning the great homes as they advanced. He did not deceive himself by imagining she had bowed to his desires.

Jeanette tells me there is work for a doctor in any city, Coniglio said. Even for a Sicilian doctor, she says. I expect there is some truth in that.

What will you do?

Coniglio looked out the window, smiled vaguely. I will imagine the very worst of fates and settle for a lesser one, he said. But my patients, I would worry for them, Don Giuseppe. It would mean, of course, many farewells.

It is always better to be the one leaving than the one left behind, said Giuseppe.

Yes. And some journeys cannot be delayed.

Giuseppe inclined his head.

Coniglio pinched the bridge of his nose and there was a sudden anguish and bafflement in the gesture. He removed his spectacles, blinked his watery blue eyes. The man's strong emotion surprised Giuseppe, left him uncomfortable. Do you know, said the doctor, for years now, whenever I am faced with a difficult decision, I think of something your mother said to me. She said, Always take the easier path, Dr. Coniglio. And yet I have never done so. I wonder what is the matter with me.

It was as though a coin flared in the cold sunlight between them.

Your mother was a powerful personality, Coniglio continued. She had strong opinions. I remember she used to talk to me about Mussolini.

She was rather confused, near the end.

She used to complain about his spats. Too many spats, she would say. Coniglio smiled, shook his head. I remember she held my hand one morning and said Mussolini had changed nothing and yet because of him everything had changed.

She was thinking of her house, Giuseppe said quietly.

A beautiful palazzo, the doctor agreed. The Americans did not need to bomb us as they did.

I did not know you knew it, Doctor.

Coniglio gave him a puzzled look. I visited your mother there. Several times.

It was hardly beautiful then.

Well.

It was a fine house once, before its ruin.

And a fine house after, Don Giuseppe. When I was a child I would pass by it every Sunday morning. My father worked a fish stall in the Vucciria. It was not the fastest route. But then I was not always in such a hurry to join him.

He said this without shame or embarrassment at his low origins and Giuseppe could only nod vaguely. It seemed all at once of supreme insignificance. His mother, he remembered now, had distrusted this doctor by the end, had coughed and grimaced and called him her good doctor Mafioso. He opened his mouth to speak, closed it. Do not gawp like a fish, his mother used to tell him. He got abruptly to his feet.

You must forgive me, he said.

Coniglio half rose from behind his desk. Of course.

I have lost track of the hour.

Certainly. We shall speak again soon, of that I am certain, Don Giuseppe. Remember me to Don Casimiro and Don Lucio, if you will. And of course to the princess.

He suddenly heard in the doctor's old-fashioned phrasing the syntax of an English novel, as if it were a sentence translated aloud from Meredith or Eliot, and he glanced at the doctor from beneath heavy eyelids. More than most this man had witnessed the tension and soured love directed by his mother towards himself as she ailed, had witnessed her bitterness, the muttered imprecations, the veiled insults. It left him, Giuseppe felt with a quick sharpness, vulnerable and foolish. But then the feeling was gone and he wanted only to absent himself from the small office with its smells of lemon gauze and varnish and camphor, smells that would forever remind him of his own death.

And so Giuseppe Tomasi, last Prince of Lampedusa, put on his hat with care, worked his fingers into his dead father's kidskin gloves, and took up his walking stick and his worn leather bag. At the door he paused.

How much time do I have, Doctor?

Coniglio's hands were clasped carefully on the desk before him and as he tilted his head his spectacles filled with light, obscuring his eyes. That will depend on you, he said. Let us pray it is many years yet.

In which case, said Giuseppe, it will not depend on me at all.

The doctor smiled, but there was a sadness in it, and Giuseppe went out, the frosted glass on the streetside door rattling softly as it closed, and he shuffled out into the cold bright air leaning on his cane as if it were still the same morning as before, and he the same man.

———

Outside in the roar he stood amazed, watching the cars and motor scooters creep through the crowds in a haze of exhaust and brake lights and shouting. It was the sudden clear knowledge of his own death that filled him. He thought of Licy asleep at Via Butera, her drapes drawn against the day, and although he knew Coniglio was right, and that he must go to her, and tell her, he did not do so. A kind of slowness had taken hold in him, so that he did not want to go anywhere, think of anything, he wanted just to stay where he was as the crowds poured around him and the drivers stood up on their Lambrettas shouting and the sellers at their tables called out their wares. The doctor's office loomed behind, shadowy, dreamlike. He told himself that to allow Licy her sleep was a kindness. He would see her in the evening.

But the evening is now, for you, always. This thought came to him unbidden and he drew his chin down to his chest and took a sharp pained breath. So. He would die before his wife. This was the true meaning of his meeting with Coniglio, he saw: the certainty that she would go on, alone in the world, after him. And he felt for a moment a kind of bitterness that he must die first; and then he leaned into his walking stick, his thick wool coat buttoned tight across his hips, and felt suddenly ashamed at the thought.

They had never had a child. What of himself would be left behind for Licy? His estate had eroded until he could no longer be counted among Palermo's first families; he had descended into a genteel poverty; the war had taken what little was left until his presence now at the Bellini Club attracted, it seemed to him, only sidelong glances and whispers. The great palaces had been sold or reduced to rubble. His mother had been the last powerful Lampedusa, the last true Lampedusa, and she had disapproved of Licy from the first.

Giuseppe lifted his face in the cold air. His mother. It was true what Coniglio said, she had believed in Mussolini. Many had. He remembered her standing on the terrace of the Casa Lampedusa in the wind reading aloud from a crackling newspaper as the dictator marched on Rome, the sharp brittle pleasure in her voice. Her maiden name was Cutò and she had been a beauty in her youth and a formidable aristocrat in age. Underneath her savage confidence, her quickness, her intelligence, lay a sadness that he understood was in him also. She had been one of five sisters, three of whom had died in quick succession and whose deaths had haunted his mother all her life to come. Her sister Lina had starved to death under the rubble after the Messina earthquake in 1908 and three years later her favourite sister Giulia was murdered by a lover in a shabby hotel in Rome, and later yet the public scandal of it led to her youngest sister's suicide. Maria had been buried apart from the family and Giuseppe could remember the cold empty church, the absence of his father, the priest's unkind prayers rustling like pigeons in the dim arches overhead. He thought of those years and of his mother's little blue bottles of laudanum and the drifting through Europe and of his own year in Naples and how when at last they returned to Palermo it was a changed city, at least to him, a city with unfriendly faces, a city of closed curtains and locked doors, only the dark leatherbound stillness of his palazzo's library remaining. Yes she had believed in Mussolini but when his government declared war in 1940 and imagined an empire in Africa she had crumpled up the newspaper in disgust and removed the little Fascist pin from her coat.

But it was her elegance, the smooth soft whiteness of her throat and her arms that he wished to keep in his memory. Her left arm extended in long sweeping strokes as she brushed her hair at night in front of a mirror, the gold hairbrush hissing at each pull. She had a long thin throat and a tiny waist and wore her hair high and her neckline low in the manner of the belle époque. He could remember walking with his governess Anna in the gardens of Santa Margherita di Belice, his mother and Aunt Giulia some twenty paces ahead, the grace and drift of their pale skirts over the white gravel under the blazing sky. Her laugh, like a silver spoon ringing against cut glass. He loved her for the great violent powerful love she demanded, and received, a creature both beloved and feared by all who knew her, himself most of all.

One memory above all others would come to him, when he thought of her. He must have been four years old. He and his mother were guests of the wealthy and powerful Florios on the island of Favignana. He would hear later the rumours of his mother and the patriarch Don Ignazio. Early one Saturday morning his Sienese governess had torn back the curtains and dragged him from sleep and combed his hair, scrubbed at his face and neck with a rough cloth, wrestled him into his finest clothes. Then she had led him outside and along the sea-stairs above the garden to the formal terrace facing the harbour. He remembered the gust and billow of orange curtains set up to cut the wind, how in the shadow of the white cliffs the light was different, the interlocking of sunlight and black water. Seated on a plush chair brought out from the gallery was an ancient Frenchwoman, her stark black widow's dress rippling around her in the wind, her black veil lifted back from her face and her startled blue eyes squinting. He would learn years later that she was the ex-empress Eugénie, wife of Napoleon III, a guest also of the Florios and soon to depart on her yacht. He kneeled before her and felt the rasp of her dry lips on his forehead, and then she set a hand light-boned and papery on the top of his head and said, *Quel joli petit*. He remembered peering across at his mother, he remembered the massive shaggy figure seated beside her, his arm loose on the back of her chair, his strong white teeth as he smiled. That was Ignazio Florio, their host, lord and magnate. Then the man stood powerfully and clapped two monstrous hands and little Giuseppe was dismissed.

That was what he would hold in his heart, somehow, always: a sense of apprehension, of windswept sunlight, a vague uncertainty as to the meaning of what he had witnessed, while great events unfolded around him and he kneeled dazed in the honeycombed light of Sicily, a child.

As he made his slow way across the old quarter, to Flaccovio's Bookshop, what he wanted was to lose himself in the aisles, unmolested, to forget Coniglio and his diagnosis and the bloom of sickness in his lungs, if only for a brief hour. Along the narrow streets he drifted, past merchants in their winter coats setting up their stalls, past the smoky Fiats with boxes tied to their roofs, their drivers standing in the half-opened doors trying to clear a path, past the blinkered cart horses creeping by, and the women in kerchiefs coming sleepily out onto their balconies to lower buckets with bills in them to the vendors on Vespas below, then draw up the morning's bread and fish. The winter light was flat, shadowless. Somewhere a radio was blaring rock 'n' roll. He felt an unaccountable strangeness in his chest, a lightness, as if he had never before seen Palermo in all its seething life. It is a beautiful city, he thought, despite all.

When he rounded the corner and crossed Via Ruggiero Settimo he caught sight of the boys, but it was too late to turn aside.

They were waiting for him in the cold. Languid and ropy with youth, leaning into the warpled glass of the bookstore windows, clapping their hands together, swinging their arms. Gioacchino and Orlando, his student friends: young, irreverent, grinning as he approached.

He and Licy had met them two years earlier at the salon of an antiquarian bookseller. Giuseppe had liked their humour, their amusing, quarrelsome, vibrant talk, the way his wife had studied their faces, nodding in approval. To his own surprise, he had invited them to visit at Via Butera, to discuss Stendhal, and Shakespeare, and Chaucer, and then last spring he had found himself preparing conversation notes about English literature and those conversations had developed into a kind of informal lecture series. Giuseppe had prepared over a thousand pages already. The boys were louche and elegant by turns, in ways he could not have imagined when he was their age. And though literature, and music, and film had first drawn them into Giuseppe's orbit, for him there was something else about them, some impossibly modern thing, which he wanted near.

Alessandra had understood it before he did: they were a part of a world that had already abandoned him, a world in which there would no longer be a place for people like him.

He had told neither of them of his morning's appointment with Coniglio and for that he was suddenly relieved. The taller of the two pushed himself upright with his foot and unfolded his arms and waved. That was Gioacchino: barely twenty, irrepressible, teasing, the son of a distant second cousin. Despite the chill the boy's coat sleeves were shoved to the elbows, his long fingers smooth, his narrow tie askew like a young photographer down from Milan. Giuseppe stared at him in the brightness of the street as if he would devour the boy whole, his energy, his rawness. For Gioacchino had become very dear to him and to Licy, and he felt a sudden gratitude to the boy simply for being there, on that morning.

Uncle! Giò was calling, needlessly loud. He waved both arms. A lady weighed down with shopping glanced up in alarm, hurried past.

We thought you might be here, said the other boy, coming up to walk alongside Giuseppe. His voice rasped, roughened as if by wine. We went by the Mazzara, but you weren't there.

So we just followed the dust, grinned Giò. I warned Orlando everything old ends up here.

Francesco Orlando shifted the heavy satchel at his shoulder, shrugging.

Now Gioacchino stepped forward, plucked a small cake from Giuseppe's leather bag, took a messy bite. You are like an English doctor, Uncle, he said, his mouth full. Carrying everything you need in your little bag.

Giò, Giuseppe said sharply. That is enough.

But he was not really angry. He was not the boy's uncle, but he accepted the title in affection. Irreverent though he was, Giò could do no wrong in his eye. The fault lay with the modern world, he felt, which bred so little solemnity into its youth.

Your cousin was there, Orlando said now. At the Mazzara. We said we would find you for him.

Casimiro is in Palermo?

Not Casimiro. Lucio.

Giuseppe cleared his throat, opened his coat, fumbled for a cigarette. Too late, he thought of Coniglio's warning, but the boys were watching him, and so he lit the cigarette and breathed in deeply. He studied Francesco Orlando: stocky, his spectacles askew, his wide round skull and pitted forehead, a student of literature with professorial ambitions. The boy was growing a thin black moustache and he kept running a finger across it as if to reassure himself it was still there. One corner of the collar of his heavy coat was bent upward, a button was missing.

Giò licked at his fingers, crumpled the paper wrapper. Tell Orlando he must come with me to the Marina, Uncle, he said. Orlando listens to you.

Because he has respect.

Gioacchino glanced up, his dark eyes sly and smiling.

What is at the Marina? Giuseppe asked.

English poker. We can still sit in, if we hurry. You are not in a gambling mood, are you, Uncle?

The grey light shifted. A decommissioned military truck rattled past in a cloud of exhaust and Giuseppe squinted, lowered his cigarette, held a handkerchief to his mouth. He feared a coughing fit and he did not reply but the youths took no notice.

I must study, Orlando was protesting. I cannot sit in, Giò.

There's plenty of time for studying. Tell him, Uncle. We are young. We should be studying the ways of the world. Didn't Stendhal say something like that?

Hardly.

No?

No.

Giò smiled, his cheeks red with the chill. Well. Usually I read an author first, before I misquote him. What is it, Uncle? Why do you look like that?

Giuseppe blinked and blinked. He was drinking in the sight of the boys with a desperation that shamed him. There was a coarse muscularity in Orlando that would always betray his middle-class origins, nothing could be done about it. He was too concentrated, too serious. But Giò was all leanness and grace, like a racing hound, his hair mussed, his eyes squinting, his teeth sharp. He thought of Licy at Via Butera, he tried to imagine how she would sit, stiffly, without interrupting, as he told her about Coniglio's diagnosis.

You always take the easier path, Gioitto, he said at last, but there was no admonishment in it. He glanced in through the clouded glass of Flaccovio's. Will you not come inside?

Giò laughed. Oh, Uncle. Even now a countess swoons somewhere and needs rescuing. If you change your mind, Orlando, you will find me at Count Alfonso's. I will be the one beside the stove with the stacks of American dollars at his elbow.

As he left, Francesco Orlando shook his head. Gioacchino is not serious, he said. He does not want to learn, he does not know what it is to have an empty pocket. He thinks the world will wait for him.

Because the world will, said Giuseppe. No greatness was ever achieved because of an empty pocket, Orlando.

The boy paused at his tone. Don Giuseppe—

Yes?

I cannot come to the lecture tonight. I must study. I have an examination in the morning.

Giuseppe had forgotten that they had moved the week's lecture to that evening. His appointment with Coniglio had chased it from his mind, and he understood now he would need the evening to sit with Licy and talk through the diagnosis. He would have had to cancel regardless. But to conceal his own embarrassment he said, gruffly: Only you can decide your priorities, Orlando.

The boy flushed. You have already prepared. Forgive me.

Well.

It is not that I do not value your lessons, Don Giuseppe. It is not that.

All at once Giuseppe regretted speaking so sharply. He patted the boy's sleeve. Go, he said, study your books, do not mind about the lessons. We will resume next week.

I will not miss another lecture. I promise.

It is all right.

Thank you, Don Giuseppe.

Go.

Orlando lingered, then went.

Giuseppe, alone now, stood in the cold shadow of the bookshop windows watching the dark shapes of the traffic ripple past. He had not wanted company but now with the boys departed he felt strangely exposed, as if his coat were unbuttoned, as if his private affairs were on display for anyone to see. He had his head down as if deciding something and then he dropped his cigarette and ground it under the toe of his shoe and started to cross the street towards the Mazzara, towards Lucio. He did not feel like his cousin's company but then Lucio with his reticence and dry self-regard was in some ways not company at all. Yet rather than crossing Via Ruggiero Settimo he did something strange, something he had not done in all the time he had walked these streets: he turned instead down Via Cerda, and after a half mile or so he turned into a warren of narrow side streets. At once the noise and exhaust of the city faded. There were puddles in the alley, garbage and newspapers blown into the doorways. Here the balconies rose up on either side and he craned his head, peered at the white sliver of sky. How elusive the world was. He noticed iron cages hanging on the balconies, empty in the cold, and on several railings were folded bright carpets, yellow, red, as if set out to dry. Was this the truer Palermo? He passed a knot of schoolboys with their hair slicked down, their shirttails untucked, kicking a football against a door, the hollow banging of each strike like the hammering of a coffin. He walked on.

Water-stained walls, rust bleeding from the hinges of street-side windows. He passed a bombed-out tenement, its plaster crumbling, the collapsed ruins visible through the shell of its door. The buildings on each side stood untouched. The alley opened into a narrow piazza and at the steps of its shabby church he paused. He could hear through the carved doors the low rumble of prayer. Across the square an old man sat on a bench, his grizzled head bowed, his hat propped on one knee, and Giuseppe shifted his walking stick and satchel to his left hand and climbed the steps, holding to the railing as he went. What he was thinking as he crossed the threshold and stood blinking in the sudden gloom was that he had arrived at his own decline.

The church was warm. He stood listening to the low drone of voices. There were figures kneeling in the shadowed pews, and he could make out the haunting rise and fall of the Ave Maria. What had he come for? He could not be counted among the faithful and had not attended mass in thirty years. His eyes adjusted slowly. The horror of the crucifixion above the altar, the twist of grief and agony in the face of its ugly wooden Christ. What troubled him was how little would stand in his place, once he was gone. How little he would leave behind. He did not believe there was life beyond the grave and when he prayed to his mother he knew the words were just that, words. She was nowhere. He watched the humble backs of the faithful in prayer and his thoughts turned to the lecture he was to have given to Orlando that evening. It was to have touched on Rousseau, and Proust, and Stendhal whom he admired above all others. Had Stendhal believed in eternity? He had written that a person, no matter how insignificant, ought to leave behind some chronicle of their time on this earth, some accretion of their collected memory and experience. That was the only eternity. He, Giuseppe Tomasi di Lampedusa, had created nothing. All that he had known, the grand houses of his childhood, his memories, his fears, the passing blossoms in the trees of St. James's Park in London in the spring, all of that would vanish with him; there would be no more Giuseppe, no boy in short pants running with a hoop, no old man fat and melancholic staring puzzled at the carved suffering of a Christ, no trace of his being in the world. The regret he felt surprised him. It did not matter how one spent one's days, time was running out for everyone. Gioitto and Orlando would not understand this. They were still so young. He, Giuseppe, was not only himself, he knew, feeling a sudden bitterness, but all he remembered, all he had done and known. And all of that would be obliterated with him.

It was strange, he thought, for Lucio to have come.

The Mazzara occupied the ground floor of a drab modern building off Via Ruggiero Settimo, very near Flaccovio's, and inside the glass doors Giuseppe stopped and unbuttoned his coat and scanned the gloom. He liked the café for its isolation and the fact that here he could work on his evening's lectures unmolested. He spied his cousin at a table in the corner, bent over a small notebook, scribbling. Several wrapped parcels tied with brown twine were stacked beside him. Giuseppe approached slowly.

Lucio, he said, his voice soft, and he set down his leather bag with an unexpected thud. The table rocked, the spoon in his cousin's coffee rattled.

Lucio lifted a finger; finished writing; raised his face.

So the Monster appears, he said, and it was as if his cousin had been expecting him. He was chewing on a toothpick like a bohemian from Paris. I have been waiting here two hours at least, Giuseppe. But I see you have been feeding. And he folded one leg over another and lifted *The Pickwick Papers* out from under the cakes in their paper wrappers and he scanned its spine.

What are you writing? Giuseppe asked. Not a poem, I hope?

Not a poem, Lucio said grandly. No.

But Giuseppe had been teasing and he sat now in silence embarrassed at his cousin's failure to realize this. When the waiter approached he ordered a black coffee, a plate of sweet pastries. Lucio had always been one to take himself too seriously. Though his cousin read Persian directly, and Sanskrit, and ancient Greek, and though he excelled in mathematics, astronomy, and musical composition, still he seemed a kind of child to Giuseppe, easily wounded and therefore, in his way, dangerous. It did not matter that he had been celebrated as a poet. When he and Lucio and Casimiro had been boys, Giuseppe remembered, it was always Lucio who suggested the games they play, the naval warships they try to build out of toothpicks, who should sit where at their hillside lunches. He had changed little. Whereas Giuseppe had become like the great bombed-out houses of old Palermo: rubbled by history, an embarrassing reminder, best left boarded up and walked past. He smiled sadly, thinking this. But now he would have to go on, as he had always done, struggling not to disappoint those who would look to him to be, still, what he had always been: unchanging, steadfast, mild.

Not a poem, Lucio said again, with a calculated shrug. I am merely recording impressions.

Impressions, echoed Giuseppe.

Mm. Notes *towards* a poem, perhaps. Which is what living is, for a poet, I suppose. Lucio turned the spoon in his coffee, tapped it with a click twice on the edge of his cup. He said: I shall scrutinize them later, Cousin. For now, I simply write. In the end we must all be responsible for our words, no?

In the end, said Giuseppe, yes.

He knew that for Lucio the world was not a sensual thing, not something that overwhelmed with powerful scents and eddies of beauty. His cousin struggled just to see its surfaces and did not trust his own heart and because of this his poetry required tremendous effort and concentration. But he had received an award from the poet Montale last summer and as a result his privately published collection of poems was to be republished by Mondadori in Milan later in the year and Giuseppe supposed, *in the end*, his cousin's limitations did not matter. He rubbed his slow hands together as the waiter set down a tray of pastries and a coffee.

Lucio was wearing a small pink tie and a grey jacket and his hair when he took off his hat fell carelessly across his forehead. He had been a sickly boy and had grown into a small-shouldered, large-headed man. Giuseppe observed his little eyes, his long nose, his high eyebrows, like a man perpetually surprised at the mournfulness of the world. His brother Casimiro had by contrast the flair of a gentleman. The Piccolos lived in the east, at Capo d'Orlando, and had not lost their villa above the sea in the war. Giuseppe loved them like brothers despite their idiosyncrasies. They believed not only in spirits and communion with the dead but conducted themselves with an artistic passion in their faith, walking by candlelight to private seances held in shrouded rooms, draping their mirrors in sheets to draw forth the dead.

All this Giuseppe admired for the magnificent foolishness of it. He felt their supreme innocence derived from their isolation, that Lucio and Casimiro and even their reclusive sister Agata Giovanna all believed that after death they would continue to live in their beautiful villa above the sea, and continue to walk among the citrus groves, the buzzards, the agapanthus, and that their servants and labourers would die with them and continue to serve their interests in the next life.

The hour deepened, the plate lightened, Giuseppe's coffee was refilled. His appointment with Coniglio receded, like a dream.

I am always surprised to see you in Palermo, Cousin, he said.

Well. I grow lonely in the east, I pine for the city.

You do not.

Lucio smiled. Casimiro is in need of paint. Where are your young friends? Gioacchino said he would be returning with you. That boy is somewhat unpredictable, is he not?

We Tomasi understand fanatics of all kinds, Lucio. Especially those who share our blood. You will stay for dinner?

Lucio's eyelids flickered. Licy is cooking?

She will insist. She will cancel with her phobics and neurotics and insist.

Then I regret I cannot, Lucio said quickly. I must return to Capo d'Orlando this afternoon. Casimiro will be wondering after his supplies.

And if Licy were not cooking?

You are from a family of ascetics and mystics, Cousin, Lucio said. We Piccolos are ruled by our appetites. Why do you smile? I am younger than you, I require nourishment.

Ah. The stones are younger than me.

He saw Lucio study him then with a softening eye. A silence fell between them.

All at once uncomfortable, and without meaning to, Giuseppe said: I was asked by Dr. Coniglio to remember him to you. I am to tell you he is well. His wife is in Marseilles again.

Coniglio?

Yes.

When did you see Coniglio?

Giuseppe stirred his coffee. It occurred to him now, since he had not told Licy of his appointment, that she would be at once suspicious when he did mention it; she would think something very wrong, and would not accept his reassurances. She would insist on becoming *involved*. He looked up and saw in Lucio's face the dark joy of a rumour taking shape and he wished he had said nothing of it.

I saw him this morning, he said reluctantly. Only briefly. In passing, really.

Something is the matter?

What would be the matter?

Lucio peered at him. You do not look well, Cousin.

Thank you.

Nothing is the matter?

Giuseppe shook his head. He let his gaze drift across the crowded tables to the brass railing of the bar. Time was a cascade of rooms, opening out like the drawing rooms of his childhood, a succession of shafts of light and dust and quiet. That is what no novel seemed able to express. Sometimes it seemed to him the world would not have had him, even had he wanted it. He tried to explain this to Lucio but it did not come out right. He frowned into the silence and studied the coffee spoon and then he asked if his cousin ever wondered what would remain of him after his death.

You mean on this side, said Lucio.

Yes.

No. I do not wonder about it.

Giuseppe studied his cousin's little black eyes and realized it must be a gift to be so untroubled. That is what faith gives one, he thought.

I do not wonder about it, Lucio said again. The poetry will remain.

He reached into the bag beside him and withdrew a slender volume and held it delicately in his long thin fingers.

You have brought your poems with you, said Giuseppe.

Lucio ignored this. Our memories, Cousin, are unusual. We are from a world that no longer exists. If I do not write that world, write it down, then what will become of it? He waved a languid hand and shrugged. An entire way of life will vanish with us. Signor Montale once said to me that I had preserved a Sicily that was already fading.

There was something composed, theatrical, in Lucio's words that made Giuseppe wonder if he had rehearsed them. It was true the world would know little of what had been lost. It pained him to think of the long decline of the princes of Lampedusa, the waste, how easily a line of historical beauty could be strangled.

He ran a finger over his upper lip, drying the coffee in his moustache. I always thought I would write a novel, he said vaguely.

Yes. Your Sicilian *Ulysses*.

He was surprised his cousin remembered.

What I remember, Lucio clarified, is you writing us from England about it. Of course that was twenty years ago. Twenty-four hours in the life of your astronomer great-grandfather, wasn't it, during Garibaldi's landing at Marsala? Lucio crossed his legs, his expression unreadable. I should always have thought his receiving of the award from the Sorbonne more fitting material. What had your great-grandfather to do with the redshirts?

Not enough, it would seem, said Giuseppe.

You are not thinking about writing it now, surely?

Giuseppe smiled. I am old, Lucio. Impossibly old.

His cousin seemed to relax. Nonsense. You shall live forever, Cousin, so long as you do not write a book. It is no way to live, I assure you. Publishing is a cruel affair.

And he shook his head, leafing delicately through the verses of his collection as he did so.

In the late-afternoon darkness he caught a bus from the Mazzara to the Quattro Canti and then trudged slowly back to Via Butera, leaning into the freezing wind, a stout shabby dignified figure, his leather bag bulky in one fist, his face carefully composed, his eyes turned away from the souls he passed. He was thinking of the day, his sickness, Licy at home preparing, no doubt, for the evening's patients. As the afternoon had deepened, after Lucio had bid farewell, a brooding melancholy had come up in him, so that he could only read fitfully while his mind drifted and did not settle. He unlocked the streetside door and crossed the stone courtyard and climbed the steps and went inside. Upstairs in the library he kissed his wife on the top of her head where she sat reading a case study on childhood depression. She paused with the book open in her lap and raised her face. A web of lines at her eyes, the steady dark inscrutable smile at her lips, her black hair with its grey drawn carefully back from her forehead. She held an opera-length cigarette holder to one side, and now she smoked and regarded Giuseppe and he felt himself start to blush, as if he had done something wrong.

You are back early, she said softly. My first patient has not arrived yet.

Giuseppe poured himself a glass of water from a carafe on the side table. This is the one with the fear of bees?

Signor Mireau. The violinist. Aggressive narcissist, history of childhood psychoneurosis.

Ah. Yes.

She watched as he settled in the armchair. What is that look? she asked.

It is nothing. There is no look.

Hm.

I saw Dr. Coniglio today.

Licy smiled. Not on purpose, I trust.

Giuseppe held out his hands in a show of resignation. Alas.

Reluctantly Licy closed the book on one knuckle, to keep her page. Did you not see him last month?

I did.

You are seeing rather much of him. What did he have to say? How grave is it?

Most grave, I am afraid. It seems I am dying.

Licy laughed. Meanwhile Coniglio tells me I will live to be one hundred. Do we suppose he knows anything at all?

Giuseppe gave her a quiet smile. Perhaps he is not even a doctor, he said.

As he said this he smoothed out the wrinkles in his trousers, crossed his legs, withdrew a cigarette from the little silver case he kept in his jacket pocket. He did not light it. He understood now was the moment to tell her about his emphysema but for some reason he did not, and then the moment had passed.

What he was thinking was how much he liked the gentleness, the ease of the conversation. All that would change. Everything would change between them when he told her. The ordinary pleasurable fact of their lives, sitting together, smoking, their faces turned away from their own deaths as if they were twenty years younger still, all of it would be different. And he saw that he was not prepared for this, not prepared to live as a man with an illness, a man who carried his own death in his pocket.

I was thinking, he said softly, about children.

The light caught on the pearls at his wife's throat as she leaned forward, tapped her cigarette into the ashtray. Children, she said. What about them?

He shrugged. The consolation that they are, he said. The future that they are.

You do not mean children of our own?

He gave her a smile.

I think we are somewhat past the age, Giuseppe.

Ah, he said, and lowered his voice. But we are not too old to try.

But she did not laugh at this and instead turned her face aside, exhaled a long plume of smoke, turned back. Her face was suddenly serious. What would we have done with a child? she said quietly. Would you have lived with us in Riga? Would your mother have permitted that?

He frowned. I thought you had wanted one.

It does not matter. It did not happen.

No.

We have Giò and Mirella now. They come and go as they please, they borrow our books, they eat our food.

It is not the same.

But he could see Alessandra resisting the unhappiness in his voice and for this he was suddenly grateful. Among her qualities that he most loved was a strong Baltic steadiness and a sensitivity to his moods and he knew she would not allow him to sink further.

I do not know what is going on in that head of yours, she said now, with a careful composure. But I do not like it.

What I need, he said, is someone to talk to.

Yes. A professional.

But who?

Who indeed.

He picked a piece of tobacco from his lips. Lucio was at the Mazzara today, he said.

Lucio!

I was surprised too.

Is he coming here tonight, then?

Ah. Well. I told him you were preparing dinner.

Licy laughed. You are wicked, my love.

Just then the buzzer rang at the front door and Giuseppe crushed out his cigarette and got to his feet and Licy too rose, smoothing out her blue dress.

Your narcissist is here, murmured Giuseppe.

My other one, she said, waving him away with her fingers.

He went downstairs to the smaller library and closed the doors behind him and stood with his back to them and breathed, his smile fading slowly. He felt suddenly tired, disappointed at himself for having failed to speak of the emphysema. It would only be the more awkward now. He loosened his tie and took off his jacket and draped it over a chair, grateful at least that Orlando would not be coming for his lectures. Let us pray, Coniglio had said. Prayer, he thought wearily. *Nunc et in hora mortis nostrae. Amen.* An image came to him, the stone church he had passed that morning in the narrow piazza, and he thought how that church had survived so many hundreds of years, how ninety-five years earlier on that same morning the same low soothing tidal drone of voices could have been heard, before Italy was Italy, before Garibaldi had begun his conquest and the Lampedusas their decline.

He sat down, opened his notebook, unscrewed the lid of his blue Biro. From his shirt pocket he withdrew his reading glasses and unfolded them and put them on. Earlier that morning, while talking to Lucio, he had found something in his mind, vivid, like a memory, though it was no memory. This had not happened to him before. It was a man, poised and reticent and powerful, a man vulnerable to sudden beauty, overwhelmed by his own sensuous nature. He would locate this man on the afternoon of Garibaldi's landing, away from the heat and clatter of rifles, and submerge him instead in the quietude and gloom of a family prayer. He had always supposed his great-grandfather to be a man who could not bear to grow old and for whom dying meant extinction but what he had not realized was that sensuousness and ruin were inseparable, and that to live overwhelmed by the past was its own kind of extinction. It seemed to him now that the man he saw, gruff, dignified, autocratic, who both was and was not his great-grandfather, this man's very passion for life must be the cause of his decline.

He was surprised at how easily the sentences came, one upon another, once he began, and he wrote with a kind of anguish, afraid he would lose the thread or that the sentences would twist back upon themselves. He had not written before with the rigorous imagination needed of art and he had always supposed a guiding intelligence necessary on the part of any artist but here the story came almost ready-made, as if certain of itself, as if he were both writing it and being written by it. His astronomer prince would stand immaculate at the edge of his sunlit terrace and stare out at the shifting world and understand that what seemed to be passing had in truth already passed. Dust and heat in a cyclone at his thighs in the golden light.

When he paused, the pen hovering an inch above the paper, his hand was aching. He was surprised to see he had written several pages. He rose and crossed to the window, an old fat rumpled figure reflected there, sleeves bunched above his wrists, and he worked through the next sentence in his mind finding the right expression and then he returned to his desk and sat and read back what he had written. He crossed out the word *lilting* and then he wrote it back in. He could hear Licy calling to her black spaniel in the hall, the scrape of claws on the hardwood, the hinges of the terrace door squeaking like the faint sounds in a dream. The evening dark was silvery and still. He worked with a sober clarity, some part of himself stripped away, a concentration rising in him that he had not felt since his youth, a thing liquid and powerful and cold and immersive and when the words slowed he slowed and waited, calm, until the words came again and his hand began to move, deliberate, steady, soft across the soft paper, his fingertips afire in the late and furious hour.

PALMA DI
MONTECHIARO

=========

SEPTEMBER 1955

He worked through the windy spring and into the summer on the long first gesture of his novel, hardly daring to breathe, dreading each day's work, fearing it would not come. The strangeness of the experience alarmed him, astounded him, made him feel, perplexingly, both frail and alive. He had thought to write a novel in the manner of Joyce, a single twenty-four-hour account of his astronomer great-grandfather during the landings of Garibaldi's soldiers in May of 1860. His prince, Don Fabrizio, would observe uneasily the passing of his world, and his class, and the coming of the new Italy. A nephew, Tancredi, handsome, charming, changeable, would see his opportunity and fight alongside the redshirts. At first he had imagined the novel's tension would arise between these two but when he sat down to write them he wrote instead with the love and baffled admiration he himself felt towards Giò and Orlando. Already by April Giuseppe had understood that it would not be a novel of easy conflict, that the story wanted something else. It flickered and shifted through a haze of time and memory like the early moving pictures he had seen as a boy, in the private theatre at Santa Margherita. By the end of May he had finished the first twenty-four hours, had traced his prince from his morning prayers in the family's oratory through his day at the palazzo, had witnessed Tancredi leaving to enlist with Garibaldi, had followed the aging prince down to an assignation in Palermo, and already returned to the next morning's prayers, and what he had imagined for twenty-five years to be an entire novel had proved, in fact, only a beginning. After he understood this he was uncertain how to continue. Something was missing. He worked and reworked his only chapter.

By the deep still fiery close of July there was a wholeness, a completion, to the chapter which he had not expected. Some evenings before sleep he would go to his small library and turn on the desk lamp and read over the pages as if they had been written by another. He told no one of the novel but his wife, although he would not read her anything from it, and when he spoke of it he did so derisively, calling it his scribbling, shaking his head wryly at his foolishness. The days lengthened, the heat thickened. In the red dust of high summer he would walk to the Mazzara and sit with his notebook and write for hours, seeing himself as others must have, a shabby mild old man writing, perhaps, a letter to a distant friend. He felt his mood darken, and would rise some mornings disgusted at the inferiority of the work, only to read over the preceding night's pages and find himself surprised, admonished by a beauty he had not realized lay in the sentences themselves.

As the weeks passed he felt, somehow, a second bloom coming up inside him. He could not think how else to describe it. He did not know if it had to do with his diagnosis, or with the novel he had set out to write, or some natural consequence of his age. But it seemed to him the world was brighter, more intense, more alive than he had remembered. Colours were more vibrant, shimmering; the scents of ordinary things, wet pavement, bricks in sunlight, unripe peaches, felt layered and dizzyingly complex. He would stare at the silver ribbon of tap water in the kitchen sink, listening to it bang and rattle off the porcelain, agape. Some mornings on his walk to the Mazzara he would glimpse an old man at the corner of Piazza Marina, eating a bowl of coarse pasta and oil, and he would linger at the smell, amazed. How long had he walked past that man, unseeing? When the public gardens came into bloom in the spring he sat for hours on the benches, his eyes closed, remembering the huge wet flowers of his childhood. He smiled more easily with Gioacchino and Orlando in the evenings, caught himself longing for their company after a day of writing.

It was true, he still had not told Licy of the emphysema; he found it increasingly difficult to raise the subject. At first it had been a matter of the right moment; then, as the weeks passed, he came to fear her anger at not having been told, and so more time had passed, and the telling became more difficult. In his mind these two—the world erupting into beauty around him, and his withholding of the truth to Licy—became one, intertwined, as if the former was sweeter and made the more delicate by his shame at the latter. Now in the already bright mornings, before the sun's heat baked the palazzo, Giuseppe would awake and at once muffle his coughing with his sleeve. Nor did he let on about his difficulties ascending the stairs, or the way he would sometimes falter at the landing, losing his balance. When he walked out with Licy on sun-drenched evenings to the confectioner's he kept his breathing unlaboured, his steps on the pavement steady, finding reasons to linger at shop windows and street corners, catching his breath as he did so.

In this way what had been, at first, merely a piece of troubling news that he had not yet shared, grew gradually into a more sinister thing, until his emphysema had developed, almost of its own volition, into a genuine and painful secret.

His evening lectures with Giò and Orlando, and even sometimes Giò's fiancée, Mirella, went on. His young friends would arrive at half-six, never late, the men in black tie, Mirella with her light brown hair up, and he would wait for them in the historical library with a bottle of wine breathing on the desk and the low drone of Licy at her consultations just audible elsewhere in the palazzo. He spoke about the history of English literature, discussed Chaucer, and Shakespeare, but also Sir Walter Scott and the Cavalier poets and Dickens and Meredith. He would walk to the courtyard window, stand smoking, turn to his young guests, continue. He spoke about vanished authors and their characters as if some part of them lived yet, as if they were almost present in the shuttered halls of the palazzo. The purpose originally had been to offer the youths a supplement to their education, a supplement that could not be obtained elsewhere on the island, but this had soon altered for Giuseppe until each lecture became an opportunity for him to live again inside familiar books, to allow unexpected comparisons to emerge, sensitivities to the current that was in the literature of his great and beloved English authors. He told his young friends that Tennyson was the finest writer of punctuation in English in part because he used punctuation as if the language were afraid of it. He said to them: If you wish to understand Edward Gibbon's sentences, you must read Montaigne's sentences in the French. He insisted that among the English only Donne and Eliot were true religious poets, although neither in his opinion was a Christian. Once while the sunlight slowly faded in the shutters he confessed he would sacrifice ten years of his life for the privilege of meeting Sir John Falstaff in the flesh and as soon as he had said this he realized it was true. I envy you, he said to the boys, turning away. You have so much yet to read.

One evening at the end of the summer he was discussing Graham Greene and religion, and how, in his strongest novels, Greene had gone back to the roots of Christianity; he felt Greene's attraction to all that is repugnant in the world was, in part, a reflection of original Christian charity. Horror for the unredeemed human being was mitigated, in Greene, by every person's resemblance to God. Though it was also true, Giuseppe conceded, that Greene's attraction to evil seemed sometimes a little too intimate, as if he enjoyed it, as if what he really wanted was simply to get closer to it.

Giuseppe had not said all he wished to say about it. But he heard a dissatisfied rustling from his listeners, and turned, and saw Orlando picking unhappily at the threads of his trousers.

Giò, eyebrows raised, had noticed also. He withdrew his arm from Mirella's shoulders, sat forward. Orlando is not happy with all this talk of religion, he said. It is the socialist in him.

Ah, said Giuseppe.

I am not a socialist, said Orlando. Please go on, Don Giuseppe.

He is without faith, said Giò.

Do not tease him, Giò, said Mirella quietly. She put a hand on his arm. He is never serious with me either, she called across to Orlando. You must not mind him.

He does not mind. Do you mind, Orlando? What do socialists mind?

Giò—

They mind only lack of progress, said Orlando. He pushed his spectacles into place with one finger. Progress is their church. There is always a church. Here in Sicily we would not know what to do if there were no church. It is not about faith. The purpose of any church is to keep power in the hands of its clergy.

Agnello would be appalled, said Giò.

No. Agnello would agree. But with one hand on the rosary in his pocket.

Giò laughed.

Giuseppe tapped his cigarette into an ashtray on the windowsill, listening. He could remember being twenty and thinking such thoughts after he returned from the prisoner camps at Szombathely, shocked at how small and petty Sicily had become in his absence. But he could not remember a time when anyone would have expressed such criticisms so directly. The world was changing. He thought of tall Francesco Agnello, who made up the third of that triumvirate of youths—along with Gioacchino and Orlando—which Giuseppe had come to think of as his students. Agnello had retreated from the heat of Palermo to his family's villa outside Agrigento for the summer. A baron, soft, heavy-set, he was a few years older than Giò and Orlando, and in person the boys treated him with the deference due an elder brother.

As the youths talked, Giuseppe watched Mirella, smoking quietly. Graham Greene had been quite forgotten. She was wearing a red dress with a plunging back and a bodice that widened out into layers of tulle at her hips, and her light brown hair was carved into curls and drawn away from her neck so that she looked, Giuseppe thought, like the new century itself. Girls had not been so self-possessed, had not contained such a clear sense of lives still to be lived, when he was young.

The conversation had shifted again.

The wind is blowing from the north, Orlando was saying. Workers are leaving the land all over. Entire villages are moving to Genoa, to Milan.

They are even taking the cows, teased Giò.

Orlando ignored him. Sicily is emptying. The south is dying.

I think it is a shame, said Mirella.

Giuseppe crushed out his cigarette. He felt a sudden pain in his chest and put a hand out to steady himself and the youths went quiet.

The pain passed.

He looked away, embarrassed; and to hide his embarrassment he started to speak. He said: The south has been dying for centuries. He clasped his hands in the small of his back, feeling the warm summer light on his face, his eyelids. He said: In my grandfather's day, the people were leaving the villages for Palermo and Messina. In my father's day, they were leaving for America. Now they leave for the north. How is it different?

Giò got to his feet, catlike, and padded over to the desk and began to open a second bottle of wine. There was, thought

Giuseppe, a sort of crooked kindness in him; it did not come out straight.

There have been too many changes, too quickly, said Orlando. Italy is not the same as it was, Don Giuseppe. Sicily cannot keep up.

Italy, yes, said Giò from the desk. But not Sicily. Sicily never changes, not really. Here in Palermo we are still living in a monarchy.

Oh, there will never again be a king, protested Mirella. Not here.

You are right, said Orlando. And yet there will always be a king in Sicily. We did not have even one district that voted against the monarchy.

Palermo did, said Giuseppe softly.

Orlando leaned forward, the evening sunlight catching in his spectacles. But Palermo is not Sicily, Don Giuseppe.

Giuseppe lit another cigarette.

Giò had returned to the sofa with the opened wine cradled in his two hands and now he set it down on the round table so that Mirella and Orlando could see the label. So the republic is a lie, he said pleasantly, and behind closed doors Sicily goes on as it always has. What of it? The referendum was ten years ago. It is done. You did not vote in it, I did not vote in it.

And I did not vote in it, said Mirella pointedly.

Giò gestured wryly at the ceiling. That is true. We are all of us products of the new republic. A republic where we are free to discuss the wonderful influence of the church, and which fascists we have locked in our attics, and what women who have a voice in our elections will say next.

Why is that funny to you? asked Mirella. She was sitting very still, her wine glass held by the stem.

Giò, catching something in her tone, paused. It is not funny, he said, suddenly serious.

Why should women not have the vote? she said.

They should, said Giò. I am glad they do. That you do.

Hm.

Giuseppe observed a delighted expression flicker across Orlando's face. There was in Mirella something that was in Licy also, he saw. Giò, being young, did not understand that Mirella's strength and stubbornness would demand he make space for her, and he wanted to tell him but he knew it was important to say nothing, that it was not something that could be learned through telling. Giò was just twenty-one; in many ways, Mirella, though younger in years, was much the older of the two.

Giò's cheeks had coloured slightly and Giuseppe understood from the hesitant way he half turned in her direction that he knew she was displeased and that their conversation would continue, later, when they were alone.

Orlando, amused, waited to see if more would come and when nothing did he said, almost reluctantly: It is not all in the past, Giò. Not really. The Fascists are still in power. They still hold positions of authority. You think just because we are a republic that anything has changed? Azzariti sits on the Constitutional Court. So does Manca.

Manca was a Fascist? asked Mirella.

Is, corrected Orlando. It is not something you put on and take off, like a shirt.

Giò smiled at that but in his smile Giuseppe saw that he was still thinking of Mirella, trying to gauge her mood.

Azzariti sat on the Tribunal of Race, Orlando went on. So did Antonio Manca. They were the ones who decided who was Aryan and who would be given over to the Nazis.

Giuseppe cleared his throat. It seemed almost in bad taste to him, going on about the war. All at once he felt very tired. Well and what is to be done about it, Orlando? he said. Who would be left, if we persecuted everyone who collaborated with the Fascists?

You would be left, said Orlando.

Giuseppe inclined his head in acknowledgement. I did not collaborate, he said, only because I did not do anything. That is not courage. A nation of Lampedusas would be a poor nation indeed.

I do not agree, said Mirella. She gave him a sweet smile.

These men were not *collaborators*, Don Giuseppe. They were *in power*. And they are still in power.

Giò poured Orlando a second glass of wine. He said, They'll all be dead soon enough anyhow. They belong to the past, Orlando.

As do we all, Giuseppe thought, the red evening sunlight filling the shutters, and then immediately he wondered if that was true.

The following evening, in the heat, as they walked Licy's black spaniel Crab down to the confectioner's, he tried to explain the feeling of irrelevance that came over him whenever his young friends talked politics. There was guitar music playing in the streets, crowds, the setting sun illuminating the red dust stirred up from the trucks and slow-moving carts. He spoke self-deprecatingly, amused at his own foolishness. It seemed to him, he said, they were describing an island he had read about once, a place and time long since vanished.

Oh, Giuseppe, his wife replied. It is not they who inhabit the past.

This was said with such unexpected regret that Giuseppe fell silent, trying to understand her meaning. Sometimes he thought she looked at him with the knowledge already in her eyes of his emphysema and at such moments he felt a complicated relief, believing he might let it go unsaid between them; but then a comment or query from her would betray the truth, that she did not know, did not even suspect, and he would feel all over again a sudden wash of guilt. Often now when he watched her he tried to imagine her without him, walking the same dusty pavements of Palermo but alone, or writing up her case studies on the terrace at Via Butera, with no one to interrupt her or to come out with a carafe of water and glasses, no one to bid her goodnight, no one to take her hand in his and tell her it was time to come inside, the light was going, it would be dark soon.

He had written her a letter. In it, he had tried to explain the diagnosis and his hesitancy in speaking to her about it. He would not get better; but he did not need to get worse. That is what Coniglio had told him. But he had torn the letter up, dissatisfied. It was not what he wanted to say. He could feel his breathing growing more laboured, and now when he smoked he felt a pricking in his lungs, in his back. Sometimes as he lay in his bed, struggling to sleep, he would decide he must tell Licy at once, but always in the mornings when he awoke he saw again how it was not the right moment, how easily it could be misconstrued.

Now Licy kneeled and collected Crab into her arms, his paws overhanging her wrist, and Giuseppe followed behind her, slowly, as she crossed Via Roma through the traffic.

Signor Aridon telephoned for you this afternoon, she said to him when he had reached the far pavement. That is twice now. You must telephone him back.

Giuseppe nodded, breathing hard. Her eyes were severe and very beautiful, he thought.

He wishes to go over the account ledgers with you. Giuseppe? Are you listening?

Yes.

She gave him a curious look, put a gloved hand to her hat, as if all at once self-conscious. Aridon says there are problems with the rents, Giuseppe. He says he has a collector in mind that he believes will be more effective, a man from Messina. The estates are in quite a predicament, it seems. He says some of the properties may need to be sold off.

Giuseppe smiled. He has been saying that for thirty years, my love.

So it is not true?

On the contrary. It has been true for thirty years.

He was still out of breath and he paused now to very slowly withdraw and light a cigarette. Licy watched him, lifting her clutch to one hip. It was of soft black leather and matched her gloves and hat and the piping at her jacket pockets and he considered again, as he often had, how strange and complicated were the rules women dressed by.

The confectioner's was only two buildings away but Licy lingered. You know I am expected in Rome, she said. For the conference.

Yes. Your psychoanalytics.

She smiled a little at the tone in his voice but he could see there was something she wished to convey to him, something that would not wait. She said: Orlando will be in Syracuse, Mirella is already in Naples with her family. What will you do while I am gone? Who will you see?

Giò will be here.

I have not seen you writing your novel of late.

Ah.

You have not given it up?

My *Histoire sans nom*, Giuseppe said grandly, mockingly. No. But it seems it does not wish to be written.

Nonsense, she said. She handed him the leash and took off her gloves and held them together with her clutch and took the leash back from him. Your writing has brought some nostalgia forward from your subconscious and it must be resolved, my love. That is why you do not know how to proceed. It is to be expected.

I shall have to study myself more deeply, said Giuseppe.

That will be of little use, Licy replied briskly. I have been thinking. The Lampedusa estate in Palma, the castle there. What is its condition?

He crushed his cigarette under his shoe. It is a ruin, I believe. I have not seen it. Why do you ask?

I am told the Ventino castle outside Enna is being converted into apartments. There are buyers down from Milan, from Genoa.

I could not sell Palma di Montechiaro, he said quietly. I could not, Licy.

Not all of it. But perhaps a part of it.

He shook his head, feeling a sudden weight on his heart. I do not think anything is left but walls, my love.

He put a hand on the small of her back then, and nodded gently, and she allowed herself to be guided into the confectioner's. They were greeted with deference by the owner, and a long glass case with ice under its trays was lit up, its little cakes and cannoli and pastries all gleaming.

They did not speak again until they were seated in the window, with their small coffees and their plates of sugared pistachio marzipans. Two ladies across from them nodded formally and Licy dipped her chin, Giuseppe touched his hat.

I will be in Rome in two weeks' time, Licy said in a low voice, so as not to be overheard. It is my opinion that you must go to Palma. Go with Giò, he is doing nothing. He will be pleased to accompany you. Examine the castle at Montechiaro. Something will need to be done, Giuseppe, according to Signor Aridon. If nothing is decided by you, it will be decided by creditors and courts.

Giuseppe put the little spoon down on his plate. He did not look up. We cannot afford it, he said quietly.

Nonsense, she said. The train is not expensive. You can stay with young Agnello. It will cost no more than a trip to your cousins.

Which we cannot afford.

And yet you see them often, she said. She studied him for a long moment.

It is my opinion, she said with finality, that a journey to Palma will help you to neutralize your nostalgia. You have been unable to write further into your novel. This is because the losses in your life continue to overwhelm you.

My losses, he murmured.

He wanted to tell her he was not overwhelmed; he wanted to say he had written no further in his novel only because he had not known what came next. He raised his face, but did not speak.

Go, Licy said gravely. She rested her fingertips on the backs of his knuckles. Go confront the seat of your ancestors. And then, my love, come back to me.

In the days that followed, his distaste for the idea only grew.

Though he was not used to resisting his wife's instructions, this he did resist. He would, he told himself, refuse to go. Simply to make such a journey might be to agree, implicitly, to the sale of his family's castle at Montechiaro. He told himself the good Dr. Coniglio would disapprove, given the delicate state of his lungs. He observed Licy as she telephoned Rome in the historical library and arranged her accommodations, as she began to lay out on a recamier her various outfits for her trip, and he thought of the long quiet days when she would be away, and how much he liked the quiet, and how little he liked the discomforts of travel.

Then, one week before her departure, Licy went looking for him between patients and told him, as he prepared a spiced tea to help him sleep, that she had noticed a change in him, a new dissatisfaction. She said this gently, calmly. He had interrupted his novel earlier that summer, at her suggestion, in order to record his impressions of his early childhood. Like the novel, it had not gone easily; like the novel, it remained unfinished. If his project of memory, his attempt to resurrect the houses he had lost, had failed to lead him back into his novel, Licy asked now, why was he resisting the trip to Palma?

It cannot do you any harm, she said. It is my experience that breakthroughs often happen in new surroundings.

He said nothing to her in response. In truth, he had been thinking much the same thing. He had spent the previous week reading through the memoir, the many pages about his mother's beloved house at Santa Margherita di Belice. Something had stirred inside him, a discovery, and he had felt his thoughts drifting back to his stalled novel. He did not admit this to Licy then. But what had been missing, he saw now, was a place of stillness and beauty for his prince that would, over the course of the novel, be lost, made irrecoverable, the way a childhood is lost.

What was missing was a journey to a great estate.

And so, on the third of September, he and Gioacchino set out by train across Sicily to visit the ancient Lampedusa estate in Palma.

The particulars, like the trip itself, came from his wife. They would journey as far as Agrigento and there meet young Francesco Agnello who would drive them to his country villa at Siculiana for the night. Giuseppe had not travelled the island by rail since he was a child and he was surprised to find how much had changed and how little. The train was still slow, and in the oppressive flat heat it swayed and clattered noisily along its ancient tracks. But the windows could be wrested, squeaking, open, and the seats though split at their seams were softer. He felt grateful for the private carriages and for the dark boy with cowlike eyes who carried a tray of refreshments looped around his neck and came staggering down the corridors every thirty minutes. Each time the boy knocked at their door, crying out in his high voice, Giuseppe would laboriously close the upper buttons of his shirt and wrestle back into his linen suit jacket before nodding to Giò. The youth thought him absurd, would tease him lightly by unfastening several buttons on his own shirt and mussing his own hair before admitting the boy, who would then stare stolidly at the floor, avoiding the strange half-dressed young man and his stiff sweating elderly companion.

When he was a boy, in the sweltering fury of July, his mother would shift the household each year from Palermo to Santa Margherita di Belice. He would rise dutifully at three in the morning at his governess's urgings and let himself be dressed, then stumble down to the courtyard, to the closed landaus looming there. He could remember the horses snorting softly in the warmth, the smell of the night flowers along the stone wall. He and his parents and Anna would clamber into the rocking enclosure and the second landau would follow with the staff and they would set off sleepily through the grey deserted streets for the Lolli station and the shabby overland train to Trapani. He had not told Gioacchino of those journeys. He watched the youth rubbing a knuckle along his moist upper lip, wondering at the world as it was. The trains in those first years of the new century had no corridors and he could remember the ticket collector clambering in his gloves and tasselled uniform along the outsides of the compartments, his hand reaching through the windows, he could remember the tracks running in the sand alongside the surf and the slow baking fire of the iron boxes they lay sweating in, trapped. He had loved those trips, the languid happiness on his mother's face, her eyes closed and the swishing of the fan in her hand.

Those journeys had taken them across the western coast but here the rails led south, inland, along and up and over the arid hilly vastness of the true Sicily. They would slow for flocks of sheep ragged and clouded with flies and hear the lazy cries of the shepherds scattering them from the tracks and watch the men in their dark clothes with their shotguns slung over one shoulder walking almost at speed alongside the train and staring black-eyed and baleful in. Those men were old. But then the unpleasantness would pass, and they would wind languidly around another stony outcropping, and the dazzling blue sky would overwhelm. There was a sad beauty to the hills, the rock-strewn defiles, and then the sudden bursts of yellow wheat or the pillars of olive trees staggering along a ridge would leave Giuseppe unsettled. Tangles of myrtle and broom and wild thyme were visible in the distance. They passed mountain villages, their streets empty in the high sun, and he thought with interest of Orlando's words, how the island was emptying, entire villages drifting north.

As the train clattered slowly inland Giò sank into a desultory silence. At last the youth began, as Giuseppe knew he would, to speak of Mirella.

She has cut her hair, he said unhappily. She has cut it all off, Uncle, into an American bob. Have you seen it yet? She looks very fashionable and fast.

Ah, he said. No.

She insists it is due to the hot weather, Giò continued. She says many girls have cut their hair and haven't I noticed them at the cafés with Orlando? It is true. But she has also taken to wearing shorter skirts, and I saw her two weeks ago with a new bracelet. I asked her where she got it and she pretended it was nothing, that she did not remember. But Mirella is not like other girls, she remembers everything. It is that student in her history class, that American. I am certain of it.

Giuseppe wiped his handkerchief across his mouth and was careful to say nothing.

Giò said: I telephoned her last weekend and her mother said she had gone to the cinema. But she had not. Where was I? Oh, just out with some friends. An innocent night. Where was *she*?

Giuseppe thought to say that Mirella Radice had a kind and loyal heart but he knew enough of love to realize the foolishness of it. The heart is neither kind nor loyal.

I think she has been angry with me, Uncle. I think she feels neglected. Do you think it is possible? Giò glanced at him and he saw now in the boy's thin face, his soft lips and dark liquid eyes, the face of an innocent. I sometimes feel like she *wants* to make me angry, Uncle, and then I get angry, and then she gets angry that I am angry. We are like an old married couple. He did not seem to notice Giuseppe's smile and he continued without embarrassment: I will have to speak to her, I will have to tell her that I will not allow her to meet with this American. I will be firm. Yes.

At Agrigento they descended into the roaring of the central railway station amid clouds of white steam and Giuseppe waited while Giò engaged a porter for their luggage and then the three of them walked through the cool building, the little wheels of the baggage trolley squeaking. The porter unloaded their cases and tipped his hat and left them standing outside in the heat soothing the creases from their clothes with the flat of their palms and squinting. In the open piazza there were slow dusty motorcars turning around but none were Francesco's.

Giò grimaced, squinting, as if looking for the sea.

Now this, the youth said. This, Mirella would not understand. This journey we are taking into your past.

Giuseppe did not know that it was true. He had watched the girl grow over the last two years into a creature of delicacy and understanding.

The piazza had emptied. The clocks stilled. Giuseppe watched a slow horse-drawn cart move like a shadow of death along the whitewashed walls of a church.

It was in Agrigento that the playwright Luigi Pirandello had been born, and also, under an ancient sun, the Greek philosopher Empedocles. Empedocles might have walked this very earth, he thought, might have drifted among the temples now in ruins above the city. He had become one of the vanished in an island of the vanished, had clambered up to the crater of Etna and hurled himself in, hoping to make his followers think he had ascended, living, to dwell among the gods. Poor foolish Empedocles. His sandal came off his foot as he jumped and was found halfway into the crater by his followers and because of this they had understood he had perished.

What do I care if she wants another? Giò was saying. Let him have her.

Giuseppe set his hat down on his heavy suitcase where it stood in the white gravel and he walked slowly the length of the concrete wall and shielded his eyes in the late sun.

I will not be made a fool of, Giò muttered.

Giuseppe regarded the buildings surrounding, their brown shutters closed, the streets sinister and still. He was thinking of his novel, how his youthful Tancredi would peel back such talk with malice. He looked at the boy.

You must beware of the hardening of the heart, Gioitto, he said softly.

My heart is like honey, Giò protested.

But miserable and scratching at his yellow knuckles as he said it.

It had been a very different journey fourteen months earlier when Giuseppe Tomasi had accompanied his cousin to the Kursaal salon at San Pellegrino Terme, in Lombardy. That expedition north in July was for Lucio to receive an honour from the poet Montale: a public introduction to his poetry and a publishing contract with the prestigious Edizioni Mondadori in Milan. They had travelled by rail with Lucio's manservant Paolo seated in third class, and Lucio in his first-class cabin had been unable to sit still. Everywhere north of Rome they had passed factories and crowded roads and hordes of workers coming out of the shantytowns. At Milan they transferred to Bergamo and in Bergamo they got off for a day waiting for the connection to San Pellegrino. It was outside Bergamo, in Scanzorosciate, that they saw Ftalital's anhydride manufacturing plant, its green plumes of smoke darkening the sun, a yellow ash settling lightly over their hair and sleeves. And in Bergamo itself they stood outside the gates of the Agnelli aluminum factory, each holding a handkerchief to his mouth, watching a filthy reddish-brown smoke pour from the huge chimneys. It seemed to Giuseppe he had entered a strange dreamscape, an Italy of power and wealth. It was the world to come.

He was relieved when they continued north, into Lombardy.

At San Pellegrino Terme they had reserved adjoining rooms at the Grand Hotel but were surprised when they arrived to see no novelists or poets in attendance, only what appeared to be journalists up from Rome. They were not early; it was the very day of the awards presentation. Then Giuseppe, embarrassed, understood.

These rooms are too expensive, Cousin, he said as they slowly ascended the curving staircase. The writers will not be sleeping here.

The writers will not be sleeping at all, Lucio said with a high nervous laugh. I have heard about the habits of writers.

They ate a late lunch in the restaurant overlooking the Brembo River and Giuseppe eyed the whitewater cataracts of its wide expanse as they ate and neither cousin said much. The wine came from a cold northern grape and was excellent and strange. When they returned to their rooms each set about dressing for the evening and although the weather was ferociously hot

Giuseppe found he had brought his fine camel-hair coat but only his second-best suit, a slightly threadbare pinstripe. He was therefore careful to button his coat to his chin despite the heat, out of embarrassment. When the two cousins descended to the boulevard that ran alongside the river they were followed by Paolo, who carried an umbrella, and they studied the directions from the hotel porter and made their way past the public baths to the auditorium where the presentations were to take place. They walked slowly, a strange trio of Sicilian manners, under a very blue sky, the river dazzling and loud and mineral green.

The presentations had begun without them. They were led through a hushed foyer and down to their seats and Giuseppe sat himself down next to a man in tinted glasses, so as to give Lucio the aisle. At the front of the hall the story writer Bassani was standing at a lectern, speaking with passion about a national publishing program. Giuseppe mumbled some politeness to the man beside him. That man he would later learn was the novelist and journalist Enzo Bettiza. Bettiza only scowled and curled a hand over his eyes and leaned away. Giuseppe, his camel-hair coat still buttoned fast, spread his knees and set his walking stick upright between them and interlaced his fingers on its crest, and then he smiled awkwardly into the near distance. In the hall surrounding would be many of the important novelists and poets of this strange new postwar Italy. He, lifelong reader and devourer of books, wondered to find himself in such company. He had known writers before, had spoken at length with Pirandello in London, but had not measured himself against the mass of ordinary living Italian writers. It struck him as both unlikely and not entirely correct that it was his cousin

Lucio who was to be feted and laureled. Lucio had for decades studied music and performed on the piano with delicacy but had worked and reworked his poems almost as an entertainment, as if to remind Giuseppe that he was not the only one of their shared bloodline to live inside language.

Now Bassani had stepped down to much applause and a slow succession of middle-aged novelists and poets stood up to introduce their sharp hawkish young protégés. Giuseppe found his mind drifting and he would close his eyes and stifle his yawns. At last he watched a girl in a green dress escort a soft dark-haired man to the podium. This was Montale, the poet. Giuseppe felt his cousin stiffen beside him and he reached across and patted Lucio's hand gently, wryly.

They had hoped to speak with the great poet before this moment but the lateness of their arrival and the rigorous clockwork of the day's events had transpired against them. The poet was talking now, in a rough Ligurian accent, about a young writer whose verses had arrived in the mail with insufficient postage. He described how he had had to make up the difference, and then began to read the poems out of a duty to the liras he had paid out of pocket.

You will understand, ladies and gentlemen, said Montale, that I receive many packages from aspiring poets. Most of these poems are earnest, heartfelt, but of no real worth. These particular poems were accompanied by an unusual letter introducing them as chronicles of a vanishing way of life, of an aristocratic world of a Palermo that is no longer. After such a letter, you will understand, I did not expect very much from them, and least of all did I expect to find in such poems anything resembling poetry.

A brief ripple of laughter in the hall.

Giuseppe shifted in his chair, feeling a heat rise to his face. He had written that letter himself.

The young poet I wish to introduce to you today, Montale continued, is a poet whose lines are marked by the intensity and musicality of the true lyric gift. His verses are rich in imagery, dense with language, but there is no struggle required to understand their meanings. This is perhaps due to their young author's study of music and Continental philosophy. I have not had the pleasure to meet young Lucio Piccolo, but if he is present today, I hope he will join me now and read to you some of his dazzling poems.

The hall filled with applause, the faces dialing palely in their seats to scan the auditorium. Lucio rose shyly from his seat and shuffled down the aisle, looking to Giuseppe impossibly dignified and aged among such a youthful crowd. He noted how the sheaf of poems under his cousin's arm trembled and how Montale stared, as if amazed, before stepping smoothly forward and taking Lucio's hand and turning him for the flare of the flashbulbs.

You gave us quite a shock, Don Lucio, said Montale later, smiling. I had thought you were a young poet. Instead I find you more accomplished than I. It is you who should have introduced me.

Accomplished, Giuseppe whispered in his cousin's ear, is a euphemism.

Lucio ignored him, flushing at the compliment. They were standing in the crowded banquet hall of the Grand Hotel.

I liked especially the poem about the sundial, said the girl in the green dress. She closed her eyes and quoted: *Regard water the undecipherable: at its touch the universe wavers.*

Lucio smiled and studied the wine glass in his hands. Thank you, he said.

Giuseppe studied this girl sidelong. He did not know if she was Montale's guest, or daughter, or lover, or if she was a writer herself. He noted her oddly accented Italian, the light brown streaks in her hair, the golden eyes. She did not even look in his direction. The talk had shifted now, Montale holding forth on some problem in contemporary English poetry, and when a pause opened he watched his unworldly cousin dare to interject some observation on Yeats. He confessed he had corresponded with the Irishman for years. He conceded some suspicion that his poems owed their muscular strangeness to his faith in the spirits. It is the unseen, Lucio said now, what lies between the stanzas, that helps to create an illusion of purpose in his poems. Or so it seems to me.

Montale took a sip of his wine, nodded. I would not have thought it, he said. But it is nevertheless true that what we believe does work upon us and force our hand. I travelled to Rapallo to meet with Pound in 1923 and Yeats was there, but, alas, we could not understand each other. You did not have that problem?

Lucio inclined his head. I did not meet with him, not face to face, he said.

A pity, I think.

We wrote each other in English.

Ah.

We wrote each other almost to the month of his death,

Lucio said regretfully. He gave an embarrassed shrug as if he had spoken too much. May I introduce my cousin, Professore, Giuseppe Tomasi, Prince of Lampedusa. Lucio's eyes flickered across to Giuseppe where he stood leaning on his cane. He added: Giuseppe wrote an essay about Yeats's poetry which was published in 1926. Perhaps you came across it?

Montale's pale blue eyes regarded Giuseppe and he felt himself beginning to blush. You are a critic, Excellency?

Giuseppe smiled shyly. Ah, no, he mumbled. Only a reader with some time on his hands.

That is no small thing, Montale said politely. We should all wish for such readers.

My good cousin is my own first reader, said Lucio. There is nothing he has not read.

Giuseppe bowed in acknowledgement.

You will excuse me, he said.

And he turned and shuffled heavily for the stairs, his expression carefully preoccupied, as if his presence were needed elsewhere. It was true, he conceded as he paused on the landing, his fingers gripping the balustrade, he had indeed published an article on the Irish Renaissance all those years ago, and Yeats had figured prominently in it, at a time when the poet was mostly unknown in Italy. It had seemed to him then that perhaps he might find his way into a life of writing. How young he had been. Only just thirty, adrift in the cities of Europe, still struggling to find a path forward in those blurred years after the war. He had submitted the article with some dread to an old friend in Genoa whose father-in-law edited a literary magazine, telling himself that it was of no consequence. An amusement only. Yet he still recalled with great clarity the pain and anxiety he had felt, waiting for word back, hearing nothing, month after month. That magazine, *Le Opere e i Giorni*, had published early work by Montale, he knew. He had felt such pride at seeing his article in print, when at last it did come. He could not now remember why he had not continued writing for the magazine, what had prevented him from publishing further. Though his mother had disapproved, that was not the reason. Some part of him had shied away, always, from the difficult possibility of exposure. He lacked Lucio's certain faith in his own genius; instead he had, in its place, made himself adept at the avoidance of failure.

He let his eyes drift across the figures below but he did not see his cousin, nor Montale. A memory came to him, then, of Lucio leaning on a stone wall in the winter garden at Villa Vina, holding Giuseppe's copy of *Le Opere* in his hands, an expression of unhappiness flickering across his face in the cold light.

And he remembered how, all those years ago, Lucio had submitted a suite of poems to the same magazine, at Giuseppe's urging: poems which his friend's father-in-law had promptly sent back.

At twenty past five Francesco Agnello came roaring down into the Agrigento piazza in a two-plus-two silver coupe, its chrome gleaming in the late sunlight, and he wore sunglasses and a white sportsman's cap and was chewing an unlit American cigarette. The coupe was a brand-new Giulietta Sprint, just built in the Alfa Romeo factories up in Milan and driven south by Francesco himself along the new coastal highways. All this he told them with pride. It looked to Giuseppe like something out of a science fiction movie.

A young woman with yellow hair was crouched in the seat beside Francesco, barefoot.

You will forgive my sister Teresa, he said. He folded his long arms over the door, rested his chin on the polished chrome. She insisted on coming.

The famous sister, Giò said gallantly.

Francesco blew out his cheeks. Notorious, more like.

Your Excellency, she said with a flash of a smile. And this must be Gioacchino.

Francesco slid his sunglasses down his nose. My sister volunteered to help stow your luggage, Lanza.

Giò started to blush.

If Francesco was stone then Teresa was fire. Giuseppe felt a sudden sensual sorrow to see her, a regret at his own advancing age. She was smooth and olive-skinned and green-eyed like a creature from the forests and was all boldness and sly beauty. She was dressed in polka-dotted cigarette pants and a loose white blouse and her lipstick was very red. Giuseppe had seen such girls only in American magazines.

Francesco, big-boned, amused and amusing, had said nothing to him of a sister. Giuseppe sat squeezed in the tiny front seat of the coupe, his suitcase on his knees, listening over the roar of the wind to a fury of laughter from the girl behind him. Her soft fingers curled over the seat at his shoulder, she leaned forward, shouted something into his ear he did not catch, and when he turned he saw Giò with eyebrows raised, face red, eyes fixed on the girl's face. Francesco drove fast.

She was the daughter of his mother's second marriage and seven years younger than Francesco and bore no resemblance. They slowed and turned onto a narrow dirt lane and when they reached the house Giuseppe watched Giò fold Francesco's seat forward and squeeze out and hurry around to hold the door for Teresa. Teresa took his hand, her blouse dipping at her neckline.

Uncle, Giò said with a grin. What are you staring at?

Francesco's mother had passed away several years before but her second husband was standing in the open door of their country house in a blue linen suit, his arms at his sides, spectacles dangling on a thread around his neck. He had a broad forehead and a small receding chin and the smooth roundness of his head made him look like a tortoise. He came down to greet them and spoke respectfully to the prince and he clasped Giò's hand and pressed his other hand on top as if in blessing. He was short, soft in the middle, with a long nose and dark rings under his eyes.

They were offered baths and a stroll among the roses and dahlias and grapevines in the garden beyond the house as the sun sank slowly towards the hills. The bedroom given to Giuseppe was large and beautiful, set above the courtyard at the side of the villa. His suitcase had been left on a divan under the window. He stood a moment studying the curtains where they glowed in soft yellow slashes, the sunlight seeping through the slats of the wooden shutters. The bed itself was old and gilded and made him long for his childhood.

Later on the terrace Giuseppe sat drinking a glass of cold water and brooding over the emptied villages they had passed that day when he glimpsed Gioacchino and Teresa under the wisteria in the garden below. Giò, pretending to drive away flies, more than once brushed the girl's blonde hair. Giuseppe had been thinking about his novel, about Tancredi slipping easily from the old world of his birth into the new forged Sicily of the Risorgimento and he saw now what was missing. Tancredi must fall out of love with Don Fabrizio's daughter. His attentions would be seized by the beauty of a rough, unlettered girl, a creature of the new breed. She would be ravenous, greedy for pleasure, a survivor, everything the old aristocracy was not. And Don Fabrizio too would desire her and that very desire would provide the measure by which he would understand his own decline.

At dinner Francesco's stepfather laughed to see Giuseppe's eyes bulge.

Steaming platters of swordfish carved shuddering into slabs and delicate wobbles of eggplant and dishes of Sicilian macaroni thick with peppers and tomatoes and pork under a golden crust. Twists of bread still hot and soft. Calamari wrapped in brown sugar.

Plato said, of Agrigento, that we build as if we expect to live forever and we eat as if we expect to die tomorrow.

If we eat even half of this, Giuseppe said dryly, we likely shall.

After they had eaten and the dishes were cleared Giò and Francesco excused themselves and Teresa followed and the two older men picked cigars from a wooden box and smoked quietly as the evening in the tall windows deepened.

Francesco's stepfather explained that he had come to Agrigento after a career as a newspaperman in Messina and had married the countess in disbelief. She wanted her second marriage to be newsworthy, he said in the manner of a man who had made this joke before. He said the coastline here still left him short of breath in the winter and that he had always found its rugged beauty more to his taste than the stillness of high summer. He said Giuseppe would be much moved by his visit to Palma. Alas, you will not be able to see Lampedusa from there, I am afraid. Not even on the clearest of days. Is it true you have never been to the island, Excellency?

He confessed it was true.

Ah. They say it has its own monster.

Giuseppe raised his eyebrows in a smile. One that lives in Palermo, perhaps?

Francesco's stepfather gave him a quick surprised look and then after a moment he returned the smile. No. No, it is said in antiquity the Arab sailors would give Lampedusa a wide birth. No trader would stop there for safe harbour, even in a storm.

Tell me about the monster.

What would you like to know?

Giuseppe held out his empty hands. Everything.

His host studied the end of his cigar, he licked his lips. An Arab geographer, Ibn al'Assad, wrote about it in the tenth century, he said. Al'Assad did not give it a name. The creature was rumoured to live in a cave under the southern part of the island and stirred only when boats set anchor. Many-tentacled and sharp of tooth, no doubt.

Giuseppe followed the old newspaperman out to the kitchen garden where a large terracotta pot stood balanced on the low stone wall. In it were the small leaves of a Sicilian basil. He smoked and studied the stars while his host, in the peasant fashion, night-watered the basil's roots.

Now that I am old, said his host, I see that there is a sharp line drawn between youth and age. And that there can be no true understanding between the two. I have no complaints, you understand. Francesco is a good son.

He is.

Teresa I do not understand. She is very modern. She intends to go to Milan to work in a fashion house there. She broke off an engagement earlier this year. The boy, I understand, was not to blame.

Giuseppe, without children himself, was careful to say nothing.

I do believe Teresa will be a success if she can sort out what it is she wishes to do. His host paused. She seems rather fond of you.

Giuseppe glanced across. Of me?

That is what she said.

But I have hardly spoken to her.

His host appeared to consider this in the darkness. Perhaps that is what she appreciates, Don Giuseppe. I do not know. She has become a mystery to me.

Well.

I look at her and at Francesco now and I do not know anything of their lives, what they are thinking. Did our parents feel this way? Were we so inscrutable also? His host laughed. I sound old.

Giuseppe smiled.

Everything here is old, his host added. I am becoming a part of the scenery. In Palermo, Excellency, it is 1955. But there is no date in Agrigento, there is no year in Palma di Montechiaro. You will see. It is a world that has already passed elsewhere.

That is what I wish to see, said Giuseppe.

Later on the way to his room a shadow detached and came towards him and he saw it was the girl Teresa. She was dressed in an old-fashioned nightgown, high-necked, like something out of his own childhood. Giuseppe blushed. The girl's apartments were not in this wing of the villa; nor were anyone's but his own; and he could not imagine what she was doing in that hallway.

He stepped to one side to allow her to pass.

As she neared, she raised her face. Her bare feet were soundless on the flagstones. There was something in the way she tilted her chin, the way the shadows played against her skin, that confused him. He had experienced only two women in his life, both girls, both during his long youth before he had met his wife, one of them a prostitute. That encounter had been in a hotel in Brussels and had left him confused in the same way, had intensified his natural shyness so that he almost could not speak. He felt now, and not for the first time that evening, as if he had stepped out of his life, into an older and stranger Sicily.

Excellency, Teresa said softly.

He swallowed. She was still, he saw, wearing her makeup. She herself did not appear embarrassed. There was in her face, rather, something that looked like a question. Her blonde hair was loose at her shoulders and under her long lashes her dark eyes were liquid. She was very unlike Mirella, he thought. And then he imagined suddenly this girl's father coming upon them unannounced, that good man, and the awkward English comedy of it. Some unhappy expression must have played across his face, for Teresa only nodded and continued past, down the hall.

He watched her go. Because of the lights in the stairwell in front of her, the silhouette of her body was visible through her thin nightdress.

Sometime after midnight he woke with a heaviness at his chest, a tightening so that he gasped and could not breathe, and he swung his feet out onto the floor with the unmistakable feeling that he had forgotten something of importance. He waited for the pain to ease. He was suddenly afraid of his emphysema, which felt more real and close to him here, in this place. In the silver light he could smell the jasmine and lavender in the villa's gardens through the open window. The past seemed a great flowing passage through which his bloodline passed, back through the wastrel grandfathers and great-grandfathers, to the saints and holy men of the eighteenth century, to the legendary civic figures of the seventeenth and the royal granting of Lampedusa in 1667 and the first Tomasi's wedding to the heiress of Palma, and deeper, back up the coast to Naples, to Capua, and further back to Siena, and then into the fog of an almost time, to Lepanto or Cyprus or the age of Tiberius in Rome. And he understood his great regret: after him would come nothing. He had produced neither son nor daughter. He had failed them all.

He woke with the sun in his eyes. He breakfasted on the terrace in the sunlight, working quietly on the notes for his novel, writing down as clearly as he could what he had found the day before, Tancredi's desire for a new creature, Angelica he would call her, while Francesco's stepfather read the morning paper across from him. Neither man spoke and the near silence of pages turning and the nib scratching in the lattice shade seemed to Giuseppe both peaceful and fine. The night's pain receded. He allowed himself to forget his fear and his determination to follow Coniglio's advice and instead he lit a cigarette and left it smouldering at the edge of the ashtray. He ate only a roll of bread with butter. There were flies on the tablecloth. Francesco, Giò, and Teresa did not appear.

Ah, but they have already eaten, the stepfather said with a rueful smile. At least young Gioacchino and Teresita have. They are in the garden, waiting on you. I have not seen Francesco.

Giuseppe shrugged his shoulders as if to say, youth must always wait on age.

Perhaps mistaking his silence as an invitation, Francesco's stepfather cleared his throat and offered, I understand you have not been to Palma before, Excellency?

Giuseppe inclined his head. I do not often come south, no.

Ah. Well the archpriest will be very pleased to welcome you. I trust you have written ahead and let him know you will be coming?

He had not. It had not occurred to him. He wondered now if his arrival would cause much consternation in the cathedral where he was still, legally, patron and prince. But Francesco's stepfather assured him he would be well treated regardless and then he took off his spectacles and said, with a laugh, You are their prince, after all. It is not for you to put them at ease.

The morning brightened cloudless and very blue. The sun blazed down out of the ether as they drove along the coast, Giò again scrunched into the rear seats, Giuseppe again clutching his hat against the open window. Francesco drove with one knee propped high against his door and his right hand loose on the gearbox. Teresa had begged off despite Giò's urgings and said she could not, absolutely could not, take the day to go to Palma. A flash of her sharp white teeth, blonde hair drawn behind the shell of an ear, Francesco rubbing the headlights of his Sprint with a soft cloth in the courtyard beyond. What is in Palma, Giuseppe had heard her whisper as he passed them, except ruins? Everything there is so *old*.

Lanza, Francesco had been calling. Adventure awaits!

Ruins, yes, Giuseppe thought broodingly. They drove without speaking for a long while and then the castle of Montechiaro appeared, vanished, appeared again around the rocky hills. It had been erected by the Tomasi at the end of the seventeenth century high on a craggy outcropping above the sea, the town clustered five miles beyond. Francesco took his hand from the wheel to point and the car drifted onto the shoulder, corrected. Then they slowed and turned up a steep rocky drive, the tires crunching in the hot gravel. Giuseppe had brought his old-fashioned camera purchased in a small shop in London in 1927 and he got out of the low-slung automobile with its strap looped over his neck, its hard case heavy at his stomach.

Welcome home, Uncle, grinned Giò.

Even from the car he could see, feeling an unexpected relief, that the inside of the castle had long since fallen into ruin. It could not be salvaged; there would be no selling it off, piece by piece, to be made into apartments, as Licy had suggested. He left his jacket in the car. The stone was pale and they followed what seemed a thin sheep track up through the rocks to the tall angular walls. The sun was hot now. Giò and Francesco walked a few feet ahead, laughing softly, but Giuseppe paused at the lower wall and set a hand on its warm stones. He felt old. He turned and stared back at the silver coupe gleaming below, its driver-side door standing carelessly open. Then Francesco called for the camera and Giuseppe posed in his shirtsleeves with Giò under an arched doorway, squinting in the sunlight, while Francesco struggled to focus the lens and then he peered up at them and took their photograph.

Excellent, Francesco said, fiddling some more. We shall call it The Return of the Tomasi.

Like a novel by Thomas Hardy, Giò laughed.

Giuseppe looked at his young companion, smiled.

And just then Francesco took a second photograph.

Giuseppe left them then to wander the cliffside and he shuffled through the broken stones, looking for shade in the castle's interior.

Away from the youths, all was quiet. He found himself in a roofless passage open to the sky where the stone walls loomed high and narrow and ended in a set of carved steps that led to a terrace. He went back down and turned right into the crumbled rooms of the tower. Outside he could hear the slow roll of the surf far below but inside in the shade all was still, muffled, silent. A melancholy was rising in him and he was suddenly grateful to have lost sight of Francesco and Giò. Here his ancestors— saints and visionaries, sons and daughters—had renounced the world and scourged their flesh in the service of greatness. Three times in their known history the Tomasi had nearly died of extinction, had relied on the survival of a single child. Giuseppe shuffled slowly forward, sat heavily on a stone block inside the ruined gatehouse. The fourth wall was fallen in, the wooden beams of the ceiling sun-bleached and scattered like the bones of some strange beast. Three hundred years ago his family had become dukes of Palma. The second duke renounced the title for a life in the church; his brother converted their palace into a Benedictine convent and ordered the building of the town's cathedral. That duke's daughter, a visionary who suffered visitations from the devil, was venerated a century after her death. It did not matter that Giuseppe thought their faith misguided. He admired the scope of what they had achieved, the intensity of their relinquishing. The world in its vanity was as nothing. These names had been seared into his memory by his father and he thought now of him, of his mother, of that slow unhappy marriage. A grey lizard flickered under the sun-heated rocks and Giuseppe rose, made his way up through the ruins, walking carefully, looking for Giò. Above in the white sunlight half the roof had collapsed but a narrow crenellated walk remained and he paused there, thinking that perhaps here his ancient forefather might have paused too, considered the emptiness of sky and sea beyond. He pressed a palm to the warm stones and closed his eyes.

A soft wind was slicing through the long grasses among the rocks far below. A gull was crying over the drop. He could not see Giò or Francesco and he supposed they had returned to the car. Through the crumbling arch of a window the coins of the sea glittered. He squinted, shielded a hand at his eyes. Somewhere beyond in the blue haze of the horizon lay a blue island, an island of nothingness.

Lampedusa.

———

It was during those three days in San Pellegrino Terme that Giuseppe came to understand his cousin's ambition. They would drift from cocktail parties to luncheons to private forays in the steam baths among the literati where Lucio would tighten the towel at his waist and grin shyly then walk out among the others, his pale sagging torso embarrassing to behold, his tiny shoulders hunched up, his wrists and hands sun-browned as if they had been stained with tea. Did the younger writers smile to observe him? Giuseppe would watch his cousin lean in to speak with Montale in the late-afternoon light and when he could no longer bear it he would turn away with a worried air and seek some balcony or window unobstructed. Literature for him had always been charged with its own self-doubt, one novel inexorably questioning a predecessor, one writer's faith scraping away at another's. This was its truth. He had learned over a lifetime of reading that no word could be the only word and that art held value precisely because it answered nothing. All it could do was ask the old questions, over and over. What Virgil had feared, Eliot had feared. Homer's longing had been suffered by Stendhal. No book made any other less necessary. Yet the novelists he met or listened to at San Pellegrino Terme asked nothing and seemed to believe the modern novel superior to what had come before. And what had come before? he would silently ask their assembled backs. He was surprised to find himself neither impressed nor intimidated by such writers and he felt a melancholic anger come up in him at the thought of their books. He would listen as they discussed their successes or spoke bitingly of the successes of others but few condescended to meet the eye of a dilettante such as himself and none asked after him.

In the evenings as the northern sun slid beneath the mountains and the river was cast into darkness the weird quick bop of modern jazz would start up somewhere near and Lucio would emerge in his fussy suits, his privately printed collection of poems poking from one pocket. Yet each night he seemed more alive, more passionate, more confident in his own convictions than the last. Giuseppe watched his cousin's transformation and slowly came to see that writing would not be a way of knowing for Lucio but rather a way of being known and when he realized this he realized he did not want any part of it. What all of the writers at San Pellegrino craved was not the self-abnegation of true literature but the admiration of those who would read it. The crowds gathered, gesturing, smoking, they dissipated into the night. Giuseppe concealed his disgust under his shyness, and mumbled his regrets, and all the while a bitterness ate away at his heart.

Had there been unkindness in this, he wondered now. Perhaps his cousin had not deserved such censure, perhaps the modern writers at San Pellegrino Terme were not to be faulted. Had it been envy, nothing more? He did not like to think so but all summer as he had set down his pen and screwed the lid back onto his jar of ink and studied his hands he had seen the flesh of an old man, a failed man. Perhaps, he thought, art could not be created without the failings of its maker. Perhaps it was the very weakness of the writer that made the writing human, and therefore moving, and therefore worth preserving. He had understood for a long time that the world was greater by far than anything he could offer it, and that what he most longed for, the creation of something to outlive him, a testament in his own hand, would most likely fail in the end. But what he had not understood before was how the strain of the attempt constituted the greater labour.

Which, he supposed, as the evenings had lightened in the shutters of his study, was not so very different from the labour of living itself.

They left the castle driving slowly under a blue-black sky and stopped for a modest lunch on a hill below Palma. Francesco had packed a hamper of sausages and cold macaroni and bread but Giuseppe had little appetite and his thoughts strayed back to the crumbling castle behind them. After eating they made their way up towards the ancient piazza of Palma but the cobblestones were bad and the winding streets very narrow and Francesco had to park some distance away. Then out of the silence they heard the clicking of horseshoes and a solitary cart came around the corner, drawn by a skeletal nag. The driver, an old peasant in a grey hat, offered them a ride. And so they passed into the deserted streets of old Palma in the heat, seeming to Giuseppe as if they had entered, at last, the world of his grandfathers. As they made their way he glimpsed, between the houses and as they creaked through the little squares, the blue sea far below. He stared down from the bench of the cart at the crescent of a beach and a lone bather walking in the surf wearing a yellow hat and after a time they reached the piazza and the vast steps that led up to the cathedral. The driver bid them farewell with a raised hand and continued out of the dream.

Although the doors of the cathedral stood open onto the

white heat of the afternoon the air hung thick and hazy around the lintel and when they walked beneath it the air turned cool and sombre and strange. Giuseppe set out a hand and held himself for a moment leaning into the stone wall below an ancient torch bracket and it seemed to him that the years were seeping away into the shadows and that he stood as a Tomasi among the foundations of the Tomasi. Here his line had distinguished itself. Here the Tomasi name had been forged in blood and faith and suffering.

Inside all was brightness and calm and hues of white and pale blue and green. The pillars had been painted to look like red marble. The cathedral was not large by Palermitan standards but handsomely proportioned all the same and they made their way up through the central aisle in silence admiring the workmanship of the stucco above. There were scenes from the life of Christ painted into the vaulted ceiling. An iron railing separated the altar and he peered through. In an enclosure to one side he could see the Tomasi family box, the seats individuated and ornate and ancient. Above the altar hung a painting of the infant Christ on Mary's knee, Giuseppe's ancestor the saint-duke kneeling in holy robes at her feet, his eyes upturned in ecstasy. The altar was covered in a white sheet and an empty silver platter shone at its centre where light from the clerestory windows fell. Their footsteps were loud in the silence, echoing up off the choir and into the brilliance. No one spoke.

Only gradually did Giuseppe become aware of being observed. He turned in place and raised his eyes to the organist's balcony but could see no one. He glanced behind him, and still he saw no one. But the feeling did not leave him.

Then he saw, standing in shadow in a side-chapel, two men, both wearing suits buttoned fast against the heat and both watching Giuseppe in silence.

When their eyes met his they stepped fluidly forth, as one, and approached. They were the archpriest, a tall thin man, white-haired, spectacled, with enormous ears standing out like saucers, and his companion, a notary, dressed in a black suit and wearing menacing black leather gloves. The notary's eyes were shadowed by thick black eyebrows and his wispy hair was combed across the pink of his scalp.

How can I help you? the archpriest asked. The notary at his side watched.

Forgive us for intruding, Giuseppe began.

It is no intrusion, the archpriest replied with a grim promptness. You are visitors to Palma di Montechiaro?

Giò came up to join them. This is Giuseppe Tomasi di Lampedusa, Father, he said. He has come to visit the Tomasi patronages.

The transformation in the two men was instantaneous. The archpriest raised his face and studied Giuseppe's features intensely, colour rising to his cheeks, and then he took off his spectacles and bowed. You are most welcome, Excellency, he said. Forgive me for not recognizing you. You bear a resemblance.

Giuseppe glanced across at Francesco, puzzled.

To the portraits, the archpriest added, seeing his confusion. Please, won't you come through? And he reached down and unlocked a small hinge in the iron gate and a piece of the wooden railing swung inward. Can I offer you and your companions some refreshment?

It was here, at last, and with an embarrassed frown, that the archpriest introduced himself and his companion. The notary, by contrast, had said nothing and he did not move. He studied Giuseppe in silence, his pale lips drawn thin. Giuseppe did not mind; he was accustomed to men pausing and reconsidering him after learning of his station in life. For many years it had seemed natural and right, and although he had come to distrust it in the years since the war and since his mother's death, a very old and deep recess in his heart also recognized it as his due.

But the notary did not linger. He excused himself with a bow to Giuseppe and a murmured word to the archpriest and then he strode darkly down the aisle of the cathedral and out into the sunlight, his black gloved hands hanging at his sides as he went.

The archpriest led them past the altar and through a cloaked doorway, inquiring politely as to their purpose and discussing some of the worthier sights within a day's drive. He was a man older than his energies allowed and spoke with a Neapolitan accent but he seemed utterly of this place. He pointed out the fine architectural underpinnings of the cathedral and spoke at length of its construction and told of a fire that broke out in the very month of Napoleon's defeat at Waterloo and how it had seemed, to the congregation, a sign. When Giò and Francesco stopped before a curious fresco of Saint Ignatius reading from a closed book the archpriest turned to Giuseppe and said, quietly, I hope you will forgive my companion. He suffered a terrible accident as a boy. That is why he wears the gloves. He has a hole in each hand from when a building collapsed on him during an earthquake. His parents were killed, his brothers. When he was dug out of the rubble they found him pierced by iron rods through each hand, his arms outspread, as if he had been crucified. The archpriest glanced at Giuseppe's face to gauge the effect of his words.

I see, said Giuseppe softly.

The people of this town have a simple faith, Excellency. They see his wounds and wish to be near them, they wish to touch them. They see a miracle.

But he does not.

For him, it is a mark of his suffering, nothing more. He does not accept that all suffering is holy.

In the sacristy they were offered iced lemon juice and sat and drank and wiped their dusty hands on their trousers. The archpriest spoke about the American movies he had seen and soon he and Giò and Francesco were quoting lines back and forth. Giuseppe crossed his legs, he let his gaze drift around the room at the oiled bookcases and the portraits of his Tomasi ancestors on the walls. The largest portrait, above the archpriest's black desk, was of Giulio, the saint-duke, founder of Palma and of the cathedral. Giuseppe studied his forefather in his ancient dignity, the angry eyes, the elaborate martial dress. He had been a great man and a man with a fiery purpose and one who had lived in the full light of a savage god. It was to this he had devoted his fortune and retired from the world, exhausted. His daughter Isabella, brilliant, implacable, learned, had enclosed herself in her father's convent when she came of age and was declared a saint within three generations. What was he, Giuseppe Tomasi, last of the Lampedusa princes, in comparison? No madness moved in him. He rose to his feet, feeling all at once drained.

Gentlemen, he said.

As they were leaving, the archpriest asked if they had yet stopped in at the convent.

Giuseppe searched the ancient priest's face. I beg your pardon?

Of course, you might have pressing business elsewhere, the priest continued. But I am certain the blessed Lady Abbess Maria will be most disappointed to have missed you, Excellency.

It is a Benedictine convent, Father, Giò interjected. Surely men are not allowed inside?

The archpriest did not take his eyes from Giuseppe's face when he replied, It is a strict enclosure, yes. But you are our prince and patron, Excellency. You are permitted to enter, along with two gentlemen from your suite, should you so wish. It has always been so. For you, and for the King of Naples.

The King of Naples, Francesco said, grinning at Giò.

The archpriest did not seem to hear the amusement in Francesco's tone, at the privileges of a king who had ceased to exist, and again Giuseppe had the eerie sensation of having stepped through into an earlier century, an era before the roar and smoke of the modern. Above him the cathedral loomed, deep and shadowy and vast. Giuseppe bowed.

Then I cannot refuse, he said simply.

That day, as he stepped back out into the white afternoon heat, and all through the weeks that were to follow, he thought of that notary with his soft black gloves, and an unsettling silence seemed to trail behind the memory, like a wisp in the air. That notary had reminded him of something he had imagined gone, had brought it back to him with a sudden clarity. As a boy the notary had been dug out of the earth, the archpriest had said, one of the lost ones reclaimed. *He does not accept that all suffering is holy*, the archpriest had explained in satisfaction, as if composing a sermon. It was not the possibility of the priest's truth that troubled Giuseppe, not the knowledge of the martyred and the saved. What he had not said in reply was that he too had known people swallowed by the earth, and there had been no design in it, no glimpse of God's hand at work, only sorrow.

Of his mother's three momentous griefs, her sister Lina's death, in the earthquake at Messina, was the first, and marked the beginning of the change that came over her. That was in December of 1908. Giuseppe had only just turned twelve. After Messina, his mother drew back into herself, and the wildness that was in her turned inward and began to eat away at itself, like a sickness. She would lie for days in the green drawing room, the curtains closed and still, a damp cloth draped over her face. His father would sigh and shake his head and drift from room to room like a man with a purpose but even as a boy Giuseppe had understood there was no purpose, the restlessness was its own reason. Some mornings he would find his mother seated in the little upstairs library, staring at the old leather volumes, wearing the clothes she had been wearing the night before. Because he was a child still, and did not understand what was happening inside her, what he remembered most vividly was the deep strangling fear that started to come over him in the night, so that he would cry out, and his French governess would come running in her nightgown with a candle. His mother had always been one who seemed to live above the turmoil and confusion that he himself, a plump shy silent child, felt whenever they went out into the world. Her name was Beatrice, like Dante's angel: Beatrice Mastrogiovanni Tasca Filangeri di Cutò.

All his childhood, Giuseppe had repeated that name like a magical ward, feeling dizzy at the thought that she had made him, that he was a part of her. He would watch her move with the grace and magnificence of a lynx, padding through the sunlit halls of the palazzo, her long pale throat extended, her dark hair up, a creature admired, adored in the light that he, her son, would shine upon her. She would lift the little songbirds out of their elaborate cages and hold them on her outstretched fingers and they would sing for her.

She was the eldest of the five beautiful and unconventional Cutò daughters, and throughout her youth she had welcomed controversy and rumour, had provoked it with her fashionable clothes and French opinions and Continental conversation. She could be bitterly sarcastic, domineering, stubborn, charming. Her dance card was always full. As a boy he had not understood that powerful men desired her, and were frightened by her, and that their very fear fascinated them. All his childhood he would lean sleepily against the balcony railings at midnight balls watching her glide across the polished floors below, seeing the other couples part and bend like long grasses as she passed. He liked to remember her seated in the soft red felt seats of the new Excelsior cinema in the Palazzo Rudinì, at the beginning of the century, how the wide folds of her dresses overflowed the seats. And sometimes still at night when he passed a brightly lit gelateria, he would see in his mind's eye his mother, leaning out of a carriage laughing, a small ice cream spoon in her gloved fingers.

But the death of Lina ended all of that. A watchfulness came over her, a slow undercurrent of sadness, so that even when laughing or dancing with some prince or another there was always a stillness at her centre, like a kind of strength, but it was not strength, he knew. The grief of her sister's death lined her eyes like kohl, shadowed her lips, and did not fade with time.

That grey winter morning when word of the tragedy reached Palermo, he had gone downstairs at his usual hour and found the grandfather clock on the landing stopped. His uncle Ferdinando, his father's younger brother, was seated in the breakfast room with the city newspaper pulled apart into sections and the sheets laid carefully around him. There had been an earthquake in Messina in the night, his uncle explained.

Your aunt and uncle, and your little cousin, Ferdinando said. We have not heard anything yet.

All that day he lurked at the windows watching the winter rains but he did not see his mother or father. He was told his mother was at the Florios' villa, seeking news, he was told his father was at the post office. The house was gloomy in the afternoon shadows, and cold, and the servants had forgotten to light the lamps. Seventy-seven thousand people died in the destruction. The grand churches held vigils, the city papers interviewed politicians, professors, survivors. Word of his aunt's death did not reach Palermo for eleven days. By then his aunt Teresa had arrived from Capo d'Orlando in despair and gone back again, and his aunt Giulia had telephoned the Florios twice from Rome for news.

Lina had died under the rubble of her magnificent villa,

with her husband at her side. The walls and roof had collapsed like a hand closing upon itself. Their bodies were recovered whole, unbroken, and from this it was understood they had not been crushed in the collapse but rather had starved slowly in the days that followed.

Giuseppe's mother started to shake when his father brought her into his study and told her the news. She had demanded the details in their entirety. Then, white-faced, stiff, she had walked very deliberately towards a chair in the corner and sat down and closed her eyes and started to scream.

All week a cold rain fell. She did not speak, did not look at Giuseppe, did not touch him. He would go to her where she sat, listless, silhouetted against the rainswept windows, or he would peer at her from the doorway, afraid to interrupt but wanting to be near. Only once during those days did she glance up, and see him. Something passed across her face then, a kind of recognition, and she held out her arms, and he went to her, feeling somehow forgiven, as if he had done something, and he felt her start to cry and he cried too.

That was the day there came a knock at their door, and his governess led into the drawing room a dark-eyed boy whom Giuseppe almost recognized. Water dripped from his oiled cloak, his hair was matted and wet, he stood with a small suitcase at his feet, and Giuseppe and his mother and his father stared at him. The house felt very quiet. His father got to his feet. Giuseppe looked at his mother and saw she had gone stiff in her black dress, and was staring with a hostile expression on her face, her fingers interlaced whitely at her lips. Then she rose from her seat and left the room.

That bedraggled creature was his six-year-old cousin, Filippo.
Lina's boy.

He was only just twelve, he would remind himself years later,
a sheltered child, shy. But he could not imagine the destruction
of his own house and so he wondered what Filippo Cianciafara
had done to deserve it. His mother would not look at his little
cousin, would not speak to him, angry and withdrawn as if his
presence in her house were an affront. Filippo himself hardly
spoke, and then only in a whisper, and his calm face never
betrayed any sadness. It is the shock, said his father. I expect the
poor boy will feel it soon enough, said his uncle. Giuseppe
heard all this and watched his mother's moods and he resolved
to close the lid of his heart.

Filippo had been dug out of the rubble on the third day,
white with dust, shaking with the chill, thirsty, like one of the
dead brought back to life. This Giuseppe was told by his governess in a hushed voice, her French accent colouring the
words. He peered at his cousin suspiciously after that. It was as
if he observed a ghost. But some part of him understood that
nothing was more living than Filippo's silences, and that the
breath in the little boy's lungs was the true affront.

Because his mother was cruel towards Filippo, he too was
cruel. It saddened him now, forty years later, to think of the
kindnesses he did not extend. His cousin's presence seemed to
embarrass his father and uncle. Only his governess, Anna, was
moved to pity the boy, who would sit alone for long periods of
the day, silent, or be called sharply into the gold drawing room

to accept condolences from some visitor or relation he had surely never met. Anna insisted Giuseppe join him, play with him, draw him out of his loneliness.

But he is so little, Giuseppe complained.

So are you, she replied.

He doesn't even speak, he said. He just sits there. He doesn't want to do anything.

One afternoon he came across his cousin in the upstairs library with a book open in his lap. When Giuseppe came in the boy wiped his eyes quickly with the sleeve of his shirt, stared intently down at the book.

Giuseppe frowned. You are just pretending to read, he said.

I am not, said Filippo.

He took the book from his cousin, which was upside down, and turned it, and gave it back.

Liar, he said.

On another occasion Anna saw Filippo in the courtyard below, his coat buttoned up against the cold, his red knuckles bare, staring at the white gravel near his boots. She opened the window. Filippo! she called. You will catch your death! Come inside, Giuseppe has something to show you.

The little boy stared up at them in the window as if he did not know them, and then slowly he trudged inside.

But I don't have anything to show him, said Giuseppe.

Anna smoothed her dress with both hands, her small freckled nose wrinkled. She did this, he knew, when she was irritated. She said, Take him to the nursery. Show him your old toys.

In the nursery Giuseppe glared at his cousin resentfully, opened the lid of his old toy chest and rummaged through it.

He took out only the broken toys. He handed across a painted white horse on a string, a toy soldier without a head.

This is broken, said Filippo.

So? said Giuseppe.

And so is this one.

You have to play with it. Anna says you have to.

And he folded his arms and watched as his little cousin turned the headless soldier in his fingers and then, slowly, sadly, he began to make the three-legged horse gallop across the carpet.

A month passed. One morning he came down to breakfast to find Filippo's chair empty, his place not set. The carriage had been taken out in the pouring rain and had not returned: Filippo had been sent to his little cousins Lucio and Casimiro at Capo d'Orlando.

It was strange, he reflected now, forty years later. He had treated Filippo with such contempt. And yet all that month when his cousin had been living with them at Casa Lampedusa he had felt no particular dislike or anger towards the boy. And after he was sent away, Giuseppe had felt no shame. He had thought only of his mother's sadness; Filippo disappeared from his thoughts completely, as if he had never come to stay with them at all. At the very end of his life, what he would recall most vividly of that time was, instead, his mother's uncontrolled grief in that first week in December, her beautiful unbrushed hair wild at her shoulders, her great breathless racking sobs, and how she had sat crumpled in a big armchair in the green drawing room where no one ever went.

———

He descended the ancient steps of the cathedral in Palma, starting his slow way downhill towards the convent. He was worried Giò and Francesco would lack the necessary respect-fulness inside. But a quick glance at their faces showed both of them lost in thought, Giò's eyes studying without seeing the wide dusty steps back down to the piazza. Francesco adjusted his collar, took off his hat, ran a hand through his black hair. Neither spoke. He was satisfied.

They turned left along the street and walked slowly, Giuseppe keeping to the line of shadow under the crumbling buildings. When at last they reached the piazza and the convent looming over it and climbed its steps, the immaculate white stone shining in the sunlight, they encountered again a sudden gloom that blinded them and made them pause at the threshold and peer in.

They found themselves in a small spare reception chamber. A raftered ceiling was centred on the ancient Tomasi crest of the leopard and there were wooden benches along the two empty walls. The third wall was built of varnished wood and a thick door stood fast and beside this were two double gratings for interviews. A little wooden wheel built into the wall allowed, Giuseppe imagined, messages to be exchanged. He stood leaning into his walking stick, uncertain, shy, as Giò stepped forward and smoothly approached the grate closest to the door and pulled a bell rope. A deep clangour rose up from somewhere beyond and they waited a long time until at last a silhouette appeared behind the grating. Giuseppe could not make out a face. An old woman's voice asked, reedily, How can we help you, young man?

After Giò had explained their purpose the nun excused her-self and they waited again, longer. A fly had come in through the open door and was buzzing the still air. Francesco peered uneasily at the walls and then he leaned in and whispered, They are watching us, Don Giuseppe. Do not think we are unobserved here.

Giuseppe was silent. He was beginning to fear it had been unwise, uncivil, to stop in unannounced. The fly swooped and buzzed.

Shortly they could hear the heavy inner door unlocking, and then with a tremendous weight it swung inward. A tiny woman—the abbess, he supposed—stood with her hands clasped before her, regarding them quietly. All three visitors got to their feet. And then, to Giuseppe's amazement, she smiled a smile of extraordinary gentle joy.

She was pretty. Giuseppe had not been expecting that. It seemed a strange quality to notice in a nun and he observed it without passion but then he thought perhaps the serenity and dignity in her distinguished her beyond it. Her eyes were green and catlike and her eyebrows were so pale as to look hairless. Her habit was an inky black, the linen wimple starched to a startling white. She looked, he thought, like a Byzantine saint. A small black mole was visible on her upper lip.

Giuseppe Tomasi di Lampedusa, at your service, he said softly. It is a privilege to be admitted here, Lady Abbess. We are grateful.

She held out her hand. It was small, and cool, its skin unusually smooth for her age. He held it a moment too long, and then flushed.

She said, happily, I am Maria Enrichetta Fanara, your Excellency. And the privilege is our own.

He stepped back. My young companion, Gioacchino Lanza. And this is Baron Francesco Agnello, of Siculiana.

She smiled but did not offer her hand again.

You must come inside, please, she said, and gestured them through into the adjacent courtyard. A statue of the virgin holding the infant Christ, a fountain dripping water, green shrubs in terracotta pots and the blue sky dizzying overhead. The door closed and locked behind them.

We have not been graced with a Tomasi for many, many years, the abbess went on. Not in all my time here.

But that cannot have been so very long, said Giò.

At that the lady abbess arched her hairless eyebrows. It is no great flattery, young Lanza, to suggest I am younger than I am. We are not vain here. Our years mark our devotion. We do not desire youth.

Giò, to Giuseppe's relief, nodded at her rebuke and said only, Forgive me, Abbess Maria. I did not mean to offend.

She was already smiling again. She led them to the right into a small office, the wooden rafters again centring on the Tomasi crest above, the whitewashed walls sparse but for a small crucifix next to a window. Through a curtain a long flagstoned corridor stretched away. There were several chairs arranged around a low table and on the table was an ancient silver tray, polished to a shine, and arrayed on a plate Giuseppe saw a pillar of almond cakes surrounded by sprigs of jasmine. A pitcher of cold water gleamed. It all looked carefully assembled despite its haste and he imagined the room must usually have stood vacant.

I hope you have gone to no trouble, Lady Abbess, he began.

But she would have none of it. It is exactly right that we do so, your Excellency. Please, I hope you will taste the cakes. They are baked by the acolytes. It would honour our house.

They are delicious, Giò said, his mouth half-full.

Giuseppe took one, hesitantly. A soft rich scent of almonds and sugar filled his nostrils and he was taken for a moment back to the childhood gardens of Santa Margherita di Belice, the shady palm trees, the white gravel pathways, the elegant wrought-iron chairs and the pastries arranged on a white tablecloth. He felt himself overwhelmed and made as if to study the crucifix on the wall with his hands clasped at his back.

After a time they were invited to tour the cloisters. They passed through a door crowned with ancient mouldings into a wide room, lined with windows, that must once have been the palace reception room. It stood now with a tidy desk in each corner, and potted ferns along the walls under the windows, and a tall elaborate wire birdcage in the shape of the Parliament in Rome. All was light, the floor a polished gold parquet. At its centre lay the Tomasi crest.

The lady abbess withdrew from her habit a tiny silver bell and she rang it before leading them through the far doors.

It is to warn the nuns that men approach, she said. Some of them are strictly isolated.

I hope we are not causing you much inconvenience, Giuseppe offered again.

She reached up and this time touched his arm, gently, but did not stop walking.

They proceeded down a long corridor, lined with small cells, and stopped at one that the lady abbess explained was not presently in use. She told them that there were fewer novices now after the war and that the convent was aging gradually but definitively. Soon there will be few of us left, she said. After that there will be only one. I am glad I shall not be the last.

They admired the sparseness of the cell, its austerity, the clean small cot, its stripped mattress turned sideways and leaned against the wall, the narrow wardrobe standing with its wings open.

Then they proceeded on. The lady abbess rang her bell and led them through the empty kitchens, a pot of tomatoes sitting half-washed in a sink, an eggplant half-sliced and the knife set down, all of it eerie and abandoned and the doors at the far end half-open as if the novices huddled beyond, peering out. They were led through the dining room with its long slabbed tables in rows of three and down a second corridor of cells, the doors closed on each. As they went the lady abbess spoke to Giuseppe about the Tomasi, about Giulio who had granted the Benedictines his palace long centuries before, about his daughter who entered the convent at the age of seventeen and who fought the devil with a fury worthy of her faith. Giuseppe had been raised on stories of Isabella Tomasi, his father relating them with a wryness that betrayed his genuine pride. She inspires us even yet, the lady abbess was saying. When I came here as a girl, there was an older sister in residence who dreamed of Prince Giulio's daughter sometimes. Some of the novices believed her mad. But the abbess at the time warned us that the spirit in the flesh can look like madness. That chastened us. She reminded us to withhold our judgment. It is not our place, she said. The good Tomasi understood that, if nothing else.

Giuseppe cleared his throat. You honour us, he said politely.

The Tomasi were intrinsically different, Excellency, she said. Like very great artists. I do not think they wished to be so, but they accepted their nature with courage. How can one not admire that?

He met her eye. I fear they would weep to see what has become of us, he replied.

The lady abbess regarded him quizzically but did not ask and he did not elaborate and instead he looked away.

And the good Isabella's cell? he said. Has it been preserved?

Isabella? Ah, Isabella. Yes. She is Isabella only to outsiders, Excellency. Here she is our Venerable Maria Crocifissa. Please, this way. Gentlemen, please. She glided silently forward and explained to them as they went that the saint's cell was used even today by acolytes. But she knew for a fact that the nun who occupied it was presently in the garden weeding and that they would not be disturbing anyone. As they went down the long corridor she rang the silver bell and Giuseppe heard the quiet clicking of doors shutting ahead of them. They saw no one but he felt eyes upon him at each step and yet there seemed nothing uneasy in it, nothing to make him anxious.

Isabella's cell was no different than the first cell the lady abbess had showed them. Narrow, bare, a single immaculate cot against one wall, a wooden dresser, the ancient wardrobe closed. Through the small window Giuseppe watched high wisps of cloud scud past in the blue. When Francesco and Giò pressed in, the space felt cramped and impossibly small.

There was one difference. Framed on the wall to the side of the door were two yellowed letters, in different spidery scripts. Giuseppe leaned in, he fumbled for his spectacles. He could not read the writing in one. Some sort of strange Cyrillic. The first paper, the abbess explained, was a letter from Isabella to the devil, exhorting him to give up his ungodly ways and come to her and walk in the light of the true faith.

And the second? Francesco asked.

That is the devil's reply, she said. No one has been able to read it. It is not written in a language known to man.

Giuseppe paused, studying the abbess, trying to determine how much she believed in such relics. She regarded the three of them serenely and betrayed nothing.

It was in the convent garden, she said, that the Venerable Maria Crocifissa was attacked by the devil. He hurled a large stone at her, hoping to strike her down. Her simplicity and faith offended him. But the stone was suspended in the air by Saint Michael and she stood her ground, unharmed.

I understand she was afflicted with visions from a young age, Giuseppe said.

Yes.

My grandfather would speak of her. He said, according to the family stories, the only game she would play as a child was pretending to be a nun.

She was touched by God at a young age, yes.

Touched?

Blessed.

Blessed, Giuseppe murmured. He removed his spectacles, blinked.

The blessings of the Lord are not to be envied, Excellency, she said and nodded as if recognizing something in him. It is a painful and lonely existence, here on earth, surrounded by all that is mortal, having felt something far greater. It is a deprivation.

In a small corner of the cell, under a glass, lay a fury's-head whip, its seven knotted lashes looking vicious even now. Francesco and Giò were studying it in silence.

As I said, the lady abbess said. A painful and lonely existence.

The poor girl, said Giò.

You do not still use such instruments? Francesco asked.

Not as you mean it.

Francesco raised his eyebrows in a question, waited.

All of living is a mortification of the flesh, she said simply. That is what it is to be alive. Our bodies are slowly giving way to the spirit. We are on earth only a short time. It is different for each of us. But that is how long we have to come to an understanding.

I fear, Giuseppe said, feeling a heaviness at his heart, that there can be no understanding for some of us.

She looked at him with great pity and he saw in it, to his surprise, a kind of love. You must have faith, Excellency, she said gently, and it might have been only the two of them in that cell, only the two of them in the convent entire. All else gradually gave way. He had almost forgotten his emphysema but it returned to him now forcefully and he wanted very much to sit down but he did not do so. He thought of his mother and how she would have been interested in these women, in this ancient seat. His mother with her stern shoulders and graceful swan's neck, whose passion for living had frightened him into shyness as a child, who had fought bitterly against her own death, hating the ugliness of growing old. Giuseppe stared now at the small surprised beauty of the lady abbess and he swallowed painfully. There was in her something absolutely unlike himself. Seeing her, he thought it might almost be possible to live unafraid of death, to live even now ready for change, whenever it should come, in whatever form, as he knew it must.

The sunlight filtered in, illuminating his grey knuckles, his grey wrists. He could hear the four of them breathing in the stillness, like ghosts.

THE TROUBLES OF
DON GIUSEPPE,
PART ONE

=====

MARCH 1911

He was fourteen years old, a child still, when the telegram with its black border arrived at the palazzo. He would remember standing on the grand staircase in the afternoon sunlight, listening as his father read out its contents in a shaking voice. His aunt Giulia, his mother's favourite sister, had been stabbed in the spine and then twice in the throat by a cavalry officer in Rome. She was dead. Her seducer, a baron, had then calmly drawn the hotel curtains against the grey light and sat at a dressing table and taken out his revolver and shot himself through the head.

All this had happened, it seemed, in a shabby neighbourhood near Roma Termini station on a morning of rain. In Palermo, Giulia's husband collapsed in the street at the news. The murderer's name was Vincenzo Paternò del Cugno, and Giuseppe, hearing it said, whispered the sinister syllables over and over, like an incantation. His aunt had met with the baron that day, it was given to understand, in order to break relations.

The seduction had begun at a summer ball in Palermo two years earlier. Giulia, pretty, almond-eyed, with delicate wrists and a slow sad smile, had been sent an unsigned letter that season warning that her husband was conducting an affair with an actress from the Scarpetta company. That letter, his mother had come to believe, was sent by Paternò del Cugno himself. Giulia was a friend of the young Queen Elena in Rome and a lady-in-waiting at court and had no one to ask for advice in affairs of the heart, and when she next saw the baron he sat with her half the night with his white gloves in his lap, drawing out her sorrows, blue-eyed, a gentleman. All this Giuseppe heard as he haunted the palazzo in those first days. He learned that he could sit quietly with a book open in his hands, the pages creaking as he turned them, and his governess would forget his presence, the servants would whisper openly, his parents would not see him at all. For his mother did not lower her voice nor care who might overhear her in her grief.

Oh reckless, reckless, his mother would weep. How could you not have known what he was, Giulia? We knew it. All of Palermo knew it. Oh Giulia, Giulia.

While Giuseppe, soft, pale, his eyes bulging, sat quietly on the second stair, and breathed.

His aunt was thirty-three years old, the baron thirty-one. Paternò del Cugno's passion had frightened her. How many times did they meet? What had entered her heart and passed from it? The baron hunted her through the spa towns of the Hapsburg Empire, begging first for one more night alone, then pleading for his gambling debts, then demanding money, threatening her with exposure. A violent man by nature, a man drawn to fast horses and fashionable salons, when his behaviour turned erratic Giulia understood he would not relent. Upon her return to Sicily, weeping, she told her sister the details and Beatrice went that very night to Giuseppe's father to beg him to intervene but the baron merely challenged the aging prince to a duel. Giuseppe's father had laughed angrily, telling it in front of the drawing room fire. The next day Beatrice had begged Ignazio Florio to confront the baron but even that man's power and wealth could not turn the baron from his course.

In the end, delicately, through connections at the Ministry of Foreign Affairs, a transfer had been arranged. The baron had, simply, been sent away. His letters from his new posting in Naples were returned unopened. His requests for leave were denied. Winter descended, like a shame, and with it came silence.

Then, two months later, the baron left his barracks in Naples for an overnight express to Rome. He carried no luggage, only a packet of Giulia's letters tied with a red ribbon in one pocket, and a loaded revolver in the other.

All of Sicily, it seemed, was outraged by the killing. The corruption of Giulia Trigona was the talk of the spring. When her body was returned to Palermo, the train stopped, in Messina, in Cefalù, at Bagheria, and was met always at the stations by weeping crowds and city mayors and ancient councilmen beribboned in black shaking their fists into microphones. His mother could not ride out in her carriage without onlookers staring in the street, removing their hats. One rainy afternoon Giuseppe discovered, in an unlocked drawer in his father's study, a drawing of the baron from the newspapers. Handsome, black-haired, black-eyed, with a sharp nose and cruel eyebrows and a full sensuous mouth. He looked, Giuseppe had thought then, like a man ruled by his passions.

His mother changed then, after Giulia's killing. A light had been extinguished in her, though it would take him a lifetime to see it. It had been two years since the loss of his aunt Lina and his mother had carried that grief with difficulty. They had been five sisters; then, grieving monstrously, four. Now, still beautiful, somehow they were only three, and the shock of this new death tore through his mother, left her reeling, overwhelmed by a fury she had not thought would rise up in her again.

She raged at first, wept, stalked the rooms of the palazzo. But gradually all that faded as she retreated into herself. She declined invitations, refused visiting cards. Drew the curtains and sat in dim seclusion, brooding. She would not allow herself to be seen, even by her sister Teresa, even by Don Florio, who called her Beatrice when he thought they were alone. Then, in the late spring, when cholera erupted in Palermo, she fled. She took Giuseppe north, into Tuscany, and later, without informing anyone, she left Italy with her son in tow to visit a sculptor she had known in her youth. That man was Spanish but he lived in those days in the south of France, in a crumbling villa in Languedoc, above a river stocked with eels and a stone windmill and sloping fields of yellow and blue flowers.

Giuseppe's father did not write. Giuseppe did not know if his parents had loved each other but he supposed it must have been so, once.

The sculptor, whose name was Ferri, drove a straw-filled mule cart into town to greet them at the platform. He was in shirtsleeves and a corduroy waistcoat, chewing at a pipe like a peasant.

Ferri's grandfather fought with Napoleon in Spain, his mother whispered. But his mother was a countess.

What do I call him? asked Giuseppe.

You call him Ferri, she said. Like everyone else.

Ferri was a giant of a man, with a thick white beard and green eyes and huge hands red with brickdust and heavy as stones. He was much older than Giuseppe had imagined him to be. Ah, Princess, he said, and his voice was like the rumble of a wagon on flagstones. So you have come to Languedoc at last.

Ferri, she replied.

He knotted his eyebrows together, suddenly overcome. And then he stepped forward and bent down and folded her into his arms and he held her a long impossible moment as if she were a child and Giuseppe stood by, his travelling case at his feet, the porter with their luggage peering slyly from the side of one eye.

And this will be Giuseppe, Ferri said at last, releasing his mother. What a handsome boy. You have both been through so much.

She shook her head. I did not think you would have heard.

The whole world weeps for her, said Ferri gravely. And then he took Giuseppe's case in his big hand and steered the boy towards the cart. We will not talk of it, he said. Not this day. Here, is life. Come, he said in a booming voice to the porter. And then, to Giuseppe: I will show you my trifles and you will tell me if they are worthless or not, yes?

They rode slowly through the countryside while the shadows grew long around them. Ferri spoke softly and slowly and his mother rode beside him with her head leaning into his shoulder and Giuseppe, unhappy, looked away.

In a barn below the villa he walked among Ferri's sculptures, as if among strange iron trees, studying the twisted figures where they kneeled or leaned impossibly as if into a strong wind, faceless, oversized. There were small angular faces carved out of stone, also, scattered on the floor, and a long plank desk under a window covered with drawings and sketches. In the mornings Giuseppe walked the rocky soil thinking of the Cathars and the crusader knights who had fought there centuries ago. He had not known the south of France before and he found its sun in June milder than Sicily's. Sometimes he would lie in the tall grasses reading while the insects clicked and buzzed around him. Mostly he waited, watching his mother. Her sadness seemed to settle around her shoulders like a shawl, and this she wore through the rooms of Ferri's villa and out onto his patio in the evenings with a new kind of grace. She seemed, for the first time in Giuseppe's young life, older. Each morning Ferri himself would vanish into his studio below the villa and there hammer away at his sculptures through the middle of the day and emerge calmly, rumpled, his beard streaked with dust, into the late-afternoon heat.

You are happy here, his mother said to her old friend one night as they sat out under the stars. The waxing moon a thin crescent high in the west, a warm still air around them.

Giuseppe raised his face, sleepy.

I am happy in my work, said Ferri. I lose myself in it. That is enough.

Nothing is enough for me, she said softly.

It is true, said Ferri.

Giuseppe closed his eyes where he lay on the granite bench, the day's heat still in the stone.

I do not think I will know happiness again, his mother said. Then she laughed sharply. Listen to me. I sound ridiculous.

You do not.

I do. I have become a figure of ridicule.

Ferri was quiet in the darkness.

But I have missed your friendship, she said. I do not have many friends in Palermo.

You are admired by everyone, Beatrice.

It is not the same. You know it is not.

You have Teresa. She will be suffering too.

Yes. And Maria.

How is she?

Still unmarried.

Ferri gave a low laugh, then stopped. We must be quieter. Your boy is sleeping.

That is not sleeping, said his mother. He heard a rustle of clothes and then felt her sit beside him on the bench, run her fingers through his hair. She said: Giuseppe listens to everything we say. Don't you, my sweet?

While he crushed his eyes shut and lay very still with the force of his pretending.

One morning in July Ferri took them high into the dry mountains to the east, to a cliff overlooking his villa, where there loomed the black ruins of a Cathar fortress. It had been besieged in the fourteenth century and put to the torch and all of its heretics slaughtered and now nothing stood but tumbled blocks of stone in the long grass, a curved half-wall of a turret at the edge of the drop. He lay out a blanket in the shade and a basket of little sandwiches and a bottle of wine.

There used to be names chiselled into the rock face here, said Ferri. The names of those trapped in the castle. But they're gone now.

After lunch in the baking heat they lay languid and half sleeping and later Ferri walked them some way through the yellow grass to a stony trail above a defile. They continued to climb. They passed a collapsed well and came to another ruin. The remains of several buildings, close together. Giuseppe stared at the three highest walls that stood yet, their roof gone, charred timbers rotting slowly in the grass, green lizards flickering away in the sunlight.

What was this place? asked his mother, picking her way through the white flowers.

A priory, smiled Ferri. It burned to the ground twenty years ago. It is said this is where the miracle happened. Others say it was witchcraft. I come here sometimes because no one else does.

It is very quiet here, said Giuseppe.

She was called Cleo of Carcassonne, said Ferri. A saint, to some.

His mother shook her head, slowly. The girl who suffered the stigmata?

You have heard of her.

She shrugged. It was talked about in the sermons, at the time. We were warned against, what was the phrase? She turned her wrists, as if to reveal her empty hands. Oh. Inappropriate enthusiasms.

Mm. The church does not like holiness that it is not responsible for.

Giuseppe felt the slow heat on his face and he ran his sleeve over his forehead. It came away damp. High up in the currents he saw a hawk turning and wheeling, unsteady in the sunlight.

She was a fifteen-year-old girl, added Ferri. A postulant. She could neither read nor write. On Good Friday her palms and the soles of her feet started to itch, then turned red. She was found face down in front of the altar with her arms outstretched, her hands and feet bleeding. There was a wound in her side.

She did it to herself? said Giuseppe quietly.

No.

But you cannot believe it, said his mother. Surely not.

Giuseppe drifted back through the rubble and the weeds. He could see behind the sculptor the valley below and the silver river with its trees and the little white villa and barn.

I do not know that it matters, said Ferri. Something happened here, something that could not be denied. The invisible world was made real. That is what interests me.

It is in your art, said his mother softly.

How did the fire start? Giuseppe interrupted. He did not like the way his mother looked at the sculptor.

Ah. Ferri stepped clinking through the charred rooftiles and stood beside him and kneeled down and sifted with his huge hands in the dirt. He said, Three days after the girl was discovered, on Easter Monday, the priory burned to the ground. The nuns all escaped with their lives. The villagers claim the flames were green and died out as soon as the roof of the chapel collapsed. It was said by some that the prioress did not believe the miracle, that the fire was her punishment. Others claimed the entire priory fell under the child's spell and a holy fire was sent to cleanse it.

Or perhaps somebody overturned a lantern while they slept, said his mother.

Ferri combed his knuckles through his beard and smiled. That is also possible.

Later, Giuseppe would take long walks along the river and through the dry fields, thinking about that day in the mountains, and the priory that was somehow both blessed and cursed in the minds of the living. The villa was often empty during the days. His mother would spend hours in the barn watching Ferri at his labours and later she began to emerge in a robe with her hair loose at her shoulders and he understood, even then, that she was modelling for the artist and that he was not to intrude nor speak of it ever.

It had not occurred to him to wonder at the nature of his mother's friendship with Ferri. He was still very young, in many ways. All his life he had drifted in carriages and trains from villa to palazzo to hotel to villa, a silent child with bulging eyes clutching a book in his lap, while his mother adjusted her hair and the ribbons at her throat, and he had never wondered at the gentlemen who greeted them at their palace gates, walking alongside the carriage with a hand on the open window. But that summer some part of him started to wonder. He looked at Ferri, standing in the door of the barn, he watched his mother gliding down towards him in the sunlight, and he thought of his aunt murdered by her lover in Rome and he was afraid.

Oh my sweet, his mother said, laughing, when he glared suspiciously at her one evening. Oh do not look at me like that, it is not like that.

But she had laughed too easily, he thought, and the laughter had not touched her eyes.

As the summer deepened into August, he became sensitive to the fact that he was living through important events, events that would affect his mother's life to come, and so affect his own. He could not have expressed it in this way, not then. But he had learned in some vague manner already, even then, that he was capable of disregarding his own griefs and that by doing so they could be diminished. It had something to do with his shyness, he would come to believe, but also the conceit of a person too comfortable with his own likes and dislikes and who saw no reason to change. He had known for a long time that he was one who could stand in a crowded room and, by artfully arranging his expression, and fixing his gaze on the middle distance, discourage anyone from approaching, and he liked to imagine he could do this with his griefs also. But he could not disregard the grief that burned in his mother.

In the last week of August the heat changed, it flattened and lost its edge and seemed to bake up out of the soil itself. He came down to the barn one afternoon in search of his mother and found the tall doors locked. He could hear low voices within. He stepped back and then, his heart beating very fast, he walked carefully around to the long window.

His mother was seated on a chaise longue that Ferri had carried down from the villa. The sculptor himself sat in a dirty undershirt on a little wooden chair turned backwards, his enormous shoulders hunched, his face slick and red, his forearms crossed loosely over the chair's back.

His mother was weeping, holding a handkerchief to her nose. I did not warn her, she said. I could have done more.

What could you have done? Ferri said in his low rumbling voice. You know Giulia would not have listened. She was like you, she followed her heart.

It was not her heart she was following.

Well.

He was a worthless man, Ferri. My god. She could not have chosen more unwisely.

It is true.

Our little sister begged her to stop. Maria told me the gossip was terrible for her. She said no one would wish to marry her, not after the way Giulia was carrying on.

Ferri cleared his throat. It was an affair, Beatrice. Giulia is hardly the first married sister to carry on. Even in Palermo.

Ah.

I do not mean it that way.

But you are right. I am to blame for that, too.

Giulia is the victim. Paternò del Cugno is to blame. That is all I am saying. Do not let your sister forget that.

Through the dusty glass Giuseppe saw his mother lift her face. It looked naked and wet and raw. She stared at a spot on the far wall.

We conducted a campaign in the press, she said. We tried to make it clear that Giulia was the innocent, that the baron had preyed on her.

And there is truth in that, said Ferri.

Is there?

I know how Giulia was. I remember.

But she *wanted* him, Ferri. It was indecent. You did not see her.

She did not deserve her death.

His mother glared at her fingers knotting the handkerchief in her lap.

Ferri's voice was low and pained when he added: Giulia was a light in the world, Beatrice. And that light should not have been extinguished.

I am so angry at her, his mother whispered. I do not know what to do with it.

I know.

Some days I hate her, she hissed, her expression twisting suddenly. I hate her and I am glad she is dead.

Many years later, while brooding in a public garden outside Paris, under a blue autumn sky, Giuseppe remembered those days in Languedoc and the fierce grief that had led his mother there, and in his memories he found something, something he did not know what to do with. His aunt Giulia's affair had begun, he saw, the very year her sister had starved to death in the ruins of their childhood home. He had not considered before whether loss had impelled her into the baron's arms. All his life he had believed she envied his mother her own discreet passions, and he had for many years presumed this envy the greater part of her straying. Giulia had wanted, he had thought, some part of what her elder sister had. He wondered now if that were true. Had she known love, with the baron, before darkness infected his heart? Giuseppe's cane crunched in the gravel where he walked under the bare trees. He wrapped his scarf tighter.

He saw, too, how completely he had tried to avoid a similar fate. All his life he had resisted the kind of consuming passion the Cutò sisters had longed for, had been ruled by, and he wondered now if the events of that spring in 1911 were the reason. The deep feeling he imagined his mother had lived by remained mysterious to him, and without it, he could not know her. He would peer helplessly at her, as if she stood in a mist and he could not quite make out the shape of her within.

He liked to imagine his mother and her four sisters as they were, in their childhood, in Bagheria. The sounds of their laughter in the gardens. The clatter of dishes and the interrupted talk at supper around the table as the girls told breathlessly their day's adventures. They were children of culture and independent thought and they learned to paint and to play the piano in the ballroom and to sit elegantly for hours in their family balcony at the theatre as the travelling players performed. But later, he imagined, after the lamps had been extinguished, they would whisper and climb into each other's beds, and act out the strange modern stories they had glimpsed in books printed a world away in Vienna and Paris and London. Together they learned to dance in each other's arms, to quarrel over the love poems of Petrarch and Dante, to hate the opera as one. In the salons of Paris they stood with their French governesses seeing the bizarre new paintings the critics were calling Impressionism, amazed, and moved. Everywhere the rooms of the world opened around them. They were famously beautiful, sharp-tongued, amusing, very much in love with their own cleverness, his mother the shining beauty of them all. He liked to imagine her, at eleven, perhaps, sitting with her four-year-old sister Giulia at the pianoforte, showing her the keys, laughing as she laughed, the crowns of their two heads leaning in and just touching. That. And Lina, eight years old, with her strong fingers, turning the pages of the score with exaggerated grace as if they were in concert and all the world strained to hear them while Teresa on a divan lifted her face from a book and little Maria, the baby, cried and cried in her bassinet in the sunlight.

But what he liked to imagine most of all was the villa itself, after the sisters had gone into the gardens and a winter light tangled in the empty curtains and the tall doors of the rooms creaked. He would close his eyes and try to imagine the spaces the girls had just been, the hollows in the air.

Their dresses and hats left strewn across their beds, the slow dap of rain starting against the windows of an upper gallery.

The long floors, gleaming in the quiet.

That.

They stayed with Ferri in his villa in Languedoc through the fall and did not return south to Sicily until November.

When they passed through Rome they found a stack of unopened letters curling from the heat, tied with twine, each awaiting reply. These Giuseppe's mother slit open and slid from their envelopes and read silently on the train as they continued south, her beautiful hands shaking. The news was disturbing. It seemed Vincenzo Paternò del Cugno had not died. He had been in a private hospital recovering from his bullet wound for nine months and had at last been declared fit to stand trial for the murder of Giulia Trigona. The trial would take place in Rome, in the new year, and Beatrice would be required to testify as a witness. Giuseppe folded his knees up onto the velvet seat and lay his head crosswise in her lap and watched the clouds scroll past the rattling windows, feeling the rumble of the tracks coming up from under his mother. He made no sound. His mother's horror was like a small bell striking in his heart and sound enough for the two of them. He felt her smooth his hair and he turned his face and studied her studying the hills south of Rome, and as they roared into a tunnel the slats of shadow and light flickered over her features and he realized, all at once, that she had forgotten him entirely.

Her calmness surprised him. Ashen, stately, she descended at last from the hired carriage into the courtyard at Via di Lampedusa and put a hand to her hair as if momentarily uncertain of herself, and then she glided past the assembled staff and allowed her husband an embrace and then she went inside. The sky was black, cold. Giuseppe could hear the dogs in the kennel, crying. Languedoc and the sun-browned face of Ferri seemed very far away. What Giuseppe felt was relief. He saw in that moment that some part of his heart had expected his mother to cause a scene, to rail against the baron, to swear and storm that she would not go to the trial, and it occurred to him that he disapproved of his mother's moods, and this disapproval felt to him like a kind of betrayal. He had already come to the end of his childhood, he would understand later, and those days would mark the end of his first happiness.

The trial in Rome was an ordeal. His mother was required

to sit in the courtroom and listen as her sister's love letters were read out loud. These letters were later published in the newspapers. Paternò del Cugno's defence painted Giulia Trigona as a woman of poor character, uninhibited, a younger sibling in a family whose beautiful daughters had all suffered from their liberal upbringing and Continental education. It became clear just how passionate Giulia had felt, at one time, about the baron. And his mother's own marriage came into question; Giulia had written obliquely about her sister's affections, and these were speculated upon freely by the Sicilian press.

More grievous, for his mother, were the letters between Giulia and the baron after their relationship had soured. She had not known just how threatening Paternò del Cugno had become, how frightening. And she had not realized the deep dread and desperation in her sister. Hearing this read out loud in front of a crowded courtroom, thinking of the private nature of her sister, she wept. Her weeping was illustrated in the newspapers the following morning.

Late in the trial the prosecution walked through the murder as it was understood to have taken place. They did not hesitate to describe in lurid detail the lovemaking between Paternò del Cugno and Giulia. They suggested the fear she must have felt, the impossibility of refusing her angry ex-lover, the implication of rape. They showed the force and strength of the first knifing, how it had fallen on Giulia's body, when her back was turned, how she had twisted as she fell onto the tangled bed, exposing her throat. How the baron must have climbed atop her to cut her throat. How long she would have taken to die.

His mother did not stay in Rome for the sentencing. She returned to Palermo to meet yet another tragedy. Her youngest sister, Maria, in the shame and grief of their sister's murder and the horrifying details that had come out during the trial, had killed herself. The funeral was held in a small church in Bagheria, attended only by Giuseppe and his parents. Because she was a suicide, the priest would not permit her body to be buried in consecrated ground, and this cruelty seemed to Giuseppe, because of its pettiness, the most appalling of all.

In the last week of June, 1912, Baron Vincenzo Paternò del Cugno was found guilty of Giulia Trigona's murder. He was given life in prison, beginning with five years in solitary confinement.

It was finished; it was not finished; there could be no end.

A lifetime later, when his wife had read through his still-unfinished novel she noticed, she hinted to him gently, his fine precision in displaying a complicated person of privilege filled with sadness and hesitation in the face of tragedy. This surprised him. But reading back through the pages he saw that it was true. That his wife, who had fought so bitterly with his mother in life, would recognize any semblance of her in his dignified and sorrowful prince, moved him deeply. He remembered the sweltering station at Palermo when he was fourteen, the crowds of weeping onlookers, and his aunt's polished coffin, littered with flowers, as it was lifted gently down to the platform. The ripple of winter light in the windows of the railway carriages was strangely beautiful. His father and mother had stood apart, not touching, and he had stared at his mother's profile thinking she looked magnificent in her sorrow.

None of them could have imagined their lives to come. For her, the long slow return of her sister's body south to Sicily was, he thought now, like a candle flame going out in a window across the street. Afterwards the darkness within was new and strange and the rooms made darker for the light that had just burned there. But the greater darkness, the darkness without, was no different from before.

THE TROUBLES OF DON GIUSEPPE, PART TWO

━━━━
━━━━

MAY 1956

All that winter Giuseppe's troubles increased. He doubted the new pages. The cold rains came then eased dripping on the terrace outside his window then came hard again, rattling the shutters. He would work shivering with a blanket at his knees until his hand had cramped for the labour of it and then he would sit and stare out at the chilly afternoon and the sea beyond with his fingers folded up into his armpits, miserable, his mind still racing, the sentences not slowing. He was old, truly; never had he felt his age so. He could not seem to catch his breath. His joints ached. The fat of his belly gathered in great fleshly folds as he leaned in.

He and Alessandra quarrelled. Her psychiatry practice slowed as the season came to its close and her patients ceased their comings in the evenings and the sudden excess of time made her irritable. The air in the streets crackled with cold. In December the modernized heat in their palazzo broke and the flue in their second chimney cracked and would not work and when he tried it a sour sooty smoke filled the rooms and would not disperse. In the grey mornings a shadow crept across Giuseppe's hands as he sat reading. In the evenings he would pinch his eyes shut, sighing, as the shadow receded. The twenty-fifth brought no joy, only an unhappy huddled dinner shared wordlessly between himself and Alessandra. A soft cough, the scraping of knives and forks on china, a faint chorus of carols from some building far down the street as Giuseppe rose from his chair to take up the wine. All month they had been alone. Giò and Mirella had gone north, to Naples, Orlando had left for Syracuse. The Piccolos stared gloomily out at the winter sea from their rooms at Capo d'Orlando and did not write.

Twice that winter he tried to explain to Alessandra about his emphysema. The first time was at the beginning of December, while she was in the kitchen.

Licy, my love, he said to her. I must tell you something. It is about Dr. Coniglio.

She glanced up from the chopping of an onion, the knife banging rapidly as if of its own accord.

But just then the telephone began to ring from elsewhere in the palazzo and she wiped her fingers in her apron. Just a moment, she said briskly.

It was a member of the Soroptimist Club, calling with urgent news, and when she did not return Giuseppe stared miserably at the half-diced onion and the tins of sardines and then turned and departed.

He had tried one other time, after Christmas, as they rode in the back seat of an automobile up Monte Pellegrino to visit Santa Rosalia's grotto. There were crowds of umbrellas moving slowly in the half darkness around them. But they were never alone that afternoon, first with the driver, then later with the penitents and the tourists inside, and in the gloomy wet as the rain rattled against the windows he had been unable to speak his thoughts.

Then in the new year Alessandra fell ill with croup. She lay in her nightgown days on end shivering and Giuseppe went to her bedside, raised a glass of water to her lips, read to her from *The Pickwick Papers*. She bared her teeth in a smile but said nothing. Sometimes she closed her eyes and slept. When Giuseppe himself fell ill in turn it was Licy, heavily blanketed, weak from her own illness, who sat with him and sang to him, sang as she had in their earliest years together. Giuseppe listened, a mountain of flesh, his thin hair sticking up, his breasts juddering under the blankets, while the winter light slid across the walls of his bedroom like a visitation. In the evenings he would hear Alessandra in the library, a record of Mozart's piano sonatas crackling on the gramophone, and he would close his eyes, and tremble, but he could not get warm.

In February their ancient stove gave out and he sat late into the night with their account books toting up figures in their columns and the following week Licy purchased a new gas stove. Two days later they collapsed with their heads swimming and only a bedroom window, opened a crack for the freshness, kept them from death. But that gas leak was sealed, the new stove repaired, and death at last packed its suitcases and left the palazzo for some other.

The months passed.

Through all this Giuseppe worked on his novel, nearing what he thought must be the end. It was to be four chapters, reworked now, denser, tighter. He had taken the cathedral and the enclosure at Palma from the preceding autumn and used it

to discover a way forward: his novel would span three twenty-
five-year periods in the Salina family. He had set his opening
chapter on a single day in 1860, during the landings at Marsala,
and the new second chapter in the immediate months following, with a journey by the Salinas to their country estate at
Donnafugata. But in the winter he began to write a third section, set in 1885, a section exploring the death of his prince. And
then, standing back and seeing that it did not yet hold together,
he had found the true ending of the novel in 1910, as the aged
and unmarried Concetta allowed her collection of holy relics to
be assessed and, to her displeasure, declared worthless.

He had been surprised at how time had compressed itself
in the novel, how utterly different his writing had proved to be
from what he had set out to achieve.

Often he would shuffle into the kitchen in his nightclothes
with the story still in his mind, then quickly withdraw a pencil
and paper and scrawl some sentence as it came to him, before
returning to the smaller library to continue. The pages would
not let him alone.

Licy watched him, a growing shadow under her eyes.

Then one night in March he came to his wife with the notebooks in his shaking fingers and he sat down and shook his head
and he smiled. She was in the historical library, where she liked
to read through her case studies, a glass of grainy wine at her
elbow. He did not open the notebooks. He felt translucent,
light, strange.

You are finished, she said at once. It was not a question.

He nodded. He found he could not speak the words.

Read it to me, she said, setting aside her own work. Read me the pages.

As he began to read, he found the sentences absorbed him, possessed him, as they had done during the writing. He paused occasionally to change a word or strike a phrase and Licy waited, breathing as if asleep, and then he read it over silently and then he went on.

Over the months he had come to a consideration of the novel that struck him now, as he read it in its entirety, as curious. He remembered how Licy had touched his face that first night, when he told her what it was he had set out to do, how she had admired him for the courage needed to create a new thing. What surprised him now was the increasing certainty he felt that it was not new but very old, that he had not created this novel but rather helped it to create itself. It was not he but the novel that had made demands. He had gradually begged off invitations, declined dinner parties, and slipped away from evenings at the cinema, allowing little concern for what his old companions must have thought. For the first twelve months of his writing, he did not tell any what it was he worked on; and though Licy might have told them in his absence, he had seen no evidence of this. All this was in his mind as he read slowly, carefully, the craggy blue scrawl in his notebook. He listened as his prince strode through the pages, a figure with his own gravity, desiring some spiritual substance in the flesh that he would not find, for it did not exist, and he found himself moved by his own words.

When he had finished, he looked up to see Alessandra regarding him with a hardness in her eyes. He had been reading aloud for two hours. She had not moved in all that time and now she sat in silence, her glass of wine still untouched beside her. She was staring at him with her eyes hooded so that he felt suddenly foolish.

Well, it is not Stendhal, he said with a sad smile. But perhaps it will do.

But Alessandra replied, almost angrily: It is a masterpiece, Giuseppe. A masterpiece.

He realized his throat was sore, his chest in pain. He sat down, blushing at her praise and at the intensity in her. He mumbled some remark about its oddness.

Not oddness, she corrected. Strangeness. They are quite different. What will you do with it now?

Ah. Well.

It will have to be published, of course. You will need a fair copy. You will need it typed.

I did not think—

Of course you cannot do it yourself. Who shall we ask. Not Giò. Orlando?

He blinked slowly and shook his head. Mirella, he said.

Yes, Alessandra said in satisfaction. Yes. Mirella.

He felt a kind of happiness then that he was not used to. He averted his gaze, tried not to betray the strength of feeling in him.

It is a wonderful novel, Licy said again, turning the rings on her fingers.

He lifted a rumpled shoulder, pleased, for in his heart he could feel it also. The sentences were strong, tensile, and when he tried to pare them away they would not let themselves be pruned. He did not say this, fearing how it would sound.

What I do not like, she said to him, switching back to French, what I do not like is how it has taxed you. I am pleased it is finished. I have not liked seeing you so frail.

He sucked his chin down into his neck, peered up at her in pleasure. He thought she was teasing. Frail! he said. I could lift the wheel of a cart in one hand.

The wheel of a cheese, perhaps.

He smiled, rubbed at the lenses of his spectacles with the end of his tie. Perhaps Dr. Coniglio will set me on a strict diet of millet and water, he said.

We shall see.

He paused, studied her expression in the electric light. She was in earnest, he saw.

I am not dying, he said.

I am very relieved to hear it.

It is a little cough. That is all.

A cough I listen to all night, she said. And you can hardly breathe come morning. I hear you. A dead man cannot finish a sentence, Giuseppe.

I should think his sentence already carried out.

Do not. Do not make light.

He closed the notebooks and held them on his lap in both hands. Show the world a man of god, he said gently, and the world will show him a cross. We all must suffer for our passion.

She snorted. Freud has a word for such a delusion.

So did Saint Peter.

You will see Dr. Coniglio then? Now that you are finished.

She looked imperious, powerful, beautiful where she sat on their salvaged sofa, Crab curled in her lap, his small ribs breathing fast. She was wearing a robe the colour of blood and her black hair with its shock of white was loose at her shoulders. Her face was suddenly in bloom with light. If you die, she said softly, it will be the death of us both, my love. Consider that.

He looked away, suddenly ashamed.

That night as he undressed in his cold bedroom and climbed into his narrow bed he let himself imagine almost for the first time how the novel might be received. He tried to banish from his mind all thought of his emphysema, of Licy's suspicions. He had told himself for a long time now that he wrote only as a distraction, an amusement, and that publication and critical reception meant nothing to him. But now he turned his face to the wall and studied the darkness there and saw in the cracked plaster the immense admiration of the literary world. He supposed if he were to try to get his novel printed he might send it to Lucio's publisher in Milan. He knew they had a reputation for literary refinement and he thought if they admired Lucio's verses, then they might admire his novel, for the two, he knew, were not so different. He liked to imagine an editor, whoever it would be, seated at a desk piled with manuscripts, setting aside some pressing work in order to read and then to finish his submitted novel. The man would have a long thin face, a sensitive mouth, fine lines at the corners of his grey eyes. He would be in his shirtsleeves, turning the pages with delicacy and care. The afternoon light would be failing but he would not have noticed. The idea made him smile. He thought of the novelists he had met in San Pellegrino Terme and he liked to imagine meeting them again, the way their heads would turn as they followed his progress into a room, the way they would approach him, casually, amiably, to congratulate him on the work. He had seen the envy in those men but too he had seen their eager embrace of what was celebrated. He turned onto his side, shifted his bulk again, the old mattress shuddering under him. His toes were cold. The window was open, the curtains billowing white and ghostlike in the night. He would take their hands, smile. He would not let on that he had met them before. What would Lucio feel, to see him so elevated? A large truck passed slowly in the street below. He did not get up to close the window, but lay very still, his fingers folded into his armpits, his eyes open as he dreamed.

One rainy afternoon at the Mazzara, after he had sat writing for several hours, he stood to go and felt a strange sensation in his head and collapsed back into his chair. The pain was startling. He sat with his eyes crushed shut, gasping. A waiter hurried over, pulled the table back from Giuseppe's heavy belly, helped to loosen his tie. At the next table a young man called for a doctor. A second waiter hurried over with a glass of water. Slowly, gradually, Giuseppe felt his head clear; his breathing eased; and then, embarrassed, he took up his hat and coat and books and he fled.

When he telephoned Dr. Coniglio the following morning he was instructed to arrive in a few days' time for another spirometer test. The new machine was different, larger, a thirteen-litre recording spirometer left behind by the American army and purchased second-hand. Giuseppe was required to breathe into a steel tube as his vital capacity was assessed and his air-flow measured. This examination was administered by an assistant and it was not until a week later, when he returned for the results, that Giuseppe saw Coniglio again. He came into his office through a small side door, his hair shining and thick, his little beard trimmed, his body muscular and lean despite his age. He was wearing a blue pinstriped suit from Milan, double-breasted and with pleated pants and he looked, Giuseppe observed, like a man fifteen years their junior. He shook Giuseppe's hand with strength and then he gestured to a little examining table in the corner.

Giuseppe rolled up one sleeve. He did not ask after Coniglio's wife, thinking it would be inappropriate, waiting instead to hear if she had returned from Marseilles; and because the doctor did not volunteer to speak of it, the two men said nothing for a time. Giuseppe felt soft, slow, old in this man's presence. Coniglio took his blood pressure, then tapped on his back with two fingers, the cold disc of a stethoscope creeping across his shirt. He asked Giuseppe to stand on a scale and he slid the little weights on their balance from side to side. At last he allowed Giuseppe to put his jacket back on.

When he spoke he did so with a new intensity and because of this Giuseppe understood he wished to impress upon him the seriousness of the disease.

The results are concerning, the doctor said. Your condition has deteriorated. I expect you know this already.

Giuseppe accepted this news calmly. Yes, that much he had known.

Coniglio sat behind his desk, turned on the little lamp. How are you feeling now?

Breathing is difficult.

You have not given up cigarettes.

Ah. Cigars were never to my taste.

Coniglio did not laugh. I see you have put on weight. You have developed a cough?

Giuseppe nodded.

It is with you always?

Except when I smoke.

Coniglio removed his spectacles, rubbed at his eyes. The orange light from the desk lamp played strangely across his face. I fear, Don Giuseppe, that you are not taking this seriously, he said.

Giuseppe felt his smile fade.

What I am concerned about, said Coniglio, is your susceptibility to a bacterial infection. You might easily develop pneumonia, or bronchitis. Why have you not stopped smoking? Do you *wish* to die?

Giuseppe understood this was not a question he was expected to answer. He sat in silence, thinking how much he disliked the man's tone, but enduring it, his two hands gripping the head of his walking stick upright between his knees. He saw through the window that it had started to rain.

I am concerned, continued Coniglio, about the likelihood of a dynamic expiratory airway collapse.

Ah.

We must take measures to keep you breathing as well and for as long as possible.

Yes.

I should like you to get an x-ray.

At this Giuseppe allowed a quick frown to pass across his face. He knew very little about such technology but he distrusted the idea of photographing his insides, which struck him as indecent, an invasion of privacy. He knew Coniglio considered him a client of prestige and he knew, despite the doctor's professional manner, that he observed Giuseppe's reactions with care.

Now Coniglio said, smoothly, softly, as if he himself were reconsidering: Perhaps the x-ray is not necessary at this juncture. We can begin instead with a treatment of tablets.

Giuseppe nodded gravely.

I shall give you a prescription for theophylline. This has been proven in America to have a sustained effect on keeping the airways open. Take the tablets with water. But they must not be combined with any other medication, that is most important. Take only what is prescribed. Too much theophylline in the blood can produce an overdose.

I understand.

I wish to be absolutely clear with you, Don Giuseppe. There is no cure for emphysema. But there are ways to slow its progression, to allow for a normal life. It does not have to be a death sentence.

Unless it turns into cancer.

Coniglio smiled tightly. It does not work like that.

It will not lead to cancer?

You might develop lung cancer, certainly. But it will not be from this.

Giuseppe studied the head of his walking stick and then he looked up, feeling suddenly hopeful. Then it is a matter of discomfort only? he said.

Discomfort? No.

But it will not kill me?

It *will* progress. And as it progresses, your discomfort will increase. But the real danger is what it will lead to, the complications. Those complications *can* kill you. You must take an active role in the management of the disease, Don Giuseppe. Quitting cigarettes is the first and most important step. But you must also reduce your stress, eat less, exercise more.

His hopefulness diminished, like the light as a door closed.

I see you have come alone again. The princess is not with you? No.

Coniglio folded his hands together on the top of his desk and he adjusted his spectacles. At last he said: How much does the princess know?

I have not wished to worry her.

Of course it is not my place to offer advice, Don Giuseppe. Indeed.

But may I suggest to you, delicately, that you cannot keep this from her? Your life will have to change, one way or the other. The princess will have to be told.

Giuseppe frowned. He wished to say that his affairs were his own concern; he wished to stand abruptly and take his hat and heavy coat down from the rack beside the door and fold them over one arm and clarify in a forceful manner what was, and was not, an allowable liberty between them. He was still a Prince of Lampedusa, dying or not.

Instead he remained seated, staring at Coniglio in offended silence.

But the doctor, if he noticed any change in his patient, betrayed nothing. Now he reached down, unlocked a drawer at his knee.

I have a little something here, which I had printed for me in Rome, Coniglio was saying.

He showed his strong white teeth in a smile. He had withdrawn from his desk a small brochure, handsomely illustrated, outlining various ways of discussing one's illnesses with loved ones, and now he began to read it aloud, taking, Giuseppe could not help but notice, considerable care with the sentences as he did so.

In the end, he told himself some days, there is only what is done and what is not done. That is a life, that is what remains behind. A man such as Coniglio had done much, and would be remembered by those he had helped. The ancient Tomasi had achieved immortality in Palma di Montechiaro by building and giving to the church their palazzos and cathedrals. It did not matter what sort of men or women they had been in life; it did not matter that Coniglio was immodest, self-serving, ambitious; his inner self would be lost to time, as he himself would be lost; but Coniglio's reputation would remain. Giuseppe, on the other hand, was a man without reputation. All his life, he saw, he had avoided any gesture that might be noticed or considered worthy of remembrance. As he left the doctor's office and hurried to join a crowd just boarding a public bus, more people pressing in behind him, while all around a cold rain came down in ropes, banging on the roof and forcing the passengers to shout to be heard, he understood with a new clarity that he must go back to Via Butera at once and interrupt Alessandra at her labours and tell her about his illness.

There was nothing grand in such a gesture, nothing worthy of remembrance. The news itself could wait a day, a week, a month and little would change. But he knew that he lacked some essential courage, and that if he delayed going to her now, he would again fail her, and the moment would be lost.

At Via Butera in the gloom he shook out his umbrella, hung his dripping coat and hat, wiped his shoes a little too carefully. He peered up the marble stairwell, listening. He could hear no sound of Licy above. His trousers were soaked halfway up his shins and he considered changing his clothing before seeking her out but he did not do so.

He found her papers spread out in the historical library, across the smaller chaise under the French biographies, as if she had been at work only a moment earlier. She herself was not any-where. The light on the walnut and cherry staves of the floor was blue, shadow-dappled from the water streaking the windows. He clasped his hands in the small of his back and waited with his face raised but she did not return and after a time, without know-ing quite why, he went to the ballroom doors and unlocked them and passed through into the ruined room beyond.

It was a place of sadness; it smelled of the past. He did not go into it often for that very reason. The long shutters facing the sea stood always closed, like a rebuke, and in the chill of the room Giuseppe let his eyes adjust to the darkness and to the memories. As he made his slow way among the old furniture his shoes clicked, clicked. The stucco ceiling had collapsed in the bombing from the last war and been swept into a pile in the centre of the floor and left there and when he raised his eyes he could see the timbers in places and the bubbled waterstains where the rain tracked through in the spring storms. The long room vanished into darkness at either end. All around him in the gloom lurked the hulking half-ruined pieces he had salvaged from his childhood palazzo on Via di Lampedusa after the war, his mother's beloved credenza, a bureau with two cracked drawers, painted in the Chinese manner, an eighteenth-century wardrobe turned on its side with one leg missing. He ran a finger in the dust.

You have been in the rain, Licy said from the doorway. Look at you. You will catch your death, Giuseppe.

He look across at her. I have been to see Dr. Coniglio, he replied.

Something in the manner of his response must have alerted her, for she stepped through the doorway into the chill and drew her shawl across her chest and folded her arms before her.

Tell me, she said.

He noticed again how much of herself she kept in reserve, and how naturally this came to her. It was a kind of discretion. It occurred to him this was a part of her that had always been there, that it preceded her long professional life of listening. He felt as he studied her there a sudden upwelling of tenderness, and was surprised to find how much he wished to tell her the truth.

It appears, he said quietly, that I am rather ill.

She stood very still and followed him with her eyes as he moved across the ballroom towards her.

You are ill, she said.

He nodded.

With? she said impatiently.

Giuseppe took her hand in his own and laid his other hand on top as if holding a small precious thing, a seashell, or a flower. His heart was hammering in his chest. He felt his cheeks grow hot but he forced himself to meet her eye when he said: Emphysema, quite advanced. That is why I have been unable to catch my breath in the mornings. Why I cannot keep up with you in the street. Dr. Coniglio is afraid it will lead to an infection in the lungs.

Her expression was empty, her voice, when at last she spoke, cautious. I do not know what that means, she said slowly. What does it mean, *advanced*?

He lifted one shoulder in a regretful shrug, uncertain what else to say.

It is from writing your novel, she said.

No.

I should have seen it. I could see you were not well.

My love—

It is because you have not been kind to yourself. You do not sleep, you work late.

It is not from the novel, my love, he said. It has been in me longer than that.

She paused. How much longer?

Well.

Did you not see Dr. Coniglio last year?

Giuseppe cleared his throat, examined the smooth pale bone of her wrist in his hands.

Giuseppe, she said.

Carefully he composed his features. But when he looked up he could see at once that his face had betrayed him regardless.

Of course, she murmured. You saw him twice, in the spring. Yes.

Licy.

But she withdrew her hand from between his and she walked between the furniture in the gloom and then faced him. She put her hands on the back of a shabby armchair. How long have you known about this? Has it been all year?

He said nothing.

All year, she said slowly.

It has worsened, he said. I did not think it was serious at first. Dr. Coniglio did not seem so concerned. I thought—

You said nothing to me.

I did not wish to worry you, he said. And you have been so busy with the Club—

So it is my fault.

That is not what I mean.

Are you dying?

Not at this very moment, he said with a small smile.

This is amusing to you.

No.

Are you dying? she said again.

He did not know how to answer this without provoking her further. It is not cancer, he said.

Not yet. Who else have you told?

No one. Only you.

She said nothing, absorbing this. When she looked at him he saw how much he had hurt her. He saw no anger in her but he knew that would come later and that although the anger would be directed at the sickness itself he had allowed her a simpler target, by having kept it from her.

You should have told me, she said.

She was shaking her head as if she would say more but she did not say more and then she turned with dignity and swept out of the darkening room.

In the days that followed, her hurt made itself felt, as he had known it would. He knew she would not speak of the emphysema to anyone—she had too much discretion for that—but he knew, also, that the private nature of what had happened would create its own pressure on them. There was no one to ease or lighten the tension. Gioacchino and Mirella called on them the very next evening but Licy, with a headache, begged off, and Giuseppe was forced to smile and laugh as if nothing was the matter. Two nights later, when Orlando arrived early for lectures, Licy rose wordlessly from the sofa in the historical library and slipped away. There were no recriminations, no shouting, no scenes of passion worthy of a Stendhal or Thomas Hardy. Instead a brooding sadness settled over the rooms of the palazzo. Lights were left off in the grey afternoons. They ate separately. Some nights Giuseppe would enter the kitchen to find Licy had just exited, a pot of hot tea still steeping on the table, her chair still warm. Doors stood closed at all hours, so that it became difficult to know which room his wife occupied. When he did glimpse her it was usually mid-afternoon, as her day was beginning, and his own ending, and she would look at him with such a clear intensity that he would blush, and look away. What he wanted, more than anything, was for this time to pass, for Alessandra to forgive him.

But her anger distracted him from his illness, and so, in its way, it was also a gift. Now that he had conceded the truth of what was in him, he wondered if he would begin to live as a sick man, or if the importance of the disease would diminish for him.

In the end it did neither. The days passed, as they had before; Licy drifted ghostlike through the palazzo; he turned again to his novel, for something to do. It did not matter that the story was finished. He walked down to the cafés in the mornings, wandered the bookstores, the sentences not leaving him alone. His work allowed him moments of pure concentration, when he could forget Alessandra, and his emphysema, and his failures as a husband.

He found any labour not a part of the novel made him impatient. Orlando continued to seek out his views on English literature Mondays and Wednesdays and, dutifully, Giuseppe prepared for both, though with each evening he grew a little brisker, a little gruffer, and he found himself lingering on minor works that grappled with a dying aristocracy, that wrestled with the problem of a faith lost, of a man's decline. Orlando grew sullen at such digressions. And though he did not complain, he did not appear interested as he once had. Giuseppe watched from the sides of his eyes and tried not to think about the typing out of his novel, or of Alessandra somewhere in the palazzo, reading in a hostile silence, or of the little flower of pain in his lungs.

At last, at the end of March, he telephoned Gioacchino and asked him to bring Mirella to the villa the following evening; he ignored the unspoken question in Giò's breathing and merely said he had a matter he wished to discuss with her. He did not mention his manuscript. Although Giò and Orlando had observed his scribbling, had interrupted him often at the Mazzara, he had confessed only that it was a story written for his own amusement, and he did not think either of them suspected what it had come to mean to him.

When Mirella arrived he sat her down in front of an ancient black typewriter he had borrowed from his bookseller friend Flaccovio. She wore a slim black sheath dress and a silver bolero jacket and had taken some care with her hair and she was clearly uncertain why she had been summoned. They were in the smaller library, the doors standing open, the great Venetian chandelier in the hallway dark. Licy's black spaniel raised his head from the rug, his long ears swinging, wet nose uplifted, and then he lay it again down.

I understand you are an excellent typist, Giuseppe began. Both Giò and Orlando have told me so.

Mirella blushed. A typist?

He liked the surprise in her face. He did not always find her expressions easy to read. There were days when he would look at her and it seemed he was staring at the surface of the sea, all was only reflected light and the shine of a surface, and impossible darkness beneath.

No, truly, she added, faltering. I am not.

He went to the room behind, withdrew his scrawled notebooks from a drawer in the desk, and returned holding them in both hands.

I have a favour to ask, he said.

Yes, she said.

She said it quickly and Giuseppe felt a sudden affection and gratitude. He cleared his throat.

But she was staring at the notebooks. Is that—? she said softly. That is not your novel, Don Giuseppe?

The princess has mentioned it?

Mirella smiled. She says it is marvellous.

A heat rose to his cheeks. He thought with pain of Alessandra's silent anger and he turned his face, almost by instinct, towards the opened doors, as if he might see her silhouetted there. He wondered when they had spoken, and what else might have been said, and suddenly he found himself wishing he had not approached Mirella. It was not her; there was nothing about the girl herself that displeased him. Mirella Radice was slender, with small shoulders, and a long soft neck with a fuzz of brown hair at the nape. He had found her quiet and submissive when Giò had first brought her to meet them two years ago but soon he had come to recognize the quick arched eyebrow, the slight lift of her lip when Giò spoke outrageously, and he had liked both the discretion and the dryness of her company. She had a habit of taking in a room as if from the side of her vision, and of turning her face slightly as one spoke so she might seem to be listening more intently. Her voice was low, her laugh deep and rich like a laugh heard from underwater. When she smiled, he felt old, but did not mind it, for there was such a purity of emotion in her. He could not recall a time when his own pleasure had been untainted by loss, by sadness. Mirella was educated, but uncultured, and it was this he and Licy had set to correct in her. No life can be lived deeply, Licy told her upon their first meeting, if it is lived outside of art. The first rule, Giuseppe had instructed her sternly, is to never attend the opera. He admired Giò for having had the good sense to see in this girl the fineness of her sensibility, not only the vessel but what it contained.

Now she was opening the stiff card cover of his first notebook, running a soft finger over the opening lines. He watched her there, studying the impossible scratch of his poor hand, and he realized he did not want her to hear the novel. What he feared was not her disapproval, but her ambivalence.

A stack of clean good white paper had been set beside the typewriter and Mirella had already inserted the first sheet and was rolling it into position.

I am honoured, Don Giuseppe, she said. Though I wonder if Orlando would not be a better typist.

He was too polite to concede this, or to speak of Orlando's lack of a sensual nature, which made his involvement impossible. He saw now there was no course but to continue. He took up the notebook, walked to the middle of the library, walked back. He was turning the first pages.

I have added and crossed out much, he said quietly.

Yes.

I will sometimes correct myself.

Of course. Yes.

If I speak too quickly, I hope you will let me know?

She nodded but this time she did not speak. She folded her hands before her.

Please understand, he said, it is only a draft. It still requires much work.

Again she nodded.

He cleared his throat. He looked from the page to the girl and back to the page and ran a wetted finger over his thin moustache and then he nodded and began. The typewriter, though old, was an excellent English machine and the punch of its keys startled in the hush of his library. At the first clatter of keys Crab bolted awake and glared reproachfully up at Giuseppe, as if understanding that this noise was his doing. Then he trotted disdainfully from the room.

Giuseppe would pause often while he read, and ask Mirella to read back to him from the typed manuscript, and he would listen and hear in the voice of this girl something sombre and strong in the story of his aging prince, for whom the old certainties had gone. He was surprised at how deeply this affected him. Though he had read the novel to Licy several weeks before, he had done so quickly, with a desire to present it in its wholeness and completion. But now, with Mirella, he hesitated and hovered over the details, altering a paragraph or considering a phrase before continuing.

They had been working already for an hour when he started to cough. He sat down, and drank from a glass of water, and when he had loosened his collar and caught his breath he looked up to see Mirella gazing at him with concern.

It is nothing, child, he said, embarrassed.

We could stop. Continue tomorrow.

But he shook his head no. He knew Licy would be listening somewhere in the palazzo, hearing his cough. He picked up the notebook, he patted its cover. He said: This seems to me, sometimes, like a creature I have created. A monster.

And she, in her discretion, did not smile.

They worked for two more hours that first night. When he stopped at last it was nearly midnight and he saw Mirella lean back, knead her palms gingerly, her eyes scanning back over the last sentences, absorbed. She had taken off her bolero jacket and it lay crumpled with her clutch on a chair and her hair was mussed and Giuseppe thought, with a strange feeling of regret, that under other circumstances their appearance in this room might be compromising.

What shall I tell Giò? she asked him. He will want to know.

Giuseppe smiled. These are not state secrets, he said. Tell him the truth.

That you have written a beautiful novel?

Ah. Not that.

It is true, Don Giuseppe. It is wonderful.

He busied himself collecting his notebooks, embarrassed. But you have not heard it all, he said.

A memory came to him then, unexpectedly. He remembered standing with Giò and Mirella at one of the many society balls last December, while the young ladies pressed past in their wide-skirted crinolines of pink and white and blue and the sound of the orchestra under the streamers and ribbons could be heard from the next room. He had been declining Mirella's insistence that he dance.

Giò was laughing, all teeth and crinkled eyes. You must forgive him, Mirella, Giò laughed. He imagines he is old, and that he has already lived.

The chandeliers had felt harsh, too bright. The unmoving air in the sitting room was hot. He had all his childhood attended such occasions dressed carefully by his governess and he remembered the ladies in their sweeping gowns and ribbons and the gentlemen in their tails like figures out of a lost age for now when he looked around him he saw nothing he recognized, no resemblance. Even the bloodlines were changing.

He had not seen his wife in hours and he wondered if she had gone home. Mirella, her dark eyes demure, was looking at him with a clear steady understanding, precisely as she looked at him now, in the smaller library, after their first evening of work. And he had raised a hand to his own eyes then, as he did now, and brushed his eyebrows lightly, as if to shield himself from such scrutiny.

He had lived sixty years on this earth and his memories had grown up around him like a garden, so that he now could walk among them and reach out a hand and crush their leaves in his fingers for the scent. His mother, his father, the eerie sunlit months of his childhood, when all was warmth and grace and solitude. The long unhappy certainties after the war, the smell of the ocean as he sailed for England.

And the war itself. Reading the opening chapter aloud to Mirella, hearing its balanced sentences and the steadiness in them, he thought of the dead soldier in the orchard, remembered by his prince, and then of the dead witnessed in his own mountain war. How young they had been, he thought. And would always be. In 1917 he had been the same age Giò was now. It amazed him to think it. That war was his first adult taste of the world beyond Sicily, a world always there in his dreams, a silent companion in any room he entered, a sliver of light beneath a door. What he felt was not fear but the memory of fear and the then unremarkable nearness of the dead. His mother would tell him years later how he had returned from the war unable to sleep, how he would wake weeping in the night, and how she would go to him, her dear baby, and rock him at her breast. He himself did not remember.

In May of 1917 he had been sent from Messina to an officer's training camp in Turin and in September of that year he had gone up to the high Isonzo front for the first time. Dressed in his laced boots and military cape and the cloth cap with its leather visor, like a hired driver. He was a corporal by then and almost shaving and they journeyed into the hills by slow train and then rode in the rattling beds of military trucks with their pistols buttoned high on their waists and then they walked for miles along steep dusty roads in that mountain country, stepping to one side as the trucks passed. There were rumours of an Italian victory weeks past at the Bainsizza Plateau though few believed it and then rumours of Germans reinforcing the Austrian lines but those rumours too eventually died away. The skies, Giuseppe recalled, were the blue-black of Palermo's sea. All around him rose loose rocky slopes, and as they climbed he began to glimpse mountains: sheared rock walls gleaming white. He remembered an officer whose pistol had gone off by accident and taken part of his foot and how the man had screamed. The medics who had carried the man by stretcher away were laughing when they returned. They had seen too much of suffering to still respect it. Young Giuseppe's shoulders were sore, the hat with its rough webbed lining scraped at his scalp. On the train he had started scratching at his wrists and ankles and knew he was already infested with fleas.

They entered the mountains and began the final climb to their forward positions in a fierce heat but by mid-afternoon a thick wet fog had descended and the men were forced to halt on the narrow path, crouching, shivering, waiting until it lifted. After that their heavy coats would not dry. Giuseppe shrugged at his damp pack, shifted his canterano across his thighs, sat staring out at the drifting grey tendrils of mist. They were halted on the edge of a steep defile. They did not speak for fear of their voices carrying to the Austrian lines across the ravines. After a time the fog lifted, and they stumbled on. And then the heat returned, like a madness. The path narrowed to a twelve-inch track, scoured and blasted rocky cliffs rising all around them. He had never been so high and he found the air thin, bad to breathe. Near the evening they walked through the site of a battle from some earlier campaign, the limestone splintered and broken, the ruins of shelters and defensive positions smashed by the shelling. Then a foul sulphuric stench struck the length of their column, and men began to cough and curse and cover their mouths: that was the rotting dead, Hungarian and Italian both, fallen to the base of the cliffs fifty feet below, irretrievable. They marched on.

At the front everything surprised him, the limestone walls, the hard faces of the soldiers his own age, the whine of a sniper's bullet and the boy next to him collapsing against the rock face. There was no straw to lie down on, no way to keep dry. He was profoundly unhappy, frightened all the time. He remembered the mule trains arriving in the night, bearing water and ammunition. The smell of their fear and misery. He remembered the great symphonic booming of the howitzers, their echoes in the mountain valleys. The way whole cliffsides would hover and then collapse in plumes of dust. Nothing was steadfast. There were no trenches, only boulders, caves, heaps of broken rocks. In those first days he was sent out in the nights crawling over the scree to repair the communications wires that had been severed or knocked apart in the day's skirmishes. He would creep out with another boy, Luigi, dragging a spool of heavy wire in a canvas sack, and scramble up and down the alpine ridges trying to remain silent. The nights were cold. On his third night he and Luigi froze at the sound of a rustling in the underbrush on a ridge to their left and after a moment a pale face emerged, blond hair rumpled, a coil of wire looped over his shoulder. The three regarded each other in the darkness. No one moved. And then the Austrian boy nodded and slowly, without turning, he melted back into the night.

That was the week of the Caporetto disaster. It was an aggressive push by the Austrians into the Italian lines twenty miles to the east and in the days before the assault Giuseppe and his fellow artillerymen would sit on makeshift benches near their own silent guns feeling the mountain shudder under them, as if a train were passing in the rock. The percussive force of the shelling rattled glasses, skittered boxes off shelves. His teeth ached, his eyes ached. He could not imagine the wasteland and destruction such fire must be wreaking. Luigi grinned and picked at his teeth and made some joke about Austrian girls and the power of the shelling and the others laughed. How astonishing, Giuseppe had marvelled, that they could sit alive and wry and anxious in their skins and only some few miles away ordinary boys from Ravenna and Turin and Milan would be exploding into clouds of blood and mist. When he had left home he had thought the war would prove a grand adventure and he remembered this now and felt ashamed. He did not know it then but thirty thousand men would die in that assault to the east and two hundred thousand would be taken prisoner and the Italian front itself would be pushed forty miles back, to the edge of the Piave.

Immediately after, he was transferred down the line to an artillery observation point in the Melette mountains, near the slopes of the Asiago Plateau. The Caporetto collapse was still underway and they found themselves cut off. He was with an Alpini unit of the Edolo battalion then, staring grimly out at a regiment of Bosnian infantry. These were older men, gruffer, and the frightened humour of Luigi was nowhere to be seen. They called Giuseppe Baby Sicily for the fuzz on his upper lip and his softness and it was not said in kindness.

It's the look of you, a mountaineer had said to him softly, at the mess one night, a short man with the thick wrists of a stonemason. You'll die fast, just like the last one, you will.

He remembered the battalion priest, a cadaverous man with bloodshot eyes, who would grip his Bible like a brick and strike a soldier over the head with it to make his points. On his first afternoon with the Edolo he had seen that priest seize a man's carbine and stand silhouetted on the parapet and shoot crazily at the Muslim infidels huddled in the beyond. They are not men but beasts, the priest cried. Kill them for your God, my sons.

The soldiers had only shaken their heads. Such exhortation had been seen before and would be seen again and they knew it for what it was. Giuseppe in the artillery was granted command of one of the 75-mm Krupp quick-firing guns and oversaw the loading of the breech and driving the huge bolt into place and the spinning of the wheels to determine the range and like the others he would crouch clutching his ears as the monstrous guns exploded and rolled backwards on their wheels in the discharge. All was fury and fear and numbness. The days passed. The guns rolled and broke and rolled again, as endless and powerful as the sea.

In the third week of November the Bosnians crossed the ravine and struck swarming through the grey daylight. And though Giuseppe's unit had known the assault was imminent, still they were overrun. Giuseppe had cowered behind a sandbagged parapet and gripped his officer's pistol in a shaking hand and when a Bosnian emerged out of the mist and flame with his bayonet lowered Giuseppe unloaded his weapon into the man's chest.

He had tried to run, then; but at the last moment came the high whine of a trench mortar, and something lifted the earth like a carpet before him, and it fell breaking back, and he was plunged into darkness.

Gradually, as March slid into April, his wife's anger eased and was replaced by a reproachful silence. When he heard her walking in the halls of the palazzo he would hesitate, standing sometimes behind a closed door with his hand on the pull, listening for her to pass. He understood he was not afraid of her but of the embarrassment caused by their meeting. What he wanted above all was her forgiveness. But she was not one to forgive. And this, too, frightened him.

He was leaving the Mazzara one afternoon with an old edition of Flaubert wrapped in paper under his arm and his notebooks in his satchel in the other hand when he saw Orlando again. Giuseppe, in the sudden roar of the street, had put a hand to his hat, hesitating.

He was in no mood for the boy. He had just met with his accountant and estate manager Signor Aridon, going over the ancient handwritten ledgers at a corner table, Giuseppe understanding little. The estates were running out of money. That much was clear. The meagre rents they collected on the few scattered properties were dwindling. He thought something could be sold off but even the sale of the old palazzo on Via di Lampedusa would ease their troubles only slightly, his old friend had informed him.

Orlando looked preoccupied: his shirt was rumpled, his collar bent and unwashed; he wore a haze of stubble like a fieldworker. He did not see Giuseppe until the last moment and then, startled, he stopped in the sidewalk as the crowds flowed around him.

Orlando, said Giuseppe, shifting his parcel and offering his hand. How are your studies?

He had cancelled his lectures with the youth two weeks earlier, to clear his evenings for dictation with Mirella. Orlando's unhappiness at this had not troubled him. I have nothing more to teach you, he had said, though the truth was Orlando had grown, he felt, increasingly petulant, increasingly distracted. The boy would arrive in the evenings with stains on his suit, his fingernails chipped, his eyes shadowed; he did not sit still; he no longer made Giuseppe laugh.

The youth was on an errand for his mother, he explained, on his way to the Piazza San Domenico. She was, he said, not well. Giuseppe observed the boy with a sudden sharp curiosity. It occurred to him to wonder at the changes going on in Orlando's life, but he did not ask; and the boy, perhaps to conceal the intensity of his own emotion, perhaps out of politeness, did not elaborate.

He began to talk, instead, about Francesco Agnello, and the terrible events of the previous autumn. His manner was distant, cool. He spoke as if Giuseppe must be aware of the baron's suffering, and Giuseppe listened in astonishment, shuffling heavily alongside him, struggling for breath as they went.

Agnello, it seemed, had been kidnapped by mafioso elements in November and held for ransom for several months. His silver Alfa Romeo had been found parked on the side of the road, both its doors standing open, Agnello's sports coat still folded on the passenger seat with his identity card in the left pocket.

The ransom letter reached his stepfather two days later. The sum they demanded was high; negotiations began in earnest; and the kidnappers held poor Agnello in miserable conditions in the hills outside Agrigento. Every few days he was moved to a new barn, a new shed, a new farmhouse. It must have been, said Orlando, awful.

Giuseppe shook his head. How is it I did not hear of this? he said at last.

Don't be offended, Don Giuseppe. None of us knew. Francesco's stepfather did not wish to involve the police or the press.

But Giuseppe felt an obscure hurt, all the same. We are a diseased island, he said.

You are angry, Orlando said approvingly.

Giuseppe did not respond.

That is good, Don Giuseppe. If more people were angrier, this would stop.

We are a diseased island, Giuseppe said again. All my life it has been this way. It is a disease that can be slowed, but not stopped.

Orlando nodded. That is what the princess said also.

Giuseppe put a hand on Orlando's sleeve. You have told this to Alessandra?

Orlando appeared puzzled. Last week, on the Corso. She did not say?

Giuseppe, suddenly embarrassed, adjusted the parcel under his arm. Ah, yes, he said. Of course. I remember now.

Orlando gave him a curious look. They had crossed Piazza San Domenico and now the youth slipped into a tiny dimly lit shop off Via dei Bambinai. It reeked of rats and mould; little pink wax legs and arms and feet and hands were strung up on a rack beside the door, like the dismembered pieces of babies. It was a display of ex-votos, to honour the saints after a miracle cure; and in a glass display case on the other side of the door Giuseppe glimpsed the flattened silver shapes of lungs and kidneys, noses and buttocks.

He had never entered such a place in his life, and was amazed to see Orlando, the socialist, who had railed against religion during their evening visits, speak with such deference to the small old lady who descended the ladder from the wooden loft, her leather apron dragging at her shoulders.

He could not imagine what had transpired in Orlando's life to bring him to such a place as this. What impressed him, and what he would not have expected, was Orlando's lack of embarrassment, the way he had allowed Giuseppe to accompany him here, to observe him paying for the little wrapped package. He wondered at a person with such strength of character and he felt, suddenly, that he had misjudged the boy.

Outside in the street Orlando said, It has been good to see you again, Don Giuseppe. Please do give my regards to the princess.

And mine to your mother, dear boy, he said.

Orlando bowed his head, then stood regarding Giuseppe with a quiet sad gaze. It was the first time Giuseppe felt the youth was fully present, and he understood that the boy would listen with great care to anything he said next.

But he did not speak. The moment passed. As Orlando turned and walked away with the wrapped ex-voto in his arms, it seemed to Giuseppe that something had come to an end, and that he would not see the boy again.

By this time he and Mirella were making progress. Giò would drive her to Via Butera and walk her to their door and holler up at the shutters and Giuseppe, quiet, reserved, would pull away from the receiving room window where he had been watching for her approach. Giò did not ever come inside and Giuseppe was grateful for his discretion. He wondered what Mirella said about the novel to him when they were alone, if Giò asked about the pages.

After that first night, Mirella did not again react to the story. She responded neither with surprise nor disapproval nor delight. Rather she was quiet and precise and wholly present, like a shadow on a wall. He was grateful for this. Some part of him understood that these were the cleanest and purest working hours he would ever know; hearing the language aloud, steady, slow, permitted him to edit as he went; and later, after Mirella had left, he would lift the new typed papers to a random page and begin making alterations almost at once, unable to help himself. There were truths inside the story that surprised him, that he had not intended. It felt at times as if he were overhearing the novel speaking to itself. His prince, he saw, whom he had always thought of as hollowed out by an absent faith, in fact was the last of the devout. But his prince's faith was a faith in tradition, in the fate of a bloodline, and at such moments Giuseppe saw that he had written his way through his own bitterness, towards the man he might have wished to be. His prince stood alone, impassive, needing no one; and because of this, and because there is no true survival in isolation, it would be his prince's very strength that destroyed him.

By the beginning of April half of the novel was typed and clean. Giuseppe would spend his mornings at the café reading over the preceding pages and listening for the music in the sentences and thinking. His head would feel light, as if the back of his skull were lifting, and he would set a soft hand on the edge of the table and grip it tightly and close his eyes.

Some Tuesdays he would walk down Via Roma, past Piazza San Domenico with its casual shoppers weighed down with brown-paper parcels tied with string, to the ancient alleys of the Vucciria. There were always too many people. The narrow streets there were soft underfoot, the refuse and rotting fruit crushed by the crowds into a slippery grime. High up the stone walls the light would darken and then filter through in the interstices of the iron balconies overflowing with potted plants and the criss-cross of laundry lines and Giuseppe would wind his way down to the market, unhurried, the crowds gradually increasing, the flatbed wagons standing with melons in tall stacks or long bolts of red and yellow cloth or gigantic silver fish laid out glistening in rows, their deep flat saucerlike eyes staring at the horrors of the world. In the Piazza Garraffello he would drift past the ruined houses, abandoned since the war, their fronts sheared off and the rubble still loose in their rooms. There were half-wild dogs trotting through the streets, small brown pigs rooting in the gutters. There were tents and swooping tarps strung up to cut out the early-spring sunlight and the smells of roasting meat and raw fish and the metallic reek of earthy vegetables. There were tables with radios of all kinds for sale and pocket watches and men's ties and everything any could imagine. Giuseppe walked slowly, his Shakespeare in the bag at his side, his good overcoat unbuttoned, and he kept his face held high. He had not been allowed as a child to walk among the market stalls but he remembered them after he returned from the war, the coils of innards and cows' heads hanging on hooks, black with blood and flies, and how the roar of it all had consoled him and brought him back to himself. He would go to the market after the crowds had eased, hoping to catch the fishmongers before they had packed up for the day.

There was a happiness in his life at this time, though he would not have known to call it that. Alessandra still said little to him. He felt tired of the guilt. His breathing was still tight, he still sat doubled over on his bed in the morning light, coughing, his eyes bleared with the pain. And yet he liked the steady work, the evening calm with Mirella clacking away in her pool of lamplight, he liked the clean thick weight of the pages in their stack and watching as they increased.

In the third week of his dictating he realized the girl was coming to their door without Giò. It had been a week at least since he had last seen him. Giuseppe did not know what had happened to the young couple and thought to ask but something held him back from doing so. He heard Licy open the courtyard door below, and the barking of their spaniel Crab, and merely stood in the centre of the smaller library beside the yellow chaise with his spectacles in his pocket and waited for Mirella to arrive. He greeted her softly, and studied her face for any distress, but could see no difference. And yet two days later in the early afternoon he walked onto the terrace and found Mirella and Licy standing together at the fountain, their heads close, murmuring to each other. He saw Licy touch the girl's hand, and both raised their faces as one and turned and studied him where he stood in the doorway. Mirella had been crying.

He cleared his throat, abashed. The sky was white and blinding and he squinted. His wife was looking at him as if he were a stranger.

Forgive me, he called across. I did not mean to interrupt.

Licy said nothing, her eyes lost in shadow. Mirella rubbed at her eyes with the insides of her wrists, looked away.

He did not ask about the incident and neither Mirella nor his wife spoke of it. He feared they had discussed his health, then reminded himself of Licy's discretion, and studied his reflection in the pier glass and shook his head at his vanity. You are not so important, he said.

Mirella arrived that night for the dictation as usual, and they worked steadily, but as she left she stood on her toes and gave him a brief melancholy kiss on his cheek. Her lips felt like flowers.

Some nights, alone in his small bed after Mirella had left, and the typed pages had been collected and set carefully away in a drawer in his study, he would lie awake and wonder at the hidden places inside him, the crevices and unswept corners of his self, and at what lay within these. It might have been his age, which weighed on him more heavily now, that led him to brood so. Or perhaps his knowledge of the shrinking rooms of his lungs. What surprised him was the nature of the fear inside him, how little it seemed to have changed. He supposed fear must be the one constant in his life. He could think back with great clarity to those fears of his childhood and see in them the seeds of the man he had become. It was fear that led to his shyness, fear that led to his voracious reading. And, too, it had been fear that led to his writing of the novel. He had been afraid as a young man in the artillery and afraid also in the prisoners' camp at Szombathely. Fear had driven him to attempt to escape and fear, too, had drawn him to seek out the few friendships he had kept. He could find inside himself several of his earliest memories, loaded as they were with his fears, and he wondered now at all those others, those that were hidden from him, and which he would not ever exhume. They too were a part of him. He did not want to die.

In those immediate years after the war it seemed to him that he merely needed to close his eyes and he was returned, again, to the prisoners' camp in Szombathely, in Hungary, where he was held throughout 1918. He had awoken in an interrogation camp several days after the Edolo battalion had been overrun. He was dragged stumbling outside and lined up against a brick wall in the cold wind with some dozen or so other captured Italians and Giuseppe had feared they were to be executed in reprisal for the battalion's shooting of unarmed Bosnian soldiers some weeks earlier. But they were not shot. They were marched to a small stone building with damp cells in its basement and there they were held for questioning. He could hear the other boys whimpering in the cold. The Austrian officer who interrogated Giuseppe wore an immaculate white uniform from the time of the Risorgimento, with gold tassels and a blue sash, and he spoke a crisp German that Giuseppe spoke back to him perfectly. When Giuseppe was stripped to his shirtsleeves the officer found the ducal coronets sewn into his cuffs and his captor's behaviour changed.

That man in white was a baron from Saxony of an old family and he sat with Giuseppe and offered him a cigarette and the two men, the one old enough to be a grandfather, the other still almost a child, smoked together and discussed literature and the museums in Paris. Giuseppe could remember studying the officer's waxed grey moustache and the ancient pink hands he folded in front of him and he remembered how he had liked the man's passion for the paintings of Jacques-Louis David. He wondered now where that man had died, if it had been on the battlefield or at his estate in Saxony. It was already December by then and winter was upon them but Giuseppe was moved from the filthy cell to a proper bed, and two days later transferred to a transit camp in Vienna. He was driven through that city in an open military automobile of German manufacture under a crisp blue winter sky with blankets on his lap and the guard and driver indicated the various sites as they passed, the opera house, the ornate train station. All this Giuseppe observed in amazement. He saw the Viennese looking tired, grim, he saw men huddled on street corners selling family jewellery, others with tables of fine china, all of them blowing into their cupped hands for warmth. The city, magnificent still, looked dreary and worn down by the war.

All that week he waited in Vienna, in a converted hotel, locked in his room but allowed use of the balcony. He sat in a faded red armchair near the window and read languidly through

the works of Goethe, in handsome leather editions. It seemed
incredible to him that the war was blazing somewhere beyond
the stillness. When he asked after his family in Sicily he was
instructed that the Italian military had been informed of his
capture and that his mother would be able to write him when
he reached Hungary. He did not see any other prisoners and
wondered at the courtesy he was receiving but did not ask.
Then the snow started to fall. All his life Giuseppe would
remember the strange silent soft whiteness of his first snowfall,
the expanse of it across the wide avenues, the luminous glow
that seemed to rise up out of it, as if a lamp were lit under the
street. At the end of that week he was taken by train to western
Hungary, to the officers' prison camp in the hard frozen fields
outside Szombathely.

In Hungary the hours slowed. All was drab monotonous
waiting, the war a vague memory. When did he first think to
escape? He thought of the boy he was then with a kind of wonder, finding it impossible to imagine. In the greater world
boys were being slaughtered by the thousands and he himself
had seen the agony a bullet could cause. The camp had been
surrounded by barbed-wire fences, the prison guards though
respectful still walked the perimeter armed. Some twenty-five
drafty wooden barracks, with four men to a building, held
the prisoners. They were Italians, English, French, and there
were two quiet unfriendly Canadians also, out of Quebec. The
hours slowed, all was drab grey skies and slow hours. In March
the first package came from his mother in Palermo. It contained
two books by Stendhal and, more absurdly, a tennis racket and
a dinner jacket and good leather shoes. Some men had started

a camp newspaper in French; others organized informal lectures on random subjects. Giuseppe watched all this with mild disapproval. They seemed to have accepted their lot. He felt no particular love for his country nor did he long to return to the war or to honour the dead. Thoughts of escape became just one way among many to pass the days.

In June as the summer settled in with clouds of blackflies and men fell to fevers Giuseppe and a fellow Italian bribed a guard with tins of coffee and sugar and acquired Austrian uniforms and tickets for the Swiss border. They slipped away in the night and crept over the rattling fences, throwing a blanket before them to cover the barbed wire. But the final fence was alarmed and as they struggled to get across it they saw lights from the guardhouse and then harsh voices and then they were seized and kicked and punched. Giuseppe cried out in Italian, feeling his ribs crack, and the soldiers stopped. In the morning his barracks guard laughed about it. They had been mistaken for Austrian deserters.

They were not punished. They were ordered to pay the value of the train tickets to the guard they had bribed and that was all. But Giuseppe would remember until the end of his life the looks of respect in the faces of his fellow prisoners as he walked the yard in the days following, as if he were a man elevated above his station, as if he had achieved some greatness through the grace of having tried at all.

The months passed. The guards thinned; fewer and fewer parcels arrived. Some evenings there would be no food at all and the prisoners doubled back their belts, rolled high their sleeves on skeletal arms. In late October Giuseppe put on his hat one morning, tied his shabby boots, and walked out in the pre-dawn light through the front gates of the prison camp and onto the long sparse grey dirt road away from Szombathely. No one stopped him. The war was nearly over by then though he did not know this. The countryside seemed deserted. But he spoke fluent German and made his way on foot over the following weeks to the port of Trieste and from there he found his way onto a vessel sailing for Greece and in the port of Athens he learned the war was over and that the German army had collapsed. An early winter was settling in, the waters of the Adriatic black with cold. He boarded a British vessel, sailing for Venice under an assumed name, and arrived in the north of Italy thin, haggard, and bruised, one of the defeated.

Alessandra still was not speaking to him when the anniversary of Giò's arrival in their lives came around. They had started celebrating that day three years earlier, almost as a joke, dressing in black as if in mourning, but that had gradually relaxed into a matinee at the cinema and then a long dinner at Mario's restaurant.

Giuseppe had not known how Licy would behave. He was dressed early and he watched her come out onto the landing in a shaped black dress, fitted through the waist, like something Mirella might have worn. She carried a cloak over one arm. He fussed in the mirror with his hat, his walking stick, his coat. When Giò rang the buzzer, he was surprised to see Licy pause on the stairs, wait for him to join her. Giò wore a carnation in his button hole, dyed black. Mirella had not come.

They left Giò's car parked at Via Butera, caught the city autobus through the flat cool light of Palermo. The day was fine, cloudless, the sky the pale blue of a Tintoretto sea. Giuseppe smoked quietly in the autobus watching the streets scroll past, the motor scooters weaving through the traffic. They got out a block from the theatre and walked with their coats open and collars rolled. Licy walked ahead with Giò as Giuseppe trailed behind. He liked how tall she was, how stately in her heels and the new cloak she had ordered from Rome.

A Rossellini picture was showing, *Viaggio in Italia*, some two years old, but he did not mind it. He had been hoping for an American western but at least, he told himself, at least it was not a musical. In the prison camp at Szombathely he had watched two-reelers of westerns over and over, every night, played against the wall of one of the barracks, and he had fallen in love with the flickering clarity of the action, the gestures of a revolver firing, a man plunging from his horse, which seemed so complete in themselves.

Giò was laughing, telling in a wry voice some scandal involving Rossellini and the actress Ingrid Bergman, something about their affair and Bergman's husband and daughter still in America. Licy did not like to admit it but she found such gossip fascinating. Giuseppe observed how his wife sat on the far side of Giò, arranging the seating so as not to draw the boy's attention to it. He squeezed himself into the theatre seat, stood, removed his coat and unwound his scarf and folded each and sat again and held them gingerly on his knees. Because Licy was speaking softly, and Giò had turned to face her, Giuseppe let his mind drift. He could hear the roar of conversation from the rest of the patrons, studied the heavy red curtains hanging before the screen. They had found seats in the second row of the balcony. He liked this time, these minutes before the theatre hushed and the curtains parted and the shine of the picture transformed the darkness. He heard Giò say something about Mirella and he turned his face but just then the lights dimmed and the audience began to applaud.

Afterwards they walked down to Mario's for a drink, though it was early yet. And there they found André, Licy's first husband, drinking, and together they shifted to the large table on the rooftop terrace. André Pilar von Pilchau was a round-faced Estonian baron, already balding, and he dressed in coral pink suits and cream shirts and wore many rings. The sunlight was long and yellow in his face, and Giuseppe wondered suddenly if the man was ill. A warm wind rippled the tablecloths around them and Licy raised her fingers to her hat. André had brought with him a companion, a young French poet the same age as Giò, who had been staying with the baron through the winter. The older man would brush the poet's hands, or hold his gaze, or lean over to whisper some instruction with gentleness and Giuseppe saw his wife watching all this with an expression of pity and something darker.

He himself had liked André from their first meeting in the castle at Stomersee all those years ago. He felt no bitterness towards him, no jealousy for his wife's affections. After all, he said to her some nights, had her ex-husband been of a different persuasion, Giuseppe could never have stolen the baroness from him. Am I property then, to be stolen? Licy would reply, smiling. In truth, André had caused her considerable pain, and yet she had come to accept that his inclinations were simply a part of who he was, and he confessed one night that he had never been happy until he had accepted himself for what he was. Giuseppe did not mind. It surprised him, sometimes, to think that he had not always thought in this way. His cousins did not understand. His mother would never have tolerated the lonely baron. Licy herself had suffered a nervous breakdown in the first years of that marriage, struggling to make sense of it. She had treated herself with insulin, then travelled to Vienna for consultations with Julius Boehm, a pupil of Karl Abraham. That man Boehm they later learned had run the Göring Institute during the war and had personally sentenced hundreds of homosexuals to death.

Giò was speaking now about the Rossellini picture, comparing its ending in Pompeii with his experiences in the ancient Addaura caves, on Monte Pellegrino.

Addaura, André announced, puzzled. How is it I have not heard of these caves?

There was a happiness in him that Giuseppe watched with fascination, wondering at it.

It is because the Americans found them, said Licy. You will hear of them when they appear in a Hollywood picture.

A picture about the war, no doubt.

Ah. About an American soldier defeating the entire German Sixth Army.

But I have heard of these caves, said the French poet. I have read about them. The Americans were storing bombs in the caves and one of them blew up, yes? He raised his hands wide in imitation of the explosion. His attention was fixed a little too intensely on Giò's lips. When they went back inside they found the back wall was gone and the cave went deeper, yes?

It is a very strange thing to see, said Giò. It is like staring across time.

You have been there?

Giò laughed. They are not really suitable for the public. There are paintings on the walls that must be ten thousand years old. There is a strange one of two naked men tied up in rather compromising positions. Figures with the heads of animals are dancing around them.

Horrific, said André, smiling.

La dolce vita, laughed the French poet.

Licy raised her face and stared out over the railing, exposing her long throat, and the table fell quiet watching her, waiting for her to speak. It was a trick she had, Giuseppe knew, when she wanted to say something that pleased her. We have always inclined toward ritual, she said now. It amazes me when people speak of our world today as if we are somehow different from those who painted such pictures. The subconscious mind is ancient. And it is still with us. Our desires have not changed. When did you go up there?

Last spring. With Francesco.

Giuseppe crossed his legs, lit a cigarette. He was sensitive, when he cleared his throat, to his wife's stillness beside him. A shadow fell across the table as a figure crossed in front of the lights, then away. Francesco Agnello? he asked, in a grave tone.

A terrible thing, André said quietly in his formal Italian. How is the poor boy doing?

Licy gave a slow sigh. We have not seen him, she said.

But we know he cannot be well, said Giuseppe. Such an ordeal is not lightly forgotten.

Licy, beside him, was quiet.

I saw Orlando last week, Giuseppe continued. He told me Francesco sees no one.

Giò nodded, reached for his glass of wine. Mirella saw him in the Vucciria last month, he said. She said he looked thin. He would not come with her back to the apartment. They made a date for dinner but he did not show up. I think he cannot bear to see anyone.

It is no wonder.

What happened? asked the French poet. Forgive me, I do not understand. Your friend is ill?

He was kidnapped by criminals last fall, said Giò. He gave a shrug as if to say such things must happen. He was held for months while his family tried to raise the money. Eventually they did. He was released.

The poor boy.

That is one thing Mussolini did very well, said André. He hunted such men like beasts.

Hitler hunted such men also, said Licy sharply. I do not hear you praising him.

Other kinds of men also, murmured Giuseppe.

Yes, said Licy, without looking at him.

I am not praising him, André said. I would not praise him. But I would like to see these criminals given justice.

I understand they *are* the justice system, said the young French poet. Or a part of it?

Giuseppe wrinkled his brow. He did not like the direction this conversation had taken.

André must have sensed his discomfort or shared in it for he suddenly shifted in his chair and touched the young poet on the shoulder with two long soft fingers and said, briskly, over his head: And what is Lucio up to these days?

Giuseppe rubbed his thumb and forefinger on the stem of his glass. Oh, writing his verses, he said.

He is a great poet, I understand.

Giò laughed. So he tells us.

Giò, said Licy.

But she too was smiling as she said it.

Something shifted in Alessandra that night. It had happened gradually, unnoticed, but later Giuseppe felt it in the easy way she walked alongside him back to Via Butera, in the way she waited with her hands lost in their furs as he unlocked the gate, stepped aside, held the door for her. It occurred to him that a long marriage allowed for the slipping back into familiar habits, and that such acceptance could lead sometimes to something like forgiveness. He knew that even during the past weeks when she had avoided him she had been watching for signs of his illness and understood that her concern had been the source of much of her anger. As he stood behind her, as she allowed him to help her remove her coat, he was filled with an immense gratitude that she would permit him such a small kindness. They were both of them still a little drunk, and he listened as she went over the evening's conversation, tentatively at first, avoiding his eye.

She also had thought André looked happy, and had felt a

deep satisfaction seeing him so, she said. Giò, she thought, had been subdued, not quite present, and this was not like the boy. Giuseppe had noticed this also and wondered at Mirella's absence, but if Licy knew anything she did not mention it. The seafood had been excellent, the rockfish watery and tasting of the sea. Both of them had found Rossellini's picture sad and resigned and they had liked this about it very much. As the film had deepened Giuseppe had lit a cigarette and let his eyes drift over the heads of the audience. He liked to watch them in the flickering blue light, smoking quietly, liked to watch the ways they shifted as one, leaning in to catch the intensity of Ingrid Bergman's anguish. He had been surprised at the number of people in the audience and wondered if perhaps there was a wider appetite for serious cinema than he had supposed. Licy thought the camera was a little bit in love with Bergman.

After all, she lived in her unhappiness so beautifully, she said.

She was very beautiful, he agreed.

Very. But it was not a picture about her, I think.

He had been bending over, putting on his slippers, and he heard a tone in her voice and he looked at her and he waited.

But Licy did not explain herself. She said instead, I think he feared her company. He feared being alone with her. I think he only ever saw her from across a room.

George Sanders?

Mm.

I expect all of Italy must have wondered if it was a picture about Rossellini's own life.

As they will about your novel.

Giuseppe recognized in the consideration of her remark a kind of reaching out, and he watched her face with attention. He understood she would not mention his illness that evening, but that everything she said was filled with it.

All of Italy will not read my novel, my love, he said to her.

Perhaps, she said. Has it a title yet? You will need a title if you are to submit it to Mondadori. Lucio will need a title.

Well.

She gave him a quick catlike smile. Go on. What is it?

You will not like it.

No?

I was thinking, Il Gattopardo.

Il Gattopardo.

You do not like it.

She paused, considering. But there are no leopards in Sicily, Giuseppe.

He cleared his throat. Not anymore.

Not ever. You will be criticized for it. Then she raised her eyebrows. But of course you mean the dying prince.

Well.

Will they understand that, at Mondadori? Will the public?

He frowned, all at once uncertain.

Licy took off her wire-rimmed spectacles and shifted the dress at her hips and held out her arms with her magnificent fingers spread wide. She did not smile but regarded him with great seriousness.

Come here, my leopard, she said softly.

LOVE RETURNS
TO SICILY

——
——

OCTOBER 1956

He had met Licy in London in the summer of 1925. She was married then, still, to André, though the baron had already broken her heart. That first evening they had walked together, not touching, through the crowds of working Englishmen, had walked from his uncle's embassy to Whitechapel speaking all the while in slow quiet French sentences about Shakespeare the man and Shakespeare the artist and the gulf that lay between the two. They were speaking in fact about beauty and the invisible world though neither would have used such words and when he remembered that first evening, Alessandra's swift low bark of laughter, the way she would look at him directly with a clear gaze, what he recalled most vividly was his own embarrassment, for some part of him had understood even then their true subject was desire.

It was his first visit to London. He had arrived from Paris, his eyes still dazed by the modern pavilions at the Art Deco Exposition, the Seine at midday, the Raphaels at the Louvre. He was travelling without his mother and on that first occasion settled in as a guest of the Italian embassy on Grosvenor Street. He was to stay with his father's brother, Pietro Tomasi, Marchese of Torretta. His father disapproved of this brother, but Giuseppe had always loved him, perhaps more so for his father's disapproval. In those days, Uncle Pietro was Mussolini's ambassador to England, and though he disliked the Fascists, somehow he had continued in his post. Pietro had served as a diplomat in Vienna, and in Russia during the revolution, and had known Lenin in Moscow and admired him. In 1922 Pietro accepted the posting to London, where he travelled with his new wife, Alice Barbi, fifteen years his senior, a retired mezzo-soprano and one-time muse of Johannes Brahms. Giuseppe remembered the expression on his father's face at dinner, the night the letter announcing their wedding arrived, how he had let the letter fall beside his chair and the hound had risen and sniffed at it and then trotted languidly back to the fire, as if no longer hungry. His mother had avoided asking; but Giuseppe rose from his chair, and walked the length of the table, and picked up the letter from the floor and read it in silence.

He had not met Aunt Alice then; none of them had. He would meet her only twice, briefly, before he arrived in London in that summer of 1925. He had remembered her as pale, and thin, like a weak flame at the end of a match; and so he did not recognize the stout matriarch who received him, a widow with two grown daughters. Young Alice, his mother called her, scornful of her sixty-six years. His aunt spoke to him in English, but to his uncle in Russian. Her black hair had greyed in streaks and she wore it cut at a slant along her jaw-line, in the fashionable flapper cut of girls a quarter her age. Her face was heavy, her lips thin and frowning, but there was a vitality in her language and gestures that Giuseppe admired from the first. She was a woman, he understood, who expected to be observed.

He had arrived without warning and on that first night, with the roar of Piccadilly still in his ears, he perched on the corner of his steamer trunk in the front hall of the embassy and listened as his aunt and uncle explained they could not receive him; he should understand, his uncle said, they had a royal reception to attend; but he would be well looked after by Alice's daughter, indeed he would like her, for she was a rather bookish creature, not unlike himself. She was without her husband, and would appreciate the companionship.

Giuseppe imagined an owl-eyed creature, both timid and miserable. He raised his eyebrows, struggled to smile. Oh yes, that is, well, yes, he mumbled. Mm. Perhaps when I have unpacked, and washed, and slept, then—? But he could not think how to finish the sentence and he looked at his uncle helplessly and then said: Really there is no need to trouble your daughter, Aunt. Truly.

Had you informed us of your arrival, you see, Uncle Pietro began. But it was said with a smile from under his waxed moustache, as if such behaviour were fitting in a young man.

Giuseppe said he had hoped to be no bother.

Nonsense. The young should always be a bother. It is your right.

His aunt, who had not spoken, now tilted her head from side to side, deftly putting on long glittering earrings. Best come along, she said in a brisk tone. I shall show you your rooms. No, leave the trunk here. Pietro will have someone bring it up. I want you to meet Alessandra before we go.

Uncle, Giuseppe protested.

But his uncle only adjusted his cufflinks and waved a hand in dismissal.

In the elevator, as the gate was folded shut with a clatter, his aunt's breasts had brushed up against his arm and something had gone through him, a violent shudder, not entirely unpleasant, and he had blushed furiously.

He could not have imagined how his life was soon to change. On his second afternoon, he would set out with Alessandra to see the Turners at the Tate, and find himself startled into speech by their atmospherics, as if a sombre music were rising out of the paint and infecting him. At a dinner on his third evening, a former viceroy of India would stand aside in a display of English courtesy, insisting Giuseppe precede him through the door. On that occasion he caught Alessandra's gaze from across the table and he felt a sudden uncomfortable heat rise to his cheeks. In London he would acquire a taste for bow ties, and spats, and he would begin to wear a small clipped moustache that he would keep for most of his life, and brush his straight hair back without a parting. All of this was done with Alessandra's teasing encouragement.

But on that first evening, his aunt had led him up into Alessandra's rooms without knocking and they had found her seated at a desk, recording some impressions into a notebook. She was writing with a slow steady hand and Giuseppe paused at the threshold of her room, noticing the heavy furniture and the thick carpets and the windows standing wide to catch the nonexistent breeze. A small metal fan was rattling in its cage on the desk.

Set that down, Licy, his aunt said in French. This is Pietro's nephew.

Arrived from Palermo, Alessandra replied coolly, as if she had been expecting him. And then she raised her eyes and looked at him, and he could not help himself, and he stared. She had the lovely sad eyes of his own mother.

Giuseppe Tomasi, he said and gave a small bow, all at once grave. At your service, Madame.

You will call me Licy, she said.

Licy, he murmured.

She looked him up and down. I suppose we are cousins then, you and I, she said.

And she stood from the desk, tall, powerful, wearing a white dress in a Japanese print and with her black hair loose at her shoulders. She had large hands and she held one out to him, ringless, he noticed, and he took it, a lightness filling his chest like water.

Cousins, he said shyly.

Of a sort, she said.

His aunt grunted from somewhere near the door. I shall leave you both, she called, and Giuseppe in his confusion did not turn to watch her go.

He had spent much of that decade already in travel, seated upon wrought-iron balconies in Viennese hotels, walking the boulevards of Paris and Berlin, standing jostled in the crowded jazz clubs of Amsterdam trying to rid himself of his memories of the war. He had little interest in the events of the world. Though he too applauded D'Annunzio's annexation of Fiume, he found the man himself ridiculous, and the nationalist passion distasteful. Weariness with the social pressures of Palermo, and disgust at his own physical frailty, led him for a time to Genoa and Turin, where several survivors from the Szombathely camp now lived. In the intervening years he travelled with his mother to Bologna, and Munich, and Paris, seeking nothing but unsatisfied with everything. He acquired a camera and took photographs of the cathedral in Pistoia, of the baptistery and the Ponte Vecchio in Florence, of the grand fountains in Rome. Always he would wait until he could photograph a building without its people present, desiring the monument in its solitude and agelessness, seeking some purity in the stone that stood outside time. But elsewhere he allowed himself to drift. He liked being no one, he liked the invisibility he found in the cities of Europe. It was the roaring twenties and gin and jazz crackled across the continent like some American fire.

And yet travel brought him no peace; he slept badly, and suffered nightmares, and did not stay away from Sicily for long. It seemed he was always either just leaving or just returning to Palermo, and to his mother, as if very much a boy still, unattached and dependent, though he was in truth approaching thirty. He understood now, at sixty, that he had been fleeing the person he was, and that, having lived through the dangers of the war, he did not trust the settled life. He knew too well that what was given could always be taken back, and how soft and disintegrating the human body could be. But at the time all he knew was a vague unhappiness, a disgust at the petty conversations of others, and a contrasting satisfaction at the companionship of books. He was no longer young, true; and yet his face remained plump, and his manner gentle, and only his large eyes, round, melancholy, slightly bulging, betrayed the horrors he had seen on the Isonzo front.

He still wished his life might resemble a novel. He was still young enough for that. He had wanted, he thought now, not only for a purpose, but most especially for a shape that might manifest itself; he had wanted for a sense of movement, of direction; he had outlived his beginning and desired whatever came next. He wished for what he had known in his childhood, but made richer, developed, brought to risk. No one is the narrator of their own life, he had observed once to Licy. A life is not a book, she had replied. Perhaps; but it seemed to him now that there were shapes, patterns, echoes in some lives that could nevertheless be drawn out, made sense of, and in this way a kind of insight might be attained. That was what he wanted. It could not be managed in the moment, only later, in just the way a narrative is shaped in a novel, by sifting through and selecting certain threads.

Among those threads most precious to him was the curious fascination of his aunt's eldest daughter. He had little experience with the female sex, but enough to know, even on that first night in London, that Alessandra Wolff's beauty was unconventional. Her expressions shifted like light on water so that her face seemed in constant motion, her aristocratic nose wrinkling, her dark serious eyes narrowing. She moved not with grace but with decisiveness, as if she were seizing opportunity, as if some obstacle might set itself in her path at any moment: prepared, always, for a sudden fierce opposition by anyone in a room. She had studied in Vienna with the world's great psychoanalysts, had wed a Tsarist war hero and baron. She was worldly, and damaged, yet somehow her losses had not changed her. The fire that was in her had always been in her, he understood, and it provoked him and frightened him both, so that the thousand ordinary exchanges that occur between men and women who do not yet know each other now left him confused, uneasy. At a café or a restaurant, he would glance up at her and hesitate, as if afraid to speak without permission, as if afraid to order on her behalf. Or he would pause at a door, uncertain if he ought to hold it open for her. And she would order her own dishes, or drag the door open with a powerful movement, regarding him all the while with a mixture of satisfaction and disgust. He had met no woman like her.

None, that is, except perhaps his mother. In his letters back to Palermo, written each night, posted each morning, he did not mention this marvellous terrifying creature, this new thing that had entered his life, this Alessandra Wolff.

Those days were much on his mind that October, as he observed Giò and Mirella, impossibly young, flush with love, while the three of them drove east along the north coast to visit the Piccolos at Capo d'Orlando.

It was a Sunday, all golden light, the end of the season, and Mirella's first visit to the Piccolo villa. Giò drove, with Giuseppe squashed into the passenger seat and his knees folded high and the girl crouched behind them, her arms spread wide, the wind pouring through her hair. The sky was very blue. He could see the ocean below at various turnings along the new roadway and he squinted down at the breakers combing inward, steady, soothing, a rolling line of foam that had always been and would always be. In the roar of warm air they had to shout to be heard. Giò drove fast, gearing down and back up as they were sucked along around the curves of the cliffsides, the sun behind them, channels of shadow and brilliant white light they raced through.

Every now and then Mirella would open her eyes and lean forward and run her fingers over the back of Giò's neck and he would grin his boyish grin and lift his eyes to the rearview mirror and look at her. Giuseppe liked to see his young companions in love and together. There was an affection between them that was both less and more than passion, something akin to friendship, and it was this that he saw in them that reminded him of his courtship of Licy. But he had never been so young, he reminded himself. He and Licy had been in their late thirties when they married, already formed in their habits, already themselves. When he looked at Giò and Mirella, on the other hand, he saw two who were still learning who they might be, leaning into each other, adjusting themselves, growing alongside.

They saw no other cars all that day as they drove and Giuseppe did not know if this was unusual but he felt an eerie solitude as they went, as if the world had receded, as if they had slipped through some fold in time and were driving now deeper into an ancient Sicily.

Alessandra had declined to come with them for the week. She had too much still to do with her patients, and could not cancel appointments at such a late hour, regretfully, etcetera, and so forth, as she told Mirella. But the girl would find the Piccolos accommodating and gracious enough, Licy insisted, though strange in their ways. To Giuseppe she offered no such excuse. They both knew she had avoided the Piccolos' villa for years now, for she could not tolerate his cousins' artistic affectations, and thought their pursuit of faeries and the occult nothing short of foolish.

They are children, she would say. I do not say this to be unkind.

And there was truth in both statements, he knew, though he dared not agree with her out loud. His three cousins had lived together, unmarried, in their family villa high above the ocean since the death of their mother. As if by magic, the war had not touched their villa, though Capo d'Orlando with its coastal road and its railways had been bombed into a fury. In the darkest months of 1942 Giuseppe and his mother had fled Palermo, rented a hillside cottage near the Piccolos. That cottage had been demolished by a bomb while they were out one afternoon. That was the month of the Allied landings in the south. The Piccolos lived on, unscathed, orphaned by then. Their father, the baron of Calanovella, had fled years earlier to San Remo with a dancer, and died before the war. His spirit, Casimiro claimed, stalked the halls of the villa, mournful, filled with regrets.

If Mirella felt nervous at meeting the Piccolos she betrayed none of it. It was late afternoon when Giò drove the long road up to the villa, through citrus groves, up delicate rocky valleys of wild strawberries, and came to a crunching stop in the gravel driveway. A pale dust hung suspended behind their car. The three Piccolo cousins were waiting together at the railing with the grand doors of their enchanted villa standing open behind them, and Giuseppe tried to see them as Mirella must see them, figures out of time, untouched, absurd with privilege: Casimiro in his paint-stained shirt, untucked, loose, a tall thin figure silhouetted against the white walls of the villa, wearing knee-high English galoshes like the lord of some manor awaiting his guests; Agata Giovanna, older, clutching a small dog in her arms, her grey hair braided into some exquisite Celtic pattern, standing some feet away; Lucio, immaculately dressed in plus-fours and shooting stockings, smaller than the others, his little moustache twitching as he smiled and frowned and smiled over the railing, as if he could not decide what to make of these three visitors, arrived in a cloud of dust like some strange ghostly doubling of their own selves.

Giò turned off the engine. Wait, love, he said to Mirella. You do not want to get out just yet.

She gave him a curious look.

And then the barking and howling began. All three stayed in the car, their arms carefully withdrawn, Giò and Giuseppe calling laughingly up to the Piccolos to rescue them, for the hunting dogs were loose and had hurtled out around the automobile, frenzied, covered in sores, and they would not let them out.

The last time I was here they drew blood, Giò grinned. And he kicked a foot up onto the dashboard and rolled up his trouser to show the scar.

Through all this Giuseppe felt a great happiness. He had sent his novel to Lucio, who had praised it and submitted it to Mondadori on his behalf. That had been five months ago. He did not know how long it usually took to receive an answer, but he felt confident. He knew it was strong work, and that he had achieved something unusual with it, something he had not expected to achieve. He tried to imagine it printed and bound, tried to imagine holding it in his hands. He tried to imagine the normalcy of that, after enough time had passed, tried to imagine no longer being moved by the physical fact of it, but he could not, and this failure made him, somehow, the more happy.

Of course I have read it, said Casimiro later.

This was after Giuseppe and Mirella had unpacked, and washed the dust from their necks and wrists, and drunk lemonade in the cool sitting room while the electric fan rotated on the television set like some wondrous living sculpture. Giò did not remove his little white suitcase from the car, for Agata Giovanna did not approve of engaged couples sleeping under the same roof. He would drive thirteen miles to the nearest hotel that night. Giuseppe took his usual room. At the bedhead hung an ancient Louis Seize showcase, with ivory statuettes of the Holy Family, salvaged from the rubble of his mother's palace at Santa Margherita decades ago. Before he went out to the others he rubbed one finger over the cowl of the Mary as he had done since he was a child, feeling the cool smooth stone like water on his fingertip.

In the dining room, Agata Giovanna had laid out a cold luncheon of fettuccine with butter and parmesan, an enormous tuna steak with sauces, liver purée, black truffles, pistachios. Lucio was already eating. The head of the table had been set for the ghost of their mother, as it was always, the chair pulled out for her spirit to survey her guests. Mirella glanced at it but said nothing. After, Giuseppe and Casimiro took their leave; now he was walking through his cousin's studio, examining the new painting, a tiny watercolour of faeries and night creatures glimpsed in the Piccolos' garden. He could hear through the windows Mirella laughing, calling for Giò. She and Agata Giovanna were touring the orchids and hydrangeas, drifting in and out of earshot, while Giò hid somewhere among the palms, teasing.

The studio, a small shuttered space, felt cool and dim in the afternoon light. A glass of water and a plate with a quartered orange lay on the deep windowsill. Now Giuseppe glanced back at his cousin without turning around and he said dryly, And?

And what?

And what is your impression of it?

Casimiro smiled. I am only a poor worker of paint, Cousin. I am no literary critic.

Giuseppe folded his hands behind him. You did not like it.

Well. I do think it will cause a stir.

But you did not like it.

On the contrary, said his cousin quickly. I found it amusing. Provocative. I do not know that I understand it all, of course. But Lucio tells me it is very fine. You must know he has recommended it to his publisher?

I have brought him two new chapters.

And also this girl of young Lanza's. My goodness, you have not packed lightly, Cousin.

Giuseppe smiled. She is very charming, is she not?

She appears to be.

Licy and I like her very much.

Well. You cannot adopt her too, Casimiro laughed. There are laws against that, surely.

Not in Sicily.

Perhaps not.

Perhaps you and Lucio will adopt her.

Ah. What would Giovanna say?

Giuseppe, who had been only half teasing, shrugged a mild shrug. She will come to love Mirella too. You all will.

Casimiro unrolled his rumpled sleeves, glanced up at Giuseppe with a suddenly thoughtful expression. So. Your novel. It is not finished then?

Giuseppe blinked. I think it is, he said slowly. I believe it is.

Yet you have brought new pages—

Giuseppe gestured at his cousin's small watercolour where it had been taped to the drafting table. His cousin was notoriously fastidious, notoriously slow. Is anything finished ever? he asked.

But he did not wait for an answer, and instead crossed the studio to where a small seascape in oil sat propped on the walnut sideboard. He stood regarding it in silence. Casimiro followed at a safe distance. After a moment Giuseppe said, reluctantly, not quite wishing to change the subject but seeing no further way to pursue it: Your sister looks tired.

Ah.

Is she not well?

Lower your voice, his cousin said. She will hear you.

She will not.

Lower your voice.

With his hands raised in defence, Giuseppe said, quieter: She is not ill, I hope.

Oh, Giovanna is always ill, Casimiro said. Being ill is what keeps her going. We should be worried for her if ever she felt well. I have my painting, Lucio his poetry, and Giovanna her health. That one there, that little seascape. It was painted by our mother. Lucio found it only last month, wrapped in oilskin, under straw in the carriage house.

Giuseppe studied it carefully. The colours were strange, oranges and reds, as if the dust from the Sahara had obscured the sun and stained the ocean with heat. Why would she hide it there? he said.

I think she feared the Americans coming through, Casimiro said. Or maybe it was put there before the war. I do not know.

I did not know she painted.

It is a strange painting for her. Not like her other pieces.

Perhaps it is not even hers.

Casimiro smiled. Perhaps she took a lover. Perhaps it is his work.

Of his three Piccolo cousins, Casimiro stood nearest in age to Giuseppe. When he looked at his cousin he felt an ember of sadness, seeing the quiet way he would keep himself apart. He had studied painting and sculpture in Munich in his youth but his fiancée had sickened and died of tuberculosis in that city, and Casimiro had returned to Capo d'Orlando, broken, estranged by grief, terrified by the touch of the living. Gracious, he would take an offered hand, but then flee at the first excuse to scrub the polluted hand with alcohol. He sat apart even from his brother and sister in the drawing room, in a corner quarantined for his own use; he would draw his chair to the dining table by hooking his feet around the legs of the table, to avoid touching common surfaces. He held a handkerchief to his nose when he stood near others, and leaned back on his heels, and averted his eyes, as if sickness might be contracted through sight.

Just then there came a soft scraping at the threshold and he and Casimiro turned as one to find Agata Giovanna and Mirella standing there, softly illuminated by the sunlight beyond, their faces sly and smiling.

I have always wondered what men discuss in my absence, Agata Giovanna said in her low voice.

Casimiro raised an eyebrow. When are you ever absent, sister?

They discuss the price of cigars, offered Mirella. Endlessly.

Truly?

We discuss you, of course, said Giuseppe. You are a mystery to us.

I am?

Ladies. Ladies in general.

You girls seem well acquainted, Casimiro said. It has not even been an hour. Has my sister pried your secrets out of you yet, child? Do not be fooled by her. Her questions are not innocent.

Agata Giovanna laughed. But I am afraid I have lost the other one, she said. We think Gioacchino has walked into the garden and been taken by the faeries.

Or the gnomes, smiled Mirella.

Or the gnomes. It is difficult to know which. I do not know that we shall ever get him back.

Or whom we shall get back in his place, Mirella offered.

Indeed.

We shall have to interrogate him thoroughly when he returns.

Hot wax on his fingertips. It is the only way to be sure he is not enchanted.

Casimiro ran both his hands through his black hair, his bony shoulders hunched. He smiled at Giuseppe and then crossed the studio and spoke to Mirella. He kept himself some five feet from her, and as he spoke he ran his handkerchief across his lips as if to wash the polluted air from them. But you have not seen my paintings, child, he said to her. Come in, come in. I shall take you on the grand tour.

She is engaged, Casimiro, his sister said.

Casimiro winked at Mirella. Her fiancé has been taken by the sprites, he said. The poor creature must need consoling.

As they moved away deeper into the studio, Casimiro keeping always his distance from her, Giuseppe turned to Agata Giovanna. She had picked up the plate and the glass as if to clean her brother's studio, held them cradled to her stomach.

And what has happened to Lucio? Giuseppe asked. He has disappeared also?

He is composing his verses, she said.

Now?

She gave him a mocking look. Oh, Lucio is always composing his verses, she said.

At dinner that first night they ate late, a heaping dinner of lasagne, vol-au-vents with lobster, cutlets in bread crumbs with potatoes, peas and ham, and a puff pastry filled with cream and candied cherries. They ate in the dining room and Giuseppe watched Casimiro carefully hook his ankles around the table and draw his chair up to his table setting. He feared for his strange cousin, whose phobia seemed not to have improved, regretting the loneliness that must accompany it. They ate under a candlelit chandelier which Giuseppe could not recall having been lit since his aunt's death and he understood then that Agata Giovanna wished to make an impression on Mirella after all. When all had eaten their fill Giò smacked his lips loudly, and laughed at his fiancée's expression, and then stood and offered to assist in clearing the dishes. The servants had been dismissed for the night and Agata Giovanna gave the boy a sober nod but Giuseppe could see she was pleased. He followed his cousins into the sitting room, Mirella at his side.

It was a small elegant space, the walls covered in Casimiro's watercolours, a corner bookshelf holding poetry and esoteric texts on the occult, the floor tiled in marble. Giuseppe went from lamp to lamp, turning them on one by one, as if he were one of the hosts. He did not go to Casimiro's corner, on the far side, which belonged to his cousin alone and held his magazines and his armchair and where his cousin sat and turned on his own lamp.

Lucio did not join Mirella on the little sofa but, to Giuseppe's alarm, sat instead at the piano bench, and crossed his legs, and cupped his hands on one knee. His toes only just reached the floor. He looked to Giuseppe's eye off-balance, distinctly uncomfortable.

You do not mean to play for us, said Giuseppe.

Mirella turned to the thickset poet. You are a pianist also? she said. A pianist *and* a poet.

Lucio shrugged modestly.

He can play all of *Parsifal* by heart, called Agata Giovanna from the dining room, a stack of plates in her hands. It is really very moving. We must have a recital later this week.

Much later this week, said Giuseppe.

Much, much later, agreed Casimiro.

But Mirella was nodding in encouragement. I think that would be wonderful, she said.

Lucio sat with his fingers interlaced, peering from face to face, his small moustache twitching, as if astonished that such as he should command so much interest.

Of course, he is self-taught, called Casimiro from his armchair. You must not expect too much from my little brother, child.

Lucio is also a composer, said Giuseppe. Didn't you know?

Mirella looked puzzled. Why do you smile?

He smiles, said Lucio in his high voice, because he thinks it foolish.

Nonsense, said Giuseppe happily. My esteemed cousin has nearly completed a Magnificat in the manner of Malipiero. And it is excellent. He held up a hand. How do I know it is excellent? I know it is excellent because he has been writing it for twenty-five years.

Forgive me, said Mirella. Is that a long time?

Casimiro laughed. It depends on the Magnificat.

Lucio writes a semiquaver a year, said Giuseppe.

Creating art takes time, sniffed Lucio, his little eyes fixed on the girl, as if to pay his cousin and brother no heed. But remember, my dear. What is created lasts forever.

Forever! cried Casimiro.

That would be a long Magnificat indeed, said Giuseppe.

I should like to hear what you have so far, offered Mirella.

Oh, but you shall, called Casimiro. Do not fear on that account.

Lucio blushed. I would be honoured, he said. It is not finished. It is true I cannot write a novel in a twelvemonth, like my cousin. But I do not—

A novel! In a twelvemonth! cried Giuseppe. You would be lucky to write a sentence a year, Cousin.

Now Giò came into the sitting room, walking with care, bearing a tarnished platter of pastries, and this he set rattling down on the low table in front of Giuseppe. Agata Giovanna followed, with a small plate of pastries for Casimiro, which she took to him across the room and set beside him without touching. A small spot of sauce was on Giò's shirtfront.

The youth sat on the little burgundy sofa and he folded his long thin arm around Mirella's shoulders and Giuseppe saw this and felt happy, seeing them like that, so young and in love. As the boy crossed his ankles Giuseppe glimpsed colourful yellow socks.

Have they told you this villa is haunted? Giò said now.

Mirella gave him a dirty look. You only say that because you are not sleeping here.

It is true, he protested. Ask Lucio.

It is true, said Lucio.

But not as you imagine it, said Agata Giovanna quickly. She was pouring English tea into tiny bone cups. The spirits are not here to trouble us, sweet. They walk among us absorbed in their own existences. *We* are haunting *them*.

Mirella glanced uneasily at Giuseppe.

Do not listen to them, he whispered theatrically. You are in a house of lunatics. There is no reasoning with them, they are incorrigible.

Doubt is also a kind of faith, Cousin, Casimiro called out from his deep armchair. We have seen the departed ones with our own eyes, child.

It is true, said Agata Giovanna.

It is true, said Lucio.

Giuseppe opened his hands in a helpless gesture. You see, he said to the girl. It is hopeless, I fear. My cousins know so much about the world of the spirits, I have encouraged them to write a Baedeker on it.

Mirella curled up into Giò's arm. Were you not afraid? she said to Agata Giovanna. Seeing them, I mean?

A little, she said.

What do they look like?

Yes, said Giuseppe. Tell us. What do they look like?

They are not frightening, said Lucio. They are like us, a little indistinct, a little blurred around the edges. They appear only at a distance. At the end of a long room, or a hallway, or across the garden. They do not mean to disturb us. Theirs is simply the next life, the world beyond this one. It is all perfectly natural.

Mirella gave a shudder.

If one is obliged to believe in an afterlife, Giuseppe said dryly, I should think the Catholic Church has a rather more convincing version.

Except the Church is all nonsense, said Giò.

Giuseppe reached for a pastry, smiling happily.

Earlier that summer, at Renato's restaurant, while a dusty heat baked down from the awning outside and the candles softened and leaned sideways on the tables, Licy dreamed up a strange idea.

You will think it is crazy, she said.

He smiled. I thought Freud did not approve of that word.

Hush, she said.

Her idea, she explained, was this: that she and Giuseppe formally adopt Gioacchino as their legal son and heir. The boy was maddening, incorrigible, and a delight to them both. In this way the ancient family title, Duke of Palma, would not be extinguished. Though the grander title, Prince of Lampedusa, could not be transferred, it was the dukedom and its history of ascetics and saints that mattered most to Giuseppe. He was quiet, thinking it over. They could offer no real inducement beyond their affection. The Lampedusa wealth was long since diminished: his great-grandfather Prince Giulio, who had died without a will, and with nine covetous children, had seen to that. What little remained of the great estate, except for the destroyed palace itself, had at last found its way into the possession of his great-aunt Concetta; and upon her death in 1930, she had left it to her widowed and childless sister-in-law, rather than permit any of it to reach her nephew, Giuseppe's father, whom she loathed. Nothing now remained. Giuseppe thought about those dead, and their bitter disputes, which made up the bulk of his inheritance. But then Giò, he knew, aristocratic, already rich, whose parents resided part of the year in the Mazzarino palace, would need for nothing anyway; wealth could be little inducement. He shifted creaking in his chair, peered around him at the empty tables.

He is like a son to us already, said his wife.

Giuseppe tapped a finger lightly on the table. You mean he eats in our kitchen without being invited.

You know what I mean. He is the very age our own son would have been.

If we'd had one.

She met his eye. If we'd had one. Yes.

In the days that followed, as he thought about it, he found he liked the idea very much. He had worried about Licy and his own failing health and he liked the idea of a son and daughter-in-law whom she could love and who would love her back. Giò would be a kindness to her in her grief. But there was some part of his wife's idea that pleased him on a level beyond reason, too. Giò was the youngest son of his second cousin Fabrizio Lanza Branciforte, Prince of Trabia and Butera, Duke of Camastra, and so that family's titles would remain secure. Giò and Mirella had come into their lives only in the last few years but they had seen the young couple nearly every week during that time, and their days, so dull and tired before, had been like a heated room in which the windows were all at once opened. The world had become sharper, clearer, more vividly felt.

When they approached Giò with the proposition the young man had grinned a sly grin and said, But then you will never be able to rid yourselves of me.

And laughed.

We are in earnest, said Licy.

The boy nodded, a happiness at the corners of his eyes. As am I, he said.

The sweetness of this struck Giuseppe forcibly, where he stood smoking at the window. The three of them were still at Via Butera, in the library, preparing to go out to dinner; they were to meet Mirella and a friend at the restaurant. Giuseppe turned his face aside and peered out at the evening light, overcome, and he did not turn back until he had collected himself.

But what will your parents think? asked Licy. That is the question, Gioitto. Will they agree to the idea?

They will think it odd, surely, adopting a grown man, said Giuseppe.

One whose parents are very much alive, added Licy.

To all this Giò smoothed out his trousers with one hand, pursed his lips in a wry half smile. But it *is* odd, he said.

Giuseppe smiled too. Yes it is.

We shall write them a letter, suggested Licy. We shall lay out our reasons.

Giò nodded. And you will have to meet with them.

I have not seen your father in fifteen years, said Giuseppe. I always did like him. He did not lose himself in the Bellini Club like so many others. He was a man of intelligence and taste.

Put that in the letter, Giò said with a grin.

Licy put a hand out on the vacant cushion beside her, lightly, as if it were reserved for some other. What will Mirella think of the idea? she asked softly.

Giò laughed. Oh, she will approve. It might even be enough to convince her I am not entirely worthless.

But if you are adopted by us, said Giuseppe, you nearly will be.

Two days later Giuseppe sat down to write the letter. He was surprised to find that his appreciation for the scheme had not diminished and the right words came calmly and clearly to him. He wrote with apologies for the strangeness of the proposal, which he hoped would cause them no distress. He trusted they had seen how fond their son was of them, and he wished them to understand how alike Gioacchino was to himself, both in his sense of humour and in his intellect. He did not know if such an adoption would be recognized by the Court of Appeal. But if it pleased the prince and princess, Giuseppe and Alessandra were prepared to set out on the arduous, difficult process of paperwork and letter writing. An official answer as to whether the adoption would be permitted—definitive, whatever its position, and whenever it came—could be received before the end of the year.

They received a summons to appear at Palazzo Mazzarino, in Via Maqueda, for tea with the prince and princess, one dazzling sunlit afternoon. They were received by a servant who took their coats and hats and then guided them up a grand staircase, along a hall lined with mirrors and velvet chairs, into a bright receiving room. There they found Giò, in his shirt-sleeves, a grin on his face, a shock of hair in his eyes.

They are waiting for you in Father's study, he said conspiratorially. Do not look so alarmed. I think they like the idea.

Very good, said Alessandra.

As they turned to go Giuseppe observed the ancient furnishings and the elegant eighteenth-century stuccowork and the cool air that smelled of the past and he thought, achingly, of his own beloved palazzo.

Giò led them through a second door and down the length of a dark ballroom, its furniture covered in white sheets, and through a second door and up another set of stairs. At the landing he paused, his hand on the brass pull of a door.

They are curious about you, he said.

They are right to be, said Licy.

Father remembers you, he said to Giuseppe.

Giuseppe smiled dryly. What does he remember?

Your silences, I think.

We shall dispel that soon enough, said Licy. Let us go in, Giò.

The study, to Giuseppe's surprise, was dominated by an enormous white ammonite fossil, set on a table in the centre of the room. Against the dark bookshelves and the huge slab desk of walnut it seemed almost a thing of intelligence, glowing with its own light.

He saw Giò's mother, Conchita, first. She was as tall as Licy, but thin, her long smooth black hair drawn tightly back into a bun, like a flamenco dancer. She wore a white pencil skirt to the knees, slit at the back, and a white bolero jacket, like the wife of an industrialist down from Rome for the weekend. There was in her something flamboyant and aggressive and as a Spaniard she had lived the life of an outsider in Palermo for twenty years and it was this, Giuseppe thought, that he liked about her immediately.

Fabrizio stood behind her, a head shorter, whiskered and leonine. He was Giuseppe's second cousin but bore no resemblance: here was a man who had retained the influence of his inherited name, and who wore his power like a heavy gold watch at his wrist, loose, half-concealed by a sleeve, barely worthy of a glance. His handshake was strong, painful.

There were three armchairs in front of the desk and after they were seated Conchita went around the desk and stood beside her husband, her face unreadable.

Gioitto tells us you wish to take him from us, she said. My sweet sweet boy.

Yes, said Licy, without the trace of a smile. May we have him?

For a long moment no one spoke. Giuseppe glanced helplessly at Giò. The boy had said his parents were favourably disposed to the idea, had he not? But then he caught the ghost of a smile at Conchita's lips: it was there and then it was gone.

Oh my poor boy, she said. Is he an orphan, that you mean to house him? Does he not have loving parents?

Gioacchino, he saw, was grinning.

Now Fabrizio cleared his throat, interlacing his thick fingers on the desk in front of him. Conchita put a hand on his shoulder in support.

The first question, said Fabrizio, is whether such a proposal is even desirable to the parties involved. It would appear our youngest son, wayward as he is, is quite convinced that he would like to abandon us and join your family. He gives little thought to the pain it causes his poor parents.

You have never been poor, Father, whispered Giò loudly.

The second consideration, continued Fabrizio in a sober tone, is whether such an adoption is even permissible. I am not certain whom one would apply to in a case such as this. I expect it would be the Court of Appeal, in Naples.

Yes, said Giuseppe. He had written as much in his letter but he did not point this out.

Fabrizio smoothed out the letter before him on the desk. Such a decision might take months, even years, he continued. The difficulty could be immense, and we must ask ourselves whether it will be worth the trouble.

Giuseppe nodded. He observed Licy where she sat, her face composed, the quiet intelligent intensity in her listening.

The third consideration is whether such an adoption, if it were to be acceptable, would affect our son's future in a positive or a negative light.

Here Fabrizio fell silent. It was not quite a question, and Giuseppe did not wish to interrupt the prince's thoughts. But it seemed he was finished.

Gioacchino would gain a title, said Giuseppe softly. As would your descendants.

Another title, you mean.

The Tomasi are an ancient family, Don Fabrizio.

I know what the Tomasi are, Cousin.

Giuseppe nodded with careful seriousness.

It is customary, said Fabrizio, in cases without an heir, to simply leave one's estate to a favoured relative. Adoption is rather extreme, is it not?

Giuseppe, who had almost no estate to bestow, and whose most important asset was an unrecoverable palazzo standing in ruins behind a padlocked gate in Via di Lampedusa, said nothing.

It is not the estate they wish to preserve, Fabrizio, offered Conchita delicately. It is the title, I think.

We feel Gioacchino and Mirella are family already, said Giuseppe. They have been a great consolation to us these past years.

We are Gioacchino's family, said Fabrizio.

In the silence that descended, Giuseppe started to blush. He glanced uneasily at Licy, hoping she would speak up.

But it was Giò who spoke. He looked serious, intense, in a way Giuseppe was not used to. He said: Nothing will change,

Father. I would just add Tomasi to my name. Of course you are my family. But when I marry Mirella, you will still be my family, though I will gain her family then also. And when I have children, there will begin a third family. It is the same for everyone, Father. This adoption would just be one more family in my life.

Giuseppe felt a powerful admiration for the boy. He started to get to his feet but then sat again abruptly when he realized no one else had stirred. In the corner of the study the hands of an English clock clicked through their radius. The light shifted. Licy smiled a sad smile.

Your son will still be your son, she said. Not ours. Not really.

It was Giò's mother who spoke first. This is what you want, Gioitto?

It is.

Prince Fabrizio, lordlike and imposing behind his desk, ran an open hand over his whiskers, his rings catching the light. Then we shall not oppose it, he said.

All this had added to Giuseppe's sense of a life in upheaval, of momentous events unfolding. He had lived a long time trying to avoid change, to move as little as possible from the place where he had begun. And now, with the completion of his novel, and the possible adoption of a son, he found himself staring into a mirror, not quite knowing the face that stared back. It unsettled him; he also found, to his surprise, that he liked it. This, he thought, is how one such as Gioacchino lived always—in the moment, alive to the possible, unprepared.

Yet he would wake sometimes still, struggling to catch his breath, as if some terror were crouched upon him in the night, and at such times he would sit leaning heavily on his knees in the bed, gasping, the little night lamp turned on at his bedside and the stacks of books there half-read and casting crazed shadows over the bedclothes. Such attacks had worsened in the last month. But at Capo d'Orlando these receded, and he would watch the young ones flirting and teasing each other across the breakfast table, or their gazes lingering too long as they wandered through the streets of the town, all this with such warmth and intensity, and which he knew was not quite love but only the fascination which might lead, in time, to love, and he tried to understand what it was that brought any two together. But he could not. The heart was a locked room. He could only marvel at it, and say nothing to his cousins, who noticed very little. It did not matter. He was happy. He watched Giò and Mirella and thought about his new pages, about young Tancredi and Angelica and their doomed hide-and-seek in the shuttered rooms of Donnafugata. He realized there would be no happiness for his lovers and that perhaps their fate needed to be explored more fully. Perhaps his novel was not finished even now.

Such an idea did not fill him with dread or darken his happiness. He was surprised by this. He had hoped his novel was complete; he had hoped that nothing remained now except the waiting. And yet each morning, throughout that week at Capo d'Orlando, he continued to find new material and to work it into sentences in his mind, sentences that he did not write down, holding the story instead up to the light and turning it, as if seeking its underbelly. He did not know why he could not leave it alone. Casimiro laughed to see him so distracted; Lucio teased him at dinner; he blushed and laughed with them but did not stop.

He still hoped to meet with Lucio privately. But whenever he tried to find a moment to discuss his novel, and to inquire after the new pages, his cousin was always just rising from his chair, just exiting a room.

On the Wednesday evening Lucio declaimed in his tremulous voice a poem from Browning. Mirella applauded; Giò stood and clapped dryly.

Though Giuseppe too admired Browning, to Lucio he had for years insisted that he preferred Browning's wife.

We would know nothing of what women think about in bed, he said now, were it not for the lyrics of Sappho and the sonnets of Elizabeth Barrett. Your dear Browning owes all of his insight to his wife, Cousin.

Lucio flushed. He glanced across at Mirella and then cleared his throat, shuffled his feet, busied himself with the glass of wine in his hand.

The following morning when Lucio did not join his guests for breakfast, because he was writing, Giuseppe rose from his omelette to seek him out. The door to his cousin's small writing room was closed. Giuseppe knocked softly, twice; then pulled on the door, irritable, for he would be departing early Saturday and he had grown anxious. But Lucio did not respond. He was lying on his pink sofa, his stockinged feet on a stack of books, a cloth laid over his eyes.

Yes, I have your new pages, he muttered before Giuseppe could ask. Casimiro left them on my desk. But no, I have not had the time to look at them.

That did not matter to Giuseppe. What he wanted to know was when a reply might reach them from Mondadori, and how the new pages might best be forwarded along.

Cousin, said Lucio, and now he took the cloth from his eyes and half raised himself onto one elbow. I am working now, he said. Leave me to my poem. We can discuss this tomorrow.

And Lucio waved a small ugly hand in dismissal, and set the cloth back over his eyes, and lay himself back down. And Giuseppe, troubled, suddenly unsure of himself, apologized, shutting the door behind him.

He did not wish to be with anyone after that. He walked down through the wild strawberries below the villa, the pale grass rippling at his shins, the bees loud in the stillness, and he twisted the tiny berries from under their leaves and turned them in his fingertips in the sunlight, feeling the fine hardness in them, remembering. Then the burst of sweetness would come to his tongue, and he would frown, and wade deeper. He tried not to think of the novel or of his cousin's rudeness and the one, he told himself, was surely not the cause of the other.

Something came to him then, an afternoon he had not thought about in many years, how the wild strawberries growing in the northern forests outside Riga, on Licy's estate at Stomersee, had tasted like Sicily on her lips. That had been their first kiss. A taste of the island of his belonging. They had been almost young then, faltering, fumbling their way into a strange and serious kind of love.

That was in the late summer of 1930, the old world of Europe only just catching, not yet on fire. He was thirty-five years old. It was his first visit north, into Latvia. He remembered now the amber light in the smoking carriage, the way it crept across the whiskers of the old Russian men. And he remembered passing through a deep snow-silent pine forest near the Soviet border while eating a pasta with prosciutto in the dining car. That. And the bite of the August air in the roar from between the carriages, and the surly Polish slang of the porters hollering to each other on the platforms of Kovno as they clattered past in the night. All that long journey he had felt like a man sliding sideways out of his own life, and it had pleased him immensely to imagine that no one on that train knew his name or history or station. A day and a night and a second day passed without his speaking to any other living soul, only meeting eyes, and nodding politely, and this pleased him too. While the tracks scrolled on northward, ever northward, as if seeking the coming winter.

Alessandra did not meet him at the station in Riga. There were large murky puddles on the ground at the edges of the wooden buildings. Though the hour was late the streets were awash with a metallic light, shining up from the horizon, a pale zinc glow that Giuseppe found indescribably beautiful. He stood on the long platform in the steam and smoke from the train, while the passengers flowed around him with their bundles of clothes, their cages of chickens, and with his gloved hands flat at his sides he peered up from under his hatbrim at the shine above like a man overwhelmed by the world.

He was quite alone, despite the crowds.

At first he did not know what to do. He felt suddenly helpless, and foolish, wondering if he had made some mistake, gotten off at the wrong station, perhaps, or come to Riga in the wrong month. He had not seen Licy in three years, not since his uncle Pietro had been recalled by the Fascists to Rome, and though they had written each other increasingly intimate letters, he feared suddenly that her repeated invitations to visit her in Latvia had grown less passionate, less sincere. Perhaps he had misunderstood? He stood stiffly beside his small stack of luggage as the platform emptied, as the train pulled away, as the railway clerk walked with his ring of iron keys the length of the track, examining the ground, as if he had lost some coins somewhere, and gradually Giuseppe began to wonder if he might not purchase a ticket right there and return to Berlin that very night.

But when he looked across in the gathering shadows he saw one other standing there, an ancient Lett in a baggy coat, swaybacked, feeble. Giuseppe knew him at once for a servant.

The man approached nervously, and doffed his cap, and said something in a guttural language Giuseppe did not recognize.

I am Giuseppe Tomasi, he said calmly. You are from Stomersee?

Stomersee, the old man repeated.

You are to take me to Stomersee?

Stomersee, ja, Stomersee.

Dipping and nodding his grizzled head as he spoke.

Giuseppe noted, first, the way the old man's knuckles were lost in the cuffs of his jacket, as if he wore a borrowed finery, and then how he stepped gingerly with his heavy boots in the puddles like a man trying to preserve them from wear.

He had come with no companion. Of course that ancient servant, if such indeed he was, could not manage Giuseppe's

trunks on his own and Giuseppe felt an unexpected embarrassment at the prospect, strange in a man who had lived his entire
life in the milieu of masters and servants, and he hurried forward to help the old man wrestle his trunks into the rear of a
long silver English motorcar.

And then the old man cranked the engine, and turned on the
headlamps, and climbed inside, and drove very slowly through
the darkening trees on the winding road out of Riga.

At the baron's *Gutshaus* at Stomersee the grand rooms were ablaze
with a new electric light. Alessandra descended the sweeping
double staircase in a blue gown with her black hair up, her naked
hand running smoothly along the wood panelling, and she was
smiling at him with undisguised pleasure. There was in her, he
saw, a calmness and an exquisite light that had not been present
back in London. He had forgotten how attractive she was. All
this surprised him and he could only smile shyly up at her and
think of nothing to say.

I did not think you would come, she said gently to him,
gliding forward. You are not in Sicily now, sir.

Ah, he said. No. Well.

Giuseppe Tomasi, she said.

He smiled, swallowed. He wanted to tell her such formality
was not necessary but did not.

You must be tired from your journey? She stepped near
and was peering intensely into his eyes like a film actress as she
said this and he felt all at once the stillness of the castle around
them, the closeness of her, and he blushed.

Giuseppe, he said at last. It is always just Giuseppe to you.

Giuseppe, she said, as if tasting the name on her lips.

He remembered himself then, and glanced up, but he did not see her husband.

André is not here this evening, she said, with a little smile that Giuseppe could not quite make sense of. Of course he sends you his greetings. He told me he would leave us to be reacquainted in private.

Giuseppe, puzzled, pleased, mumbled some politeness.

Oh, don't look so frightened! she laughed. You will meet him in the morning. André is many things but a gentleman first and always.

And she looped an arm in his and led him through into a brightly lit drawing room, past fine antique furniture and blond oak bookshelves filled with works in German and French, into a round study at the base of a turret, and then into the castle's elegant dining room, its four deep windows overlooking the twilit gardens, its delicate Empire plasterwork craggy with shadows from the electric lights. As they walked, she said: But for this evening, my dear Giuseppe, it will be only the two of us. You have not eaten?

Ah. Only a little something on the train.

I have taken that train. That is not eating.

Then I have not eaten, no.

Alessandra beamed at him. Very good. So we will eat first. And then you will tell me all about living with your mother in the hot south.

With my mother? That is not living, Alessandra.

And she laughed wickedly.

All those long two weeks it was the same, he remembered. As if some part of Licy's boldness had infected him, had entered him and changed his character, so that he spoke more openly with her and allowed himself to laugh sharply at the ridiculousness of his own situation. They woke early and sought each other out and spent the mornings walking the grand lawns, picnicking on the sloping edge of the lake, talking all the while. Giuseppe had known only one other woman in his life whose mind fascinated him so completely, and that woman was his mother. But Licy was a linguist with a wide knowledge of European literature and with her he could speak about Stendhal, Dickens, Balzac, Yeats and feel no discomfort. On the second morning she told him how a German lieutenant in the first war had taken her on long walks and described to her a new modern field called psychoanalysis. She had loved that officer, she confessed, though he had returned at the end of the war to his wife in Berlin and this had devastated her young heart. That was the same year she married André. She was twenty-three then and had not yet understood she might live as she wished rather than as she ought. She had known Freud personally and had studied psychoanalysis in Vienna and while there read poetry in a circle of ladies, each of whom claimed to have been a lover of Rilke's before the war. This scandalized her; and then it did not; and then, it seemed, nothing could. She had a habit of drawing a loose tendril of hair from the nape of her neck and twisting it around her finger when she spoke about the past and Giuseppe found this surprising, and charming, as if he were glimpsing the girl she had once been in the woman she now was. Her father had been a baron and she herself felt a deep loyalty to the old collapsed Russian regime. André had been one of the few Tsarist officers to survive the German victory at the Battle of the Masurian Lakes and it was this perhaps she had fallen in love with, but their marriage had not been a happy one, though he glimpsed a great gentleness between them yet. They slept apart, Licy told Giuseppe one morning as he blushed furiously.

And then she said quietly, to his mortification: I do not even need to lock my door at night.

She loved her baronial estate at Stomersee, its turrets, its grand staircase, the fairylike gables of its roofs. It had been rebuilt by her father in the first years of the century, after a terrible fire, by local craftsmen true to the ancient craftwork of the Letts. Those Letts she spoke of contemptuously, especially the old servant who had driven Giuseppe from the station that first night. That man had served Alessandra's family for seventy years, had known her great-grandfather.

Of course he is lazy, and he does not wash, she said in disgust. I do not know what to do with him.

But later when she thought she was alone he saw her stoop over the old man, where he had drifted asleep at a wash basin, and gently lift a scrubbing brush from his wizened hand, and settle a small pillow behind his neck.

André himself was all Estonian grace and courtesy. He sat with them some mornings out in the sunlight of the courtyard and drank his coffee and smoked his Russian cigarettes with two soft fingers like a gentleman just returned from the baths at Baden-Baden. Giuseppe, to his surprise, enjoyed his company very much. The three of them drove to Marienburg, and in the soft grass of the famous island in its lake they lunched on a *kulebyaka* of duck, celery, and a delicate white pastry goldened with butter and herbs. The following afternoon they drove again down to the village of Stomersee, and Giuseppe felt himself moved to silence by the sweet-smelling forests that stretched on forever. In his second week they attempted to drive to Pechory, in Estonia, to wander through the Russian monastery there, but André could not produce the papers for his motorcar and the Russians turned them back at the frontier.

But in the evenings the baron would often go out, and Licy did not speak of his nocturnal excursions, and Giuseppe did not ask.

He understood her reticence, though not its cause, and he had all his life believed any such form of secrecy deserved discretion. He was not above secrets himself: he had not admitted the reason for his journey to Latvia to his mother, and he did not tell this to Licy, though he suspected she knew. He had told his mother instead that he was to meet an old companion from the Szombathely prison camps, and that they would travel by rail to see the new Soviet borderlands, to learn what the Bolsheviks had preserved of the old order, and what they had torn down for the new. If she did not believe him, she did not say.

Licy had kissed him among the wild strawberries that first week. He knew this but he could not now remember the moment, whether it was morning or afternoon, or where they had been going, what he had been thinking. What he remembered in its place was the paved sunlit courtyard, the little wrought-iron table they breakfasted at, which felt like it had come from a café on the south bank of the Seine, and how Licy in a white dress had paused in the middle of a sentence on his last morning and reached across and—to emphasize some point she was making—touched the knuckles of his hand.

A shock had gone through him, the shock of a sudden intimacy he had not imagined. He had gazed at her in wonder, hearing nothing.

Months later, back in Palermo, he would catch himself staring dreamily down at where she had touched him, thinking nothing at all, reaching across with his other hand to press his weight upon the spot, feeling the heat of her fingers in his own.

One day in the breakfast room at Stomersee, when the maid had delivered the post, and he had opened in surprise a letter from his uncle Pietro discussing his mother and her grievances towards her son's disagreeable *Russian expedition*, he found himself trying to account for her to Licy.

He had said little of his mother before this. He knew Licy would have heard about her difficult nature from her own mother, whom Beatrice had gone to considerable lengths to offend after his uncle Pietro had announced his betrothal.

It is because she has suffered terribly, he said. It is her grief that makes her difficult.

We all have lived with grief, said Alessandra.

Not like hers, he said.

Perhaps it is because she does not face it directly, she said.

Well.

There is a process to grief. It is perfectly natural. One cannot just ignore it.

He was quiet a long moment and then he said, She lost three of her four sisters within a few years. They were very close. And when I was born, my only sister died of a fever at the same time. You cannot imagine how she has suffered.

You are right.

She does not mean to be so severe, he said. He gave a brief smile. But my god, she can drive a person crazy.

Licy cleared her throat, took a sip of her strong morning coffee in its tiny cup. She was too intelligent to acknowledge his last sentence, he understood, and be drawn into a position he did not really wish her to take. He at once regretted saying it.

Your mother has a profound heart, Licy said simply. There must be a great love in her.

Why do you say that?

To overwhelm her so.

Yes, he said, and he looked at her with a feeling of gratitude. I believe that is true. I do not think she would agree with you. I think she would find the notion ridiculous.

You mean because it would be coming from me.

He gave a confused half smile. I do not understand.

No?

Why would it matter if you said it?

Oh, Giuseppe, your mother has lost so many that she loved. She will not relish losing you as well.

Licy might have reached across the table and slapped him, for all his surprise. The directness of her meaning made him look away, through the sunlit windows towards the trees across the lawn, flushing. Nothing in Palermitan society had prepared him for such social clarity. With Licy, what ought to be left unspoken was seized and shaken out openly, like a wrinkled shirt. He felt suddenly shy, and feared to lift his coffee cup to drink in case his hand shook unnaturally, and so he sat with his fingers interlaced in his lap, his legs crossed, unable to think of what to say. Gio grinned.

Licy meanwhile stirred her coffee with its tiny spoon, and sipped it pleasantly, and changed the topic, as if a shining door had not just opened onto what might be.

Stomersee, that first winter, felt oddly near. He had not been returned to Palermo a fortnight before Licy's first letter arrived. His mother had presented it to him one morning at breakfast without a word and he had looked at the blue ink, the elegant looping hand, and the envelope had started to tremble in his grip. He had felt the heat rising to his face. When he raised his eyes his mother was looking at him with a kind of satisfied disgust but she offered no rebuke and that, he thought now, had been the worst part. Her weapons had always been silence and shame.

He could, he was told by Licy in that first letter, make the journey north again in early spring with little difficulty. *It would please me to see you again soon*, she wrote in French. *For my part, I have not ceased thinking of your Stomersee and its beauty*, he wrote back in German. *You write like Kleist*, she replied, teasing. *O the days have begun to pass by, all the same, one after another, grey and stupid and slow like sheep*, he wrote in German, encouraged. *You must come to me again*, she replied in her imperious handwriting. *My dear Licy, it has been nearly two days since I last heard from you, I hope nothing is wrong,* he wrote her the following spring. *Giuseppe! Two letters from you yesterday!* she wrote back; *I think we are singlehandedly keeping the European postal services from bankruptcy. Oh Licy, here in Palermo I live as I please, at least in the afternoons,* he wrote to her in English, not daring to criticize his mother directly. *My dear Sicilian, though you will be arriving in Riga in two days and I know you will not read this until you have left me again, still I could not wait, I had to write,* she wrote later that summer, breathless. And after that second delirious visit, after his return to Italy, nothing in his letters was the same: *O my life, my beauty, my angel, my sweet beloved; my good one, my beauty, my adored: your thoughts are as sweet as your kisses and as the beauty of your body in the rain.*

And so it went, across the months, the years, in letter after letter.

Even after they were married.

That was in Riga, in August of 1932. He had feared telling his mother and wrote her the news on the very day of the wedding. She did not reply. They had married late, yes, and had married for love, but because in the end he could not bear to live away from his mother and the island of his birth, and because Licy could not bear to live with them, they lived apart until the dark years of the Second War. Instead, his new wife had drifted through the rooms of her mind at Stomersee, studying her psychoanalysis, writing Giuseppe daily about her discoveries. And Giuseppe had lived with his mother in their palazzo in Palermo, reading voraciously, thinking, writing letters. Gradually his desire had cooled, had quieted into something else, a kind of counterpoint, a cast and drift and return, until what he had come to treasure most was the knowledge that somewhere in the cool green northern forests there lived, like something from a fairy story, a creature of sensibility and understanding and beauty, to whom his fate was tied. He was not alone in the world.

As the week slid past, and Friday arrived, it brought with it a thick late-summer heat.

Casimiro had arranged for an outing on a private motor yacht. It had been commissioned in France four years earlier by an industrialist count with painterly inclinations, a gentleman with property in Sicily, and Giuseppe admired the clean mahogany planks, and the brass fittings, and the French crewman in his pressed whites who helped them up the plank and aboard. Its owner had flown from Rome to Paris just the month before, Casimiro explained, which was a pity, as he suspected Giuseppe would have found him rather diverting.

He has a wooden leg, he said with a smile, settling himself onto the cushioned bench at the back of the boat.

Giuseppe paused on the ramp, a book under one arm, a small hamper in the other. From the war, I imagine?

Agata Giovanna came up behind him, slipped nimbly past. Over one shoulder she said, Don Franzetta was in Arabia in thirty-eight, before the war started. His jeep overturned and caught fire. He was trapped underneath it.

The poor man, said Mirella.

Agata Giovanna shook her head firmly. Poor? He should have burned.

Giuseppe followed her up the ramp, lurched awkwardly over the railing and into the boat.

Casimiro smiled across at Mirella. She was wearing pink capris and a white collared shirt tied off at her smooth belly and Giuseppe thought she looked, in her dark glasses, like a movie star.

Casimiro said to her: Franzetta can swim faster than Lucio and I would bet he could outrun you, child. And that leg kept him out of the war. No need to pity the man.

Giuseppe had been pleased with the day's plans. He wished very much to speak with Lucio about the new pages, and to determine what should be done regarding his novel. He had found his younger cousin occupied all week, eager to avoid his company, but there would be no place for Lucio to hide on a small yacht. He was disappointed not to see his cousin already on board.

Lucio? said Agata Giovanna, when he asked. But he is back at the villa, suffering another headache.

Better his suffering than ours, smiled Casimiro.

I suspect he just wishes to work. You know how he is.

All this Giuseppe absorbed in silence.

He is always writing, said Mirella.

And making sure we hear of it, laughed Giò, swinging up from the cabin in shorts and an open shirt.

Agata Giovanna went below deck to stow the lunch hamper, settling the bottles of water into place, and Mirella followed, pressing unnecessarily close past Giò as she went. On the steep ladder she held carefully to the brass railing with one hand, her other keeping her hair from her eyes. The men sat in the rear of the boat and Giuseppe adjusted his hat in the glare and peered up at the crewman as he started the engines and double-checked the lines and slowly, cautiously, reversed them out of the marina and into the harbour. The sun on the water was hot, the breeze cool. The black ocean slid viscous and thick in the shadow of the boat, the canvas top crackling in the wind. As the hull lifted, smacked, lifted again in the slight chop Giuseppe closed his eyes, the yacht catching speed. Some part of him had always loved the ocean and this part, he suspected, was the ancient and truer part of him that had come down through his father's blood.

Later, after the heat had started to beat down upon them, and Giò had crept nimbly to the front of the yacht and lay out on a towel in the sun, like a cat, Giuseppe rolled up his sleeves and stretched his arms wide and lay his head back and closed his eyes. What was this Franzetta doing in Arabia? he asked his cousin, as if no time had passed.

Franzetta? Casimiro squinted across at his cousin.

Your friend. The owner of this.

He was exploring, his cousin said. Franzetta considers himself an amateur archaeologist. He had a notion that a city lay under the sand there and he set out to find it.

And did he?

What?

Find it. His city.

That is not what he found, said Casimiro. He withdrew a folded pair of sunglasses from his pocket and put them on.

The blue sky was cloudless and the distant haze of rocky islands could be seen across the sea. Far to the west a heavy cargo vessel was underway in the shipping lanes.

A city under the sand, Giuseppe murmured.

———

He slept and awoke to find the light had shifted, the sun high overhead. They had entered a channel of small rocky islands, nameless, rising pocked and inscrutable up out of the sea. Casimiro too was asleep on his bench. As they motored among the cliffs, the world of man seemed ancient and very far removed and Giuseppe glimpsed a solitary stone fisherman's hut at the peak of one island that might have stood for millennia but no other sign of life. The air was quiet. There were no birds.

Giò was stretched out golden on his towel at the front of the vessel. Giuseppe rose, groggy, and went down below. It was cooler in the tiny cabin. Mirella and Agata Giovanna were playing cards at the table, and Giuseppe crushed himself into the hatchway and watched awhile in silence until Agata Giovanna said, abruptly, Do you remember the disappearance of that scientist before the war?

He shook his head. Who do you mean?

Marjorana. Who jumped from the ferry. Mirella never heard of it and I could not remember the details.

Mm.

Was it not around here that he disappeared?

Giuseppe wiped at his forehead. He was struggling to recall. He was a physicist, I think, he said. Living in Naples.

That's right.

Working on government secrets.

Agata Giovanna frowned. I do not think so, Giuseppe. Perhaps they wanted him to.

Is that why he killed himself? asked Mirella.

If he killed himself, said Giuseppe. No body was ever found. He simply disappeared.

That is right. There was some uncertainty.

They hunted for him, there was a reward for any sightings of him.

Yes.

Giuseppe raised his face, peered out through the little windows at the shining sea, the passing islands. Was it near here? he said. I thought it was nearer Naples.

Agata Giovanna shrugged and lay down a card and smiled across at Mirella. Another game? she said. The younger woman scooped up the cards, began to shuffle. No one offered for Giuseppe to join them and after a moment he went back up and returned to his seat in the rear of the yacht. Casimiro was awake.

You were hoping Lucio would be here so that you could ask him about your new pages, his cousin said. You have still not managed to speak with him. Casimiro ran his hand lightly over his throat. You have not asked me what I thought of them.

Of what?

The new pages.

The pages I brought for Lucio? Has he read them?

Casimiro adjusted his sunglasses, turned his face languidly in the heat. That I cannot say, he said. Are you not interested in my opinion?

Giuseppe, suddenly irritable, closed his eyes. The blue shadows of his lids seemed to swim with the rocking of the yacht. Your opinion, he said. You told me you have no opinion.

That does not sound like me.

You said you were but a poor worker in paint—

His cousin snorted.

—and that you were no literary critic.

I do not think it is quite what I said.

Giuseppe opened his eyes and sat up. He watched the blue sea, the clean white froth of the wake behind their yacht. They were nearing small rocky islands now and the crewman cut the engines and they began to drift sideways in the warm sea.

Here is a good spot for swimming, the crewman called down. Giò and Mirella rose stiffly at the front of the vessel, stripping down to their bathing costumes.

What did you think of them, then? he asked at last.

Casimiro's mirrored sunglasses turned in his direction. They are interesting, they add to what was only suggested before. It is a shame they were not ready when Lucio sent the novel out. Your Donnafugata, it is our mothers' palazzo, is it not? No matter. But this exchange your prince has with the politician from Turin, the man Chevalley. When he declines the man's invitation to the Senate, I think it is very provocative, I think it will get you into trouble. You will make enemies, Cousin.

Enemies!

Enemies, yes. Do not laugh, Giuseppe. I think it will interest the rest of Italy, certainly. The rest of Italy is curious about us. But here in Sicily you cannot write about the old order and the new in such terms. You will look like a reactionary. Sicilians will not stand for it. It is the despair in it that will offend them. Not only the idea that the new Sicily is bankrupt, and corrupt, but the idea that it cannot be otherwise, that we are to blame because of something inside us.

It is the prince who says such things, not me. It is a novel, Cousin.

But the prince is you.

Nonsense.

He is of your class. He will be understood as being you.

By the foolish, perhaps.

Are his views not your own?

Giuseppe did not respond.

You must know I agree with you, Casimiro continued. Yes Sicily is asleep, yes it wants to remain asleep, yes its sleep is its own desire for death. I see it too, I feel it too. And the scene is magnificent, as a scene. But it does not matter. I must urge you to rewrite that passage. It will bring you only criticism.

Just then Mirella dove from the boat and surfaced into a clean backstroke and Giò, crying out and beating his chest, leaped in after her. The water was so blue as to appear black, the foam very white, and in the harsh sea light everything appeared impossibly beautiful and alive. Giuseppe watched the youngsters swim laughing in a long slow arc through the stillness, Mirella's red rubber haircap turning this way and that in the sunlight, Giò's hands rising and falling like pale blades. He had laboured long hours at that exchange between his prince and Chevalley, written and rewritten the dialogue until he had found what seemed to him a true expression, both clear and acute. His prince, both cynical and filled with regret, had come to seem to him as complicated and bottomless as any living person. Thinking this, weighing Casimiro's concerns, he felt a curious heaviness come over him, clouding his happiness. He set a hand to his chest, breathed.

Giuseppe? Casimiro said. Are you all right?

I cannot change it, Cousin, he said quietly. I would not know how.

———

The difficulty, he knew, lay in the fact that he had never been a man absorbed by politics, as other men were.

That evening as the yacht motored quietly into the harbour, all of them tired, lost in their own thoughts, and later that night under the trellis in the gardens at Capo d'Orlando, while the sun smouldered behind the hills, he considered again his conversation with Casimiro, wondering if his cousin's worries could be correct. He had not imagined his novel might be controversial. He had tried to make clear how little there was to admire in both the old order and the new, because of human nature, because people are no different today than they were yesterday, and no reason else.

His own feelings about the monarchy and its abolition after the war were ambiguous; he did not, unlike his cousins, regret their removal. Yes, he had voted for the monarchy in the referendum of 1946, and had observed Umberto's expulsion to Portugal with unhappiness. But his vote had been to preserve an ancient order, one which he understood, and not for the disgraced king himself.

Umberto was said to have blamed the women and the communists for the result. It was the first vote in which women were permitted to cast ballots. That was the influence of the Americans. But Giuseppe was sensitive to how Umberto's father, Vittorio Emanuele III, had allowed Mussolini and the Fascists to co-opt his authority; not only allowed it but in fact endorsed it; and he understood the country's anger. That same anger had been in him also.

Of course the new age ushered in by the American libera-
tors, the age of the economic miracle, of the industrial north,
was no less corroded, cruel, or wasteful than the vanishing feu-
dal age of his novel. Was it possible, as Casimiro had intimated,
that his novel was not really about the past at all? Certainly he
had witnessed the dying of a social order, no less than the
prince in his novel; certainly he had witnessed the rise of a new
republic; and he had watched the sweet world of the belle
époque vanish, though the old families could not see it.

Truly vanish, he knew: because everything had changed,
changed utterly, so that his childhood no longer seemed admi-
rable, or even worth recovering, if such a thing were possible.

All that week he had found himself watching his cousins,
thinking with his eyes, letting his mind drift. He wondered
about the nature of their memories, how the past pressed itself
upon them, where it was they found themselves now in their
lives. He had already started to think about a new story, a story
in which a character's past has destroyed his happiness in the
present. That past would be the past of his island, of a classical
Sicily, something Homeric and alien to the spirit of the modern world. His protagonist would be an aging artist, perhaps
a writer, perhaps a scholar, a man who had encountered the
Greek tradition in his youth and known first-hand the vibrancy
of it, its life, and this had paled all else for him until he had
grown bitter and disillusioned. He did not know what form
this disillusionment would take. It was while he was studying
Casimiro's paintings of night creatures, the faeries and shrunken

gnomes of his garden visions, that Giuseppe found what he had been looking for. The past would be made physical: his protagonist, his old man, would have loved a siren in his youth.

He knew even as he walked through the gardens, as he ate quietly in friendship, as the week passed and November neared, that it was not enough for him to have written his novel. It was the second work that would prove the true test, the second book that would determine whether he could call himself a writer. He felt confident as he let this new story turn inside him. He thought about the mysterious disappearance of that physicist from Naples, and he let this account run alongside his siren until he began to find a connection. All this while, as he dreamed and thought and brooded, he said nothing to Lucio or Casimiro. He felt a clean pleasure in a story that did not yet exist. The possibility in it felt powerful, and he felt as if he were taking part in something that was both original and true, and he wanted to preserve it, unspoken, for as long as he might.

On the last night of their visit he went out into the back garden in the darkness and sat beside a small lily pond and stared back at the house, blazing with light, the sound of Mirella's laughter mingling with the piano. The full moon was high, the air sweet and warm, and in the silver moonlight the grass and leaves looked tipped with frost. Far below the lights of Capo d'Orlando glittered. He heard the scrape of heels on the flagstones and then he saw, uneasily, Agata Giovanna's silhouette appear at the base of the steps. He had been expecting Lucio but she came across the grass and sat beside him on the stone bench and he offered her a cigarette. He had always found her inscrutable. Her grey eyes were capable of a flat pale coldness, her knuckles were hard, the turn of her head could silence her brothers. It was she who commanded the villa. She frightened them all.

He did not know why she had come to him now. They sat in silence, smoking. She sat with her knees together, a shawl hugged tight across her shoulders, and as he looked at her he saw the profile of his own mother, like a reproach.

You must not worry about your novel, Giuseppe, she said quietly. Lucio says August in Milan does not end until October, and they do not work in August. He will hear back soon now, he is confident.

I am not worried, Giuseppe said.

But he said this too quickly, and crossed his legs, and busied himself with tapping the ash from his cigarette so that he would not say more. He felt embarrassed that she had come to him. He wondered just what his cousins said about him, when he was absent.

It is just as well, perhaps, she continued in her gruff voice. Your new chapters can be added in without trouble.

All at once he understood that he would not get Lucio alone on this visit, that Agata Giovanna had come as a kind of emissary. He swallowed, uncertain. Does Lucio mean to send them on, then? he asked after a moment.

I am sure he does.

But he has not said?

She cleared her throat, hesitated.

Giovanna? What has Lucio said?

Sometimes it is best to leave one's publisher alone. To not be a nuisance.

As I am being?

She turned now towards him in the moonlight and he could see the faint outline of a smile. Lucio and I talk about many things, Giuseppe. Your novel is only one of them.

Of course.

She finished her cigarette, dropped it, a small ember of light, and crushed it under her toe. Lucio is to travel to Milan next month, she said. I will suggest he meet with Federici then and ask about the novel, if he still has heard nothing back. He can use the new chapters as an excuse for the journey.

If you think that is best, he said.

I do.

Giovanna—

Hm?

Should I be concerned? That I have heard nothing back?

She raised her face to the moonlight. They could hear Giò plunking away at the piano inside, Lucio protesting noisily. A tinkle of glasses. Laughter.

No, she said.

But he was not reassured.

You are leaving tomorrow, she said after a moment.

In the afternoon. Yes.

We shall be all at once alone again.

Yes.

She looked directly at him. That is good, she said. It is good to be alone.

He smiled at her. Another guest might take offence, he said.

But not you.

Not me.

Because you understand us, she said. Then she got to her feet and stood in front of him, smoothing her skirt with her hands. My mother used to say, We have lost everything but we will recover everything. She raised a hand to her hair, brushed it back from her face. She was peering off into the garden as if at some other there.

And did you? Did you recover everything?

Nothing can be recovered, Giuseppe. There is no going back. That is what life is.

What?

Loss.

Giuseppe too rose to his feet. My mother used to say, To every problem there is a solution. He frowned. She had so many friends, my mother. But she was always sad, always alone. To the problem of loneliness I don't believe she ever found a solution.

You were her solution, Agata Giovanna said quietly. Just as Gioacchino is yours.

He looked at her and started to speak but then did not.

How strange our parents are to us, no? she said. We can live our entire lives alongside them and still they will be closed to us.

Not only parents.

Mm.

It is a very bleak view, Cousin, he said.

Not bleak. Lonely, perhaps.

Well.

He was standing very still in the stillness of the garden and he finished his cigarette and crushed it into darkness and then they stood silent, solitary, subdued, while the warm stillness pressed in around them and the nightsounds of the garden rose up around them. The sky was porous with light, the stars in their milky gauze of galaxies. The sound of laughter, of a glass shattering in the house came to them.

Listen to them, he said. They are like children.

You all are, said Agata Giovanna, turning away.

He woke the following morning late, to find the house deserted. It had been a long time since he had slept so deeply. The Piccolos and Giò and Mirella had already breakfasted and had walked to town, leaving an amusing handwritten note on the table beside the fruit bowl, complete with drawings of sprites tugging at Giuseppe's moustache while he slept. He stood reading it at the open shutters in the dining room and he leaned his face into the sunlight, at peace. He could hear servants adrift in the house, like ghosts. Far below the sea was a watery eggshell blue, the white sun millionfold and turning on the surface like blades. They would be leaving that afternoon.

He felt calm. He put the water on to boil and poured coffee beans into the grinder and sat grinding with the small machine folded under one arm. He was not hungry.

When it was ready he took his coffee into the guest room where he had been sleeping and he packed his few clothes and his notebooks and blue fountain pen into his old suitcase and this he carried back into the front hall. He rinsed and set upside down to dry the small coffee cup and then he paused, his hand folded in the tea towel, all at once overcome.

What he was recalling was a time from his childhood. This was after the terrible earthquake at Messina. They had come to

Capo d'Orlando where his little cousin Filippo, who had been buried alive and hauled from the rubble, was now staying. He recalled it was a winter's afternoon, the rain coming down, the light in the villa blue with shadow. Filippo had been seated under a window, drawing battleships and dreadnoughts, and speaking happily about naval guns. He remembered the whiteness of the boy's skin, the translucent look of his hands, as if he had not been outside in years. The boy had very long beautiful eyelashes and small square teeth. He spoke with a lisp. Casimiro had lifted a single bored shoulder when Giuseppe gave him a look. Lucio had absented himself. Filippo said nothing of his grief, expressed no sorrow, though his parents had not been dead a month.

Aunt Teresa, as they were leaving, whispered to his mother that the boy was still in shock. He will feel it soon enough, the poor thing, she said.

But now a second memory came to him. He remembered seeing Filippo at the end of the hallway, as he was leaving, a tiny solitary figure silhouetted in the winter light of the windows beyond. With his white skin and very black eyes, the boy had looked dead. And Giuseppe had quickly turned away.

Such a recollection must be of little interest to any save himself, he knew. He suspected, if he were to ask Casimiro or Lucio, that neither would even recall that time. What was it the prince in his novel had said of his decline? He was among the last to have had any unusual memories. Giuseppe took off his jacket, slowly rolled his shirtsleeves up, then stepped out in his naked feet onto the warm flagstones of Agata Giovanna's terrace, like a much younger man.

All that he was remembering now, he knew, was long vanished from the world. And there was silence now in the gardens of Capo d'Orlando, neither birdsong nor the trickle of the fountain. Only the sound, like a dry whisper in the green leaves, of his own solitude and his blood moving inside him, alive, hopeful, while the full possibility of his novel drifted towards him in the warm air, and he raised his face in the radiant sun to greet it.

LUCIO PICCOLO
PAYS A VISIT

═══

NOVEMBER 1956

Lucio's wrist pained him. It had started in Capo d'Orlando as he wrestled his suitcase down to the motorcar and had sharpened on the drive to Messina and then worsened in the rattling train compartment north of Rome. He had listened to the rain on the windows and folded the book he was reading over one finger and stared gloomily out at the passing landscape, his shoes unlaced and set beneath his seat with the toes together. Later as he walked through the cold station in Milan, rubbing at his wrist, peering around him, he thought in disgust: There is not enough poetry in you, Lucio, to make this beautiful.

His sister had told his cousin of the journey. So be it. He briefly considered going directly to his friend Federici at Mondadori but changed his mind. The day was waning; Lucio was tired; let his cousin's business wait. He stood in line for the taxi and got in and fumbled in his various pockets until he found the hotel address.

He understood his presence in Milan would, in some way, be seen as a tacit approval of his cousin's writing. He was eager not to risk his own reputation; he was eager, that is, to make of his cousin's novel a success.

But not too much of a success. What was it Casimiro had said, on that morning of his departure? If you feed the Monster, Lucio, it will only get hungrier.

How they had laughed at that, the red sun in their eyes, the boom of breakers rolling in far below.

At his hotel he sat by the cold window, turning the pages of his book, unable to concentrate. Though it was still afternoon he needed the lamps to read by. In Sicily the sea is our lamp, he thought. At last he rose. At the washbasin he shaved using one of his cousin's English razors, he smoothed down his hair, he added a dab of scent to his neck and his wrists. Lastly he changed his suit and collected up his umbrella and raincoat across one arm and studied himself in the mirror. A small homunculus, little black eyes too close together, the long nose of a bandit. He wondered what Casimiro would say, to see him dressed so. The suit had been tailored in Rome last year, a modern cut, but Lucio had not worn it and instead hidden it in his wardrobe in Capo d'Orlando, embarrassed. But Casimiro did not know, as Lucio did, how the fashions of the world were changing, and how men were judged in the north. Craftsmanship did not matter, only newness.

He went down. Under the dripping awning of the hotel he lit a cigarette and studied the street and then he punched open his umbrella and started to walk. The smoke curled into the umbrella's shell, lingered. He passed a café with American music jangling loudly from a jukebox, turned left down an ancient alley that had somehow survived the war. There were boys in soaked shirts standing around a motorcycle, admiring its curves. A tattooed man in an undershirt stood in a doorway, wiping a cloth at his throat, while someone hollered from within. Lucio crossed the street, passed a shuttered cinema, walked on.

He turned left onto Via Bagutta, towards the trattoria. There the city's literati ate, argued, even some nights slept, and there Lucio felt, as a visiting poet, that he ought to be seen. But his modern suit, with its narrow shoulders, tugged and crushed at him, so that he felt distinctly not himself, and the fact was he knew few writers in Milan and, worse, feared none would know him.

Outside the trattoria he shook out his umbrella, wiped his shoes unhurriedly, and then went in. Jazz was playing somewhere in the smoke. Two men shoved past Lucio, arguing loudly, vaguely familiar. He caught a glimpse of a long horse-like face, wrapped in a fur stole, peering down at him in interest. Was she an actress? The entrance was dim, smoky, a wall of noise and hot spices from the kitchen. He pressed through the crowds and introduced himself and was shown to his reservation. The other tables were full, the restaurant roaring. Only Lucio sat alone. At such times he felt acutely his own isolation, how apart he stood from the literary world. He was seated at a small table in the far corner and he sat with his back to the wall and busied himself lighting a cigarette and studying the wine selection and adjusting his table setting.

Did he admire his cousin's novel? Giuseppe, soft-spoken, ironic, bitter, had a talent for synthesizing his reading, for juxtaposing writers and languages and cultures. He was an enthusiast. But was he an artist? Lucio grimaced. He had seen how tired his cousin looked of late, how ill, had heard him coughing in the mornings during his stay at Capo d'Orlando, and he understood how the writing had exhausted him. The novel itself was shocking, amusing, a delicious send-up of their shared ancestors and class, but Lucio could not imagine its appeal to readers beyond Sicily. It did not help that he knew Giuseppe had only started writing it after Lucio's own success as a poet. If I am certain of nothing else, Giuseppe had told him dryly, it is that I am no more of a fool than you, my dear cousin. Envy, and competitiveness, Lucio felt, were ugly wellsprings to draw poetry from.

He was being unkind. He caught a glimpse of himself, warped, haggard, rippling in the tarnished mirror beside the door. It was this errand, it was being in the north, it was being here at the trattoria that made him think such thoughts.

He thought of Casimiro as he had bid farewell, the slant of the sunlight across the tiles in the villa. His brother and sister, he knew, did not take his reputation as a poet seriously. They viewed it at a distance, as if from a great height, ironic and detached: they smiled condescendingly down at their younger brother. He suspected they thought him affected, his verses insincere. And then Capo d'Orlando came to him, unbidden, the low hiss of the gardens in the evening, and he understood how much his poetry depended on that place. He was no Verga; he would not be able to leave Sicily without losing the poetry. It would fade slowly, like a bowl of water left out in the sun, but it would fade all the same. It would not keep.

He should not be here, he thought unhappily; he should be at home, in his garden, writing. He glanced around the room, at the tables filled with laughing diners, and felt a quick low loathing. Would any of them have read his *Canti Barocchi*? But he knew it did not matter. He would always only be a guest in such rooms, a stranger begging acceptance; and beg he would, for he had no pride, he thought in shame, and what he wanted could be given by no one.

A darkness was cast across the table, interrupting his thoughts, and he looked up in alarm. The poet Montale stood with his hands in the pockets of his suit jacket, his black hair slicked back, his frown jowled. His eyes were very pale.

Don Lucio, he said, with a bow. You are very far from home, my friend.

And Lucio stared at the man feeling suddenly grateful, and flattered, and ashamed of his own desperation. Signor Montale, he said, with a polite smile. I hope you will join me.

You are the only one, Don Lucio, whose company I could bear tonight.

Nothing is the matter, I hope?

Montale sat, grimaced. No, nothing. Only exhaustion. Too many poets, too little poetry.

Lucio smiled. He set his cigarette into the corner of his mouth and held a hand high for the waiter to bring a second table setting. What brings you to Milan, signore? he said.

Business at Mondadori. And you?

Business at Mondadori.

Now the poet, too, smiled. He lit a cigarette, sat wreathed in fire.

You are not here for the Premio Bagutta, then, Lucio said.

Montale's cool eyes took in the room, the oblong light in the frames on the walls, the ladies in their sleek black dresses turning the stems of their wine glasses like cut flowers. A low bopping jazz drifted through the partition. No, he said. No, Mondadori wishes to discuss my new collection of poems. I, like you, suffer Milan only for my art. I will be leaving as soon as I am able.

Lucio smiled a pained smile. I did not know there was a new book, he said.

There is not. At least not one worth publishing yet.

Does it have a title?

Montale studied him. He tilted his head, ran a weathered hand smoothly, carefully, over his hair. *La bufera e altro*, he said, reluctant.

Yes. I like it.

Montale grunted, but Lucio could see he was pleased. Waiters were drifting through the smoke like shades of the gathered dead and Lucio thought of Dante's infernal whirlwind, la bufera infernal, che mai non resta, and wondered secretly at the man's bravado.

Pozza printed a run a few months back, Montale continued. Privately, you understand. But Mondadori wishes to bring it to the commercial market. I do not know if the poems are ready. He waved an irritated hand. But you, you are writing more lyrics, I hope? You cannot know quite what a strange sight you cut here, Don Lucio, with your sunburnt hands. You are like a memory of our August. How is that cousin of yours, the one you brought to San Pellegrino?

Giuseppe? Oh he still scribbles, when he thinks no one is watching. The offhanded cruelty in his reply surprised him. He felt the heat rise to his face, as if he had betrayed some ugliness about himself, and he uncrossed his legs and leaned forward and folded his cigarette smoothly into the ashtray. I do not mean to tease, he said, all at once serious. Giuseppe is a gifted writer.

A critic, was he not?

A novelist.

Montale smoked in silence, absorbing this. Lucio watched him. The lamp's shadow fell aslant his face so that his eyes glittered. At last he said, The Sicilian aristocracy must be more careful, dear Lucio. All of Italy will learn of its abilities.

Lucio smiled, shrugged a rumpled shoulder. For shame, he said.

Later, in the shadows of his hotel room, he would lean into the windowframe and shake out his aching wrist, wondering that he had not mentioned his cousin's manuscript. Montale was a man of taste and a critic of influence. In the street below a car would pass, its brake lights sleek and glowing. Lucio would shake his head, reach up, draw the curtains closed. No, he would tell himself, the novel was under consideration already, it would do Giuseppe no favours to distribute it on the sly. And if Montale were to feel it inferior, or weak? In that late hour Lucio would run a thumb lightly over his moustache, considering. Such a judgment might devastate his cousin.

And embarrass yourself, he would think, before he could stop himself. He would leave the window, stand at the foot of the small bed, suddenly unhappy. And he would wonder if his cousin appreciated the trouble he was going to.

The following afternoon he met with his friend. Count Federici was a tall man, balding, impeccably dressed in a blue suit and yellow tie. His face grew craggier each year, more melancholy, like the face of a man with a secret, his voice rougher and softer, all this in sharp contrast to the warmth and kindness of his manner. He was, Lucio considered, almost Russian in this way. There were not such men in Palermo.

My dear friend, Federici was saying now, in his hoarse whisper. He unfolded himself from his seat, all knees and elbows, six and a half feet of refined breeding, and he stretched his long arms wide and embraced the Sicilian without embarrassment. For a moment Lucio's cheek was crushed up against the count's ribs, he caught the quick warm scent of sweat and cologne, and then he was released, held again out at arm's length. How well you look, Federici rasped, how wonderful. Come, sit. I have ordered us a bottle of the Regaleali—

Lucio, already flustered, felt his face twitch. I shall forget I am in the north, Don Federici, he said.

—and then we shall discuss the poetry. A wide magnanimous smile opened the count's face to acknowledge Lucio's comment and then his face closed again upon itself. You are well? Of course you are. Tell me what you are writing. I wish to know all about it. A new collection, I trust?

Yes—

I expect you must be curious how the *Canti* are selling. You should know we are pleased, my friend. The collection has received several fine notices. Shall I send them to you? Well, consider it. No need to answer now. Let me know.

They sat beside a window with the restaurant's name painted in gold letters and through the glass the rain in the street billowed and swept in sheets. The daylight was cold, feeble. The table had been set for three and Lucio observed this as his friend spoke, feeling uneasy, but his friend did not comment on any guest joining them and Lucio, out of politeness, did not inquire. His gaze strayed to a small purple stain next to his water glass and he wondered that the cloth had not been changed.

Across the room a fire had been lit and the restaurant, despite the weather, struck Lucio as mild, sedentary, and cozy.

The wine arrived, chilled, golden. Federici raised his glass. Have you given any thought to the anthology?

Lucio stared at his friend. He could not recall anything about an anthology.

Did I not mention it? The Sicilian collection? Ah. Federici smiled, his smile fell again away. We are thinking it might be time, with the recent interest in the Mezzogiorno, for a collection of writings on the south. Sicily in particular. It occurred to me you might have an essay or a poem—?

He felt all at once pleased, but eager not to betray his delight. I might be able to locate something, he said. Yes.

Wonderful.

A poem, perhaps.

Very good.

He crossed his legs, picked at his threads as if considering. You will want an unpublished piece, a new piece?

Oh, I do not think it matters, my friend.

They sat then in companionable silence for a long moment.

Don Federici, Lucio said, clearing his throat.

Yes?

What is the news of my cousin's novel? I sent you two further chapters, last month, but heard nothing.

Your cousin's novel.

Il Gattopardo. Yes. Lucio felt a sudden alarm, wondering if his friend had failed to bring it to Mondadori's attention, if he had already dismissed it from his mind. But then Federici raised his chin and nodded.

It is an interesting account, he said. What is it your cousin wishes to achieve with it?

To achieve?

Who does he imagine its audience to be?

The sharpness of this comment struck Lucio forcibly, so close was it to his own uncharitable assessment. He felt himself beginning to blush and rubbed at his chin. What do you mean, Federici? It is a novel, it is written for readers of novels.

I have not finished it yet, you understand.

You should.

I fear it is rather old-fashioned.

It is inspired by Joyce.

Federici raised his eyebrows. He leaned back in the cane chair. Perhaps I have not reached that part in the manuscript yet, he said gently. You do know that it is not my decision. I offer only a reader's report. Vittorini is reading it also.

I would not think this to his taste.

Federici frowned slightly. In the end, Mondadori will decide for itself, he said.

Lucio nodded.

Tell me honestly, Lucio, Federici said. What is your opinion of it?

Lucio paused. He took the lemon from the rim of his ice water, crushed it into his glass. Then he looked up. It is a masterpiece, he said.

A RECEPTION
IN THE HILLS

═══

DECEMBER 1956

The rejection came through in the second week of December. Mondadori, with regret, would not be publishing the novel.

Lucio brought the letter to Giuseppe one evening at a friend's palazzo in Palermo and Giuseppe swallowed dryly and put on his reading glasses and studied it with cautious deliberation. He was sensitive to his cousin's attention and he raised his eyebrows in mild amusement when he had finished and he smiled and handed the letter, wordlessly, back. A heavy rain was blowing against the windows.

The book has interested us a lot, Mondadori had written, *and has had more than one reading. Nevertheless, the opinions of our advisors, though favourable, were not without reservations, and for that reason, bearing in mind our current burdensome commitments, we have come to the decision that it is not possible for us to publish it.*

At home on Via Butera Licy lowered the letter and glared over the top of it. I have never read such rubbish in my life, she said to him. You have written a work of genius, Giuseppe. They will regret this.

Indeed, my dear, he said. A bitter day will come.

But something shifted inside him after that, some presentiment of honour or respect, and he caught himself instead sometimes staring out of a window, at the rain, thinking nothing at all. His work would amount to nothing. So.

Time wobbled, elongated, slid past.

There was more and more of the monster about him now.

It was the sickness in his lung; it was the winter cold; it was his age. He could not tell which. But his eyes were pouchier, deepset into folds of purpled skin. His hands like any old man's hands looked ugly, but the flesh gleamed a strange translucent blue-white of late, his fingers spectral, except where they had yellowed from the tobacco in his English cigarettes. A great exhaustion would come over him unexpectedly. His weak shoulders were narrower than before, his waist wider, as if, he joked, he had swallowed a child whole. His eyes bulged. He shuffled along in the gloom, breathing heavily, his cane gripped like some ogre's club. When he caught a glimpse of his reflection, it amused him for a time to grimace horribly, and then it no longer did, and he merely looked away. Each morning he would comb his thinning hair smoothly back from his forehead, barbering his little moustache in the fashion of a gentleman out of his youth, as if to make himself invisible, that no one might look at him twice. In the streets the dark rain of Sicily fell and fell.

He had continued to write throughout the autumn: a short chapter about his prince's priest, Father Pirrone, making a visit to a village in the interior; a chapter about a ball, the liveliness of the dancers around his prince underscoring his prince's approaching death. And he had wrestled with an unfinished chapter, his *Canzoniere*, in which his prince at the Hôtel des Palmes intercepts Angelica and her lover, who were to be ambushed, and so saves Tancredi from embarrassment, although he saw too early how much of his murdered aunt Giulia's tragedy was in that story, and her liaison in that shabby hotel near the train station in Rome, and after that he was overwhelmed by memories of his mother in her grief, and those months with Ferri in Languedoc, and the cruel baron Paternò del Cugno, and he could not continue.

After Mondadori's letter he turned his glance away from the novel, like a man shouldering a grief, and instead tried to focus on the impending adoption of young Gioacchino Lanza. The Court of Appeal had consented to the adoption; the title Duke of Palma could be passed on, though not the princedom of Lampedusa; and the legal details were, at last, finalized. The boy's mother, the Princess Conchita, was preparing a celebration at a villa in the hills for the occasion. Alessandra, quietly aglow with satisfaction, dressed that morning in her good white skirt and jacket from her seamstress in Rome, like a bride. And so he found it less difficult than he would have supposed to put aside his particular sorrow, as if it were a plant only half-potted, or a letter opened but unread, and to pick up instead this happier thing.

It was a rainy afternoon in the third week of December when he and Alessandra and Giò met in a notary's office in the old quarter of Palermo. They had come to a third-floor office in a once grand palazzo, now carved into apartments, and leaned their dripping umbrellas in the ancient stand, and folded their damp coats over their knees, and sat—Giuseppe and Alessandra with the stiff dignity of age, Giò all knees and elbows and dripping black hair.

A gold fountain pen turned nervously in the notary's fingers.

I am pleased to call you here this day, he said, fumbling slightly in his formal Italian. He was a small man with a thick beard despite his thinning hair and a severe underbite that made him appear, Giuseppe thought, like a psychoanalyst from one of Licy's conferences. His low voice rasped as he explained the complications in the line of succession and how the passing on of the Tomasi title would work, blinking often as he spoke. Giuseppe thought suddenly of the rough-born Don Calogero in his novel, the man's oily manner, and then he remembered the letter from Mondadori, and he sighed.

Will this take long? Alessandra interrupted, as if sensing his dissatisfaction.

The notary hesitated, met her gaze. Ah, no, Princess. Not long.

Very good.

He glanced at Giuseppe, as if seeking permission to continue. A hard rain was rattling against the windows. No overhead light had been turned on and the small office deepened in the winter gloom. If you will allow me, then, I am instructed to explain the implications of the adoption to you both—

Gioacchino will be our legal son? said Alessandra.

Again the notary looked up. Yes, Princess.

Is that not the implication of the adoption?

Yes, Princess, although—

Let us get on with it then.

On a little table below the windows Giuseppe could see the papers arranged in six surprisingly small stacks. These would be the fair copies. A slim document, he thought, for the significance of its substance.

The notary stood and invited Giuseppe to seat himself at the table with his back to the room and he offered his gold pen in three damp fingers, turning the sheets of paper as he said, You will please sign here, Excellency. And here. And here.

Giuseppe did so.

No one spoke. The rain on the glass cast slow shadows across the documents, across his knuckles. As he signed, the nib scratched softly. The ancient clock on the wall ticked, ticked. This near, he could smell the notary's aftershave, glimpse the faint yellow stains at his collar. When he had finished signing he leaned heavily back in the chair, peered up. He felt mildly ridiculous, having the notary lean over him in such a fashion, while he sat like a child before his tutor.

That is all? he said. The boy belongs to us now?

The notary looked at him in dismay, swallowed. Belongs, Excellency, is not the phrase—

He is teasing you, sir, called Giò.

Ah. Yes.

Now Alessandra rose to her full height. And what do you need from me? she said.

Only a signature, Princess. Here, and here, and again here.

And when Giò too had signed his name away the notary at last seemed to relax. Not twenty minutes had passed. The rain was still falling steadily in the street outside. Giuseppe knew that beyond those windows glowed the rooftops of the old quarter of Palermo. If he were to peer west through the purple light he would glimpse the streaked traffic of Via Roma shouldering through the rain and then the grand reconstructed edifice of the Palazzo delle Poste. And to the east along the shadowy Via Valverde in the other direction he would see the sharp cornerstone of the Oratorio di Santa Cita, with its rococo cherubs celebrating victory over the Turks. That chapel had somehow survived the American bombings. And yet his gaze would pass first over the dark entrance of a street he knew too well, and it was here that the old quarter lost its beauty for him and became something other than a part of an ancient city on a quiet coastline of Sicily. For Via Valverde opened onto Via di Lampedusa, and he knew that there lay the crumbling plaster and stone of his beloved palazzo, where his mother had lived out her final years, thin, sullen, solitary, a faint reflection of the dazzling creature she had once been, where she had been discovered dead one morning in a ruined armchair in the bombed-out drawing room, under an open sky, one more casualty of a war that had been ended for two years already and yet would not ever end, having destroyed both the past and the future and leaving in the present nothing but devastation and grief.

The notary had risen to his feet, he was rubbing his little hands together.

I must congratulate you, he said. He reached across and shook Giò's hand. You are, as of this hour, Gioacchino Lanza Tomasi. Excellency, may I present to you your son.

My son, he murmured.

Hello Father, said Giò, and he gripped Giuseppe's shoulder. But there was in his voice a catch, and he saw the boy swallow.

He followed his wife and son down into the raining streets of Palermo in silence, all three of them changed somehow, moved immensely by a shared happiness, and in the sudden cold their umbrellas bloomed open and crowded together, rustling exquisitely, a family.

It surprised him sometimes to think about the nature of blood, and title, and how his name Tomasi did not belong to him but was only borrowed from those who had gone before, to be held in trust for those who would come after, like the great houses themselves, all of which were gone now. What these things had meant, how they had mattered in his life, was not something he felt equipped to comprehend.

His mother had understood such truths about the world. Last week he had gone to visit her grave, stirring his painful memories, like a hand trailing in slow water. Licy had come with him, steadfast, grim, the set of her mouth betraying her own brooding thoughts. A strong wind was up but the skies were a light grey, almost blue, and the light seeping through the clouds meant it would not rain. They walked the white gravel paths, past the ancient monuments and marble angels and the dirty drooping yellow flowers in little glass jars inside the iron fences. He was one who ought to have liked cemeteries, he thought. But he had never liked them. They passed his aunt Giulia's grave, a creature of light once and wit and grace whom no one would now remember. His mother was buried in the ancient Tomasi ground, beside his father, though he knew she would not have wished it so. He would lie in that enclosure someday, perhaps soon. Alessandra too. He felt the wind tug at his hat. He could not get warm.

He opened the gate with a little iron key and much struggle. The grasses had overgrown and tangled in the hinges. At her graveside he took his hand from his pocket and leaned with both hands into his walking stick, gasping, trying to slow his breathing. A cough had developed in him of late, had sunk its little claws in his chest, and he was sensitive to Coniglio's concerns about bronchitis and bacterial infection and tried to betray little of it to his wife. But he could feel Alessandra's eyes on him, watchful, as he swayed.

He felt faintly ridiculous. He had come because Mirella had asked it, suggesting he might tell his mother and father that the family name would go on. And the sweetness in the gesture had touched him, and his wife, though neither of them believed any part of a person went on after death.

I will go to her, he had said despite this. I will tell Mama about you and Giò.

And yet here at the grave he found he did not know how to begin, what to say. It was not only that Licy was with him, although that was a part of his embarrassment. It was also the memory of her last years, how she had died alone in the crumbling halls of Casa Lampedusa, like a mad old anchoress. That was in the winter of 1946, long after the island had been declared liberated and the war had ended in the fires of Berlin and the shabby Palermitans had returned, unhappily, to their ruined streets. He and his wife and his mother had been left with nothing.

She died alone, yes. Her physician, Coniglio, had found her.

She would have hated that. Had it been one day, two days? He creased his eyes shut at the bitterness in him, trying not to imagine it. Not long, that much was certain. Her body had not started its corruption. He was to have visited her that morning but put it off until the afternoon and he returned to his little apartment to find his wife waiting with tea on the stove and news of his mother's death. When he arrived at the ruined palazzo he found her already composed, laid out on top of her neatly dressed cot, her cold hands crossed at her breast and her eyelids drawn shut. Her lips were partially open, her skin sucked back over her cheekbones and eye sockets. His first thought had been that this was not his mother, there had been a mistake.

She was seventy-six years old. She had seen the end of the war, the rise and collapse of her modern nation. Her Europe, the Europe of the belle époque, was not even remembered now. Motorcars, aeroplanes, moving pictures, the terrifying new American bombs which could obliterate cities, all marked a strange otherworld, one she did not comprehend. She complained ruthlessly but circumspectly, observing with displeasure the little differences, the quality of the wine, of lady's fashions, the expense of travel. She had witnessed across the decades the final decline of her family, until nothing remained, no heir, no fortune, no grand houses. She had outlived her own existence.

He tried to remind himself of the woman she had once been, fearsomely modern, shocking in her views, a woman who startled and alarmed the new century as it dawned. But that was a creature from his childhood, and not a perspective he could trust, she being magnified by the lens of his adoration into something incomprehensible and magnificent. During the war he had fled with her to a little house in the Vina district at Capo d'Orlando and then, when even the coastal towns grew unsafe, they had followed the Piccolos inland to the banks of the Naso stream. He, a shabby soft man of privilege, and his ancient dowager princess mother. What a sight they must have been. At Naso they rented a tiny cottage in the plains below his cousins' house and lived poor, in the quiet of birdsong and wind. Then in the late fall of 1942 Alessandra was forced to flee Latvia and crossed the Axis countries by rail on her Italian papers and arrived shaken and ill at her mother's villa in Rome. Giuseppe joined her for Christmas. He had not seen her or touched her in six years. Seated beside her in his uncle Pietro's garden, holding her hand in his, he felt like he was meeting a stranger.

In the new year he returned to Sicily, alone. That was a strange time, the entire country in a panic. Everywhere he saw the machinery of killing. The raids on Palermo intensified. Giuseppe returned every month or so to check on his beloved Casa Lampedusa, to make certain it had not fallen to looters or been taken over by squatters. He would leave his mother alone and wonder what would remain upon his return. In March a ship exploded in Palermo's harbour, blowing the doors and windows out at the palazzo, peeling back the roofs of the library and two other rooms. In April the grand front steps were struck directly and demolished, so that Giuseppe could not enter the house, even by the tradesmen's entrance, a heap of rubble two storeys high blocking the way. Then in May the palazzo was struck again and its walls collapsed and the destruction was, at last, total. There could be no saving it, even had he the money to rebuild. He walked through the rubble weeping and alone until the sun had gone down and the air turned cold and then he sat down in the stones and closed his eyes.

He could not bring himself to return to his mother. He understood that explaining what he had seen would make it forever real, irrefutable, and this he did not want to face just yet. He walked into the hills outside of Palermo, to a cousin's villa, and there he stayed, a strange disconsolate wild-eyed figure, unable to speak, even to explain the nature of the loss that had befallen him. He did not shave. He did not sleep. Only after two days of silent grief did he make his tortured way back across a Sicily at war, his pockets turned out, his head bare, his suit covered in dust.

When he arrived at Capo d'Orlando, his mother came out to the stoop to meet him and walked down the dirt path to where he stood, trembling, and enfolded him in her arms without reproach, as she had always done, and it seemed she already understood.

It is all right, my little one, my little bird, she said. Oh my sweet sweet boy, it is all right.

What changed in him then with the obliteration of his palazzo was gradual, and soft, and pliable as knuckled dough. It was a kind of giving over, he saw now, to fate and its destructions. He did not know what to do with himself. In July of that year Licy at last travelled south to Sicily. In the week before she arrived the Americans landed on the south coast, and a few days later the little house in the Vina district was struck by a bomb and demolished. Giuseppe stood in the lane, while the dust and smoke threaded into the sky, and shook and shook. They could save nothing; and he and his wife and mother took refuge inland at Ficarra, in a tiny one-room hut, with only the clothes on their backs. The two stubborn women had met only twice before and both meetings had been disastrous. In the strain and heat of that little hut, Licy had little patience for his mother's imperious manner, and his mother disliked her Baltic forwardness and her too-affectionate manner with her son. She disliked that Licy had been married before, she disliked that Licy was too old to beget children, she disliked that Licy was not a Sicilian. *She is my wife*, Giuseppe had replied in anger. It was the closest he came to confronting her.

In October of that year Giuseppe returned to Palermo with Alessandra. His mother had gone to live with her sister Teresa, at Capo d'Orlando, to sharpen the letters to her son.

He resisted the thought that came to him then, at her grave, with Alessandra in black at his side and the cold wind rippling his coat. All around them the crooked stones and monuments of the dead crowded close. He preferred to remember his mother as a woman of force and conviction who lived inside a solitude of her own making, not lonely but alone. She had been clear and direct in her demands all her life, he told himself. But he now began to wonder if that was true. She had chosen to live in the rubble of the bombed-out Casa Lampedusa after the Americans had swept Palermo because it was her home, she said, and because she was a Filangeri and a Cutò, and ruined families belonged in ruined houses.

Oh do not look at me so, Giuseppe, she had scoffed in impatience. I am not one to succumb.

He had not protested much. This must have surprised her. After three years torn between her temper and Alessandra's angry silences, he was tired. She had been caught, he came to believe, by her own powerful tides, misled to think she held a stronger grip on her son than she did. He did not believe she imagined him a child still, merely one who would not abandon her to her own wilful nature and so, to prove this wrong, to himself as much as to her, he had taken lodgings with his wife on the far side of the old quarter, in Piazza Castelnuovo, in a miserable one-room apartment without water or heat, near the barricades. Licy traded her furs on the black market for tins of expired American food; he accepted a position as a provincial president of the Red Cross. In the cold months that followed his mother's arrival he did not visit Casa Lampedusa often. It was not Licy's heart that kept him away. He felt his mother, chilled and miserable at her little portable cookstove in the old stables, increasingly dishevelled, had failed to understand his own sadness.

Entering the courtyard of his childhood house devastated him anew, each time. Picking his way among the clinking masonry, he would begin to tremble, and fall silent, unable to speak at all some days when at last he found his mother. It seemed to him profoundly foolish, next to the vast world of suffering all around, and yet he could not discuss it, not even with her, who had lost all also and yet who continued to drift through their palazzo, not like a ghost, but like a squatter. She did not understand that a house could be not only one's past but also one's present and one's future; what she grieved for was already gone. He could peer into the distance and see his own grief still approaching. Only Licy, he realized, who had lost her castle at Stomersee to the invading Soviets, had understood. Had he moved into Casa Lampedusa with his mother, had he insisted on it, she might have survived that winter. She might have lived. But it would have taken something from him he could not spare, and left him desolate. Had she asked, and he refused, what he felt now would have been simpler. Instead what remained was a vague suspicion that he had failed her, that he might have acted differently.

Ten years had passed now; more. Yellow grasses grew long at her grave. He did not often go to that cemetery, he saw, because he did not like to think of her body there. She had elected to die in the freezing shell of a ruined palazzo, without fresh water, without heat, in a winter of starvation and death. He wrote to old friends who had known her, to Corrado della Fratta, to Guido Lajolo, to his uncle Pietro, insisting that his mother had died satisfied and at peace at Via di Lampedusa, as she had wished. He did not allow himself to speak, even to Alessandra, about his feelings. He avoided the ravaged palazzo, could not bring himself to go through his mother's scattered belongings, feeling that her ghost, or memory, or presence remained strongly in that place and would not be dispelled. He did not need to speak the words out loud; the truth of it was clear. She had wanted her son to choose her. She was willing to die if he did not.

And he had allowed this. He stood alone on the terrace at Via Butera one morning, staring out at the flat grey sea, his collar rolled high, unable to lie to himself any longer. It had angered him that she would place him in such a position, and he had refused to choose. He had known the cruelties of that winter, the frailty that was in her, how common were the frozen dead in the doorways and alleys of the old quarter. He had abandoned her. He could have saved her, preserved her, shown her that she was loved and one of the living.

What she had wanted, he came to see, was for her son to come to her, to enfold her in his arms, to insist that she mattered still. Death had nothing to do with it. She wished to preserve the spell of her own younger self. She had chosen annihilation over obsolescence.

He had not understood that then. It had seemed to him a kind of madness. She had arranged the complications in her life the way a novelist would arrange a book, he felt now, had shaped them and structured them and sought not answers but conflict and density. And so too it would follow its own logic, through to its completion. He believed her inner life had been tumultuous and beautiful and no one quite like her would ever live again. The influenza she suffered in that last winter, the medicinal cocktails prescribed by Coniglio, the deep brown rings around her eyes, all of this he knew was a part of the story she had been prepared to write, and he remembered now the restless cruel laughter she was capable of, but also her curiosity, her generous love, her fragility and easy woundedness. All that was gone now, sunken from her bones, crumbled into dust.

Now he thought about her dead body, and the unbroken sunlit palazzo she had once walked through with the gliding footsteps of a god, and the intelligence in her liquid eyes. She had become a part of his loss, a second great house, a loss he could inhabit that was his and his alone and that could not be taken from him again for it no longer stood in the world of the living. She had become memory, and this he could not reject, for it was not separate from his self, and so she had achieved what she had desired in the end.

He had never dared imagine a son.

That was the wonder of it. Now he walked slowly back along the hazy street in the rain with one hand on his son's shoulder, the other on his walking stick, the notary's office behind them vanishing into grey. At Via Butera, Mirella had let herself inside and was waiting in the white sitting room with the terriers in her lap and Giuseppe poured cocktails and the four of them drank to their new family. It felt strange, and fine, a moment in time utterly lacking in regret or sorrow, and because of this he found he did not know what to do with it. Giò's parents had arranged a reception at a friend's villa in the hills outside the city later that evening to celebrate and so the young couple took their leave and he and Alessandra sat together in the white ballroom nursing their cocktails and smiling vaguely at each other. And in the early winter evening they began to dress, and went out.

It was a modern house in the hills beyond the city, all angles and concrete, like the mansions of the industrialists in Milan. The big windows were ablaze with light. Alessandra drove slowly up the long driveway and parked on the still-wet grass with the other automobiles and Giuseppe got out and adjusted his tie and stood waiting for his wife.

It is very quiet, she said.

He nodded.

Shall we just go in? she asked.

They walked slowly up the concrete steps and passed through the glass door and entered the house, wiping their shoes carefully with his handkerchief. They did not see any other guests. The house was lit and brilliant against the cold blackness, the long wide living room looking strange with its low sofas and its minimalist sidetables. Alessandra gave him a look, and Giuseppe raised his eyebrows in agreement.

They could hear voices now, and passed down a bright hallway and up a short flight of stairs into a kind of mezzanine. A glass wall stood open before them, and a grassy park was lit with dozens of small lights beyond, and they could see a crowd of guests standing massed near an emptied swimming pool. A quartet of musicians in winter coats sat on chairs in the grass, their instruments at their knees, waiting.

Giò's father, Prince Fabrizio, was standing on a little folding chair, making a speech.

They stopped at the top of the descending steps and Giuseppe felt the cold December night on his face. Just then a tall figure detached itself from the guests and made its way up towards them and Giuseppe recognized the dark Spanish profile of the Princess Conchita.

Come, come, she said with a shake of her bracelets. I will introduce you.

Giò is not here? asked Giuseppe.

You will see. He is eager and nervous. Mirella has not arrived yet.

That night would prove an anxious one for Giò, he knew, for it was not only a celebration of their adoption but also, for Giò's parents—Giò's *other* parents, he corrected himself, feeling the strangeness of it inside him—this would be the first time Mirella was introduced to their social circle. It was to be, he understood, her entrance into society. He caught a glimpse of Giò standing in a group of young men, poised, alert, in his narrow black suit looking like an adder. He kept turning his face with its sharp cheekbones and squinting eyes to the house to watch for her arrival.

Giuseppe? a man said softly at his elbow. I thought it was you. How long has it been?

He stared at the man—tall, thin, nearly bald but for a crown of grey hair encircling his skull like a medieval monk's. The man was holding a cigarette in his left hand, his right, as if of its volition, opening and closing the buttons on his coat.

Giuseppe shook his head.

You do not remember me, the man said.

He smiled shyly. It has been a long time?

You know each other, Alfredo? said Conchita now.

The man smiled, not taking his eyes from Giuseppe. We played together as children. You do not recall? You hid from me at Santa Margherita once and I found you in the ballroom, reading. I was very angry, I tore your book in half, I think.

Some vague recollection of a boy, a sunlit afternoon, a feeling of dread. He inclined his head. Alfredo, he said, yes, of course. This is my wife, Alessandra.

Alfredo cupped the cigarette inside his curled fingers, bowed. Princess, he said.

Whom I am going to steal from you both, Conchita said now. Alessandra, there is a doctor I want you to meet, Dr. Moreno. He too practises psychiatry. I think you will find him most interesting.

Licy gave him a curious look as she was led away, a look he did not understand. He felt a wave of uneasiness pass over him.

I have always regretted that day, said Alfredo.

Which day?

When I tore your book. I was so angry.

Well. We were children.

I have been living in Morocco, Alfredo said. I fled from this life as soon as I was old enough.

And how do you spend your days in Morocco?

There was applause, laughter. Fabrizio had finished his speech, and he climbed nimbly down from the chair. The party began to break up, to drift towards the house, its warmth. Giuseppe took a glass of champagne from a passing waiter but he did not drink it.

Alfredo laughed. I am a publisher of books, he said. Art books. I run a press in Morocco. Small printings, but beautiful reproductions. Mostly of architecture. Some sculpture.

Giuseppe studied the man with interest. You work for a living, then.

If you can call it that.

You do not call it that?

My wife does not. She thinks it a hobby.

Mm.

And you, have you ever been to northern Africa? It is another world. They live more richly there, more completely. We are so stifled here, so strangled. I could feel it the moment I returned.

And when did you?

Last July. To settle my father's estates.

Ah. I am sorry.

He nodded his head. He was old, he lived a good life. He died in his sleep. There is nothing to be sorry about. And your mother?

After the war. In her sleep.

Alfredo nodded a gentle condolence, easily, with a kind of grace which Giuseppe found himself observing for signs of falseness, or strain. But he saw none. He wondered if his astronomer prince might have been so companionable, had he been real. But his prince was all weary politeness and deflection, and that was the difference: there was in his prince too much of himself.

Tell me, Alfredo was saying, how has your life been? You were not ruined by the war, I see.

Giuseppe smiled sadly. Nearly so, he said. But not quite.

Across the lawn the musicians were playing. A young woman in a red dress was dancing alone in front of them, her shadow long on the grass from the brightly lit house, her breath visible in the cold.

The war devastated my family, said Alfredo. We cannot rebuild. My father did not recover from it. I do not mind myself, I have no interest in the old estates. I will be leaving Palermo as soon as his affairs are settled.

In Sicily, nothing is ever settled.

Alfredo winked. He took a long drag of his cigarette and then flicked it away and said, It is easy to escape anything, if you do not wish to preserve the past.

Giuseppe truly did not remember this man as a boy. He was trying to dredge up a recollection of his face, of that afternoon at his mother's palace, but could not find anything. As he let his gaze wander into the middle distance, he noticed that he and Alfredo were being observed by a young woman in a black shawl who stood some distance away, alone, beside the concrete shell of the pool. She was turning the stem of a wine glass in her fingers. He thought she must be an acquaintance of Alfredo's. And yet soon he was overcome with the feeling that it was he himself she studied with such concentration. The woman had long white hair, almost silver in the darkness, and yet she seemed very young. She wore only a thin necklace, no heavy jewels, and because of this he knew she must be very wealthy, the daughter of some industrialist in the north perhaps. She might have been a dear companion of Giò's and Mirella's, he supposed, wanting to congratulate him. But he knew somehow with certainty that this was not the case. She had none of the relaxed charm or easy laughter evident in his son's friends or in the other young people gathered there at that party. She seemed rather to radiate a kind of sober distance, a solitude, almost angry in its intensity, which prevented anyone from approaching her. Her face was lined, as if she had lived a long time in fierce climates, and her long narrow features were not beautiful. When at last Giuseppe allowed himself to hold her gaze she stared back at him boldly, and did not smile, nor raise her glass in greeting. There was no hostility in her, only a directness that left him uneasy, as if she were one who would ask after his novel, or his health, or his unhappy heart, knowing the truth in his answer before he spoke. He resolved that he would avoid her. But when he looked back she had turned and was drifting with the crowds towards the house and was gone.

Tell me, said Giuseppe, turning back to Alfredo. Whose house is this?

Alfredo laughed. It was my father's, he said. He and Fabrizio conducted business together. Investments. There was a factory in Naples which they purchased and converted into flats, I think. Alfredo shrugged. I'm not that clear on it all, to be honest. I understand congratulations are in order.

Thank you.

Gioacchino is a wonderful boy.

Mm.

But Giuseppe was now feeling distinctly uncomfortable. He did not know what his host knew of his circumstances but could only imagine that Giò's father had told him much. The quartet had started up again from somewhere inside the house, a piece by Mozart, and Giuseppe heard the laughter of the guests and the steady clink of glasses and silverware on plates. They were walking now on the terrace past long tables of food and wine and Alfredo paused to offer some refreshment but Giuseppe, still clutching his untouched champagne, shook his head no.

And then his host was gone, moving fluidly among the guests, smiling at some, brushing others on the shoulder as he passed, all with an ease that Giuseppe could only marvel at. The house above him was ablaze with light, the rooms illuminated, figures moving through in twos and threes. There was a rough garden of country plants descending alongside the concrete steps to the grass, and lanterns hung from the branches of the small trees.

He discovered Alessandra, alone, brooding, in a study. Two young women were balancing on the railing of a balcony beyond, laughing.

You do not look pleased to be here, he said.

She shook her head. Did Giò find you?

He is looking for me? Has Mirella arrived?

Yes.

They will all love her, he said. They will be as charmed by her as we have been.

Perhaps.

I am certain of it.

In the grand hall Giò's father found him, urged a glass of wine into his clumsy fingers, left him. He walked outside to the garden paths trying to look preoccupied, as if he had somewhere to be. Giò and Mirella found him near a fountain, pulled at his sleeves, teasing. He saw Licy in deep conversation with a small man near the food tables on the terrace and he turned and peered in the opposite direction. The party went on. The musicians laid down their instruments, ate from little plates. He slipped back into the house and went upstairs and stood for a time on an upper balcony watching the guests on the lawn below, wheeling through the lights, singing. Inside the house the musicians began to play a waltz and he saw Giò and Mirella sweep across the grass, elegant, youthful, beloved.

In the gardens below he glimpsed a secluded corner with a little bench near a leaf-choked fountain and he made his way down but when he reached it he saw he was not alone.

Forgive me, he said, bowing and turning away.

Don't go. Please.

The figure was seated on a little swing that hung from the dwarf pear and she stirred and leaned forward and he saw that it was, of course, the white-haired woman in the black shawl. They had found each other, as he had known they would.

It is quiet here, she said. She gave a little laugh. I do not like so many people.

He stood uncertain for a long moment and then blushed realizing the rudeness of this and he sat. The bench was very cold. A mazurka reached them, faint, far away, as if it were a dream receding.

You are not from here, he said at last.

Is it so obvious?

Well. Your accent.

He was staring at the woman in the winter darkness, her white hair shining and haloed in the electric lights from the garden beyond. He could feel the skin prickling at the back of his neck.

Where I am from, all of this is not even imagined, she said.

Where is that? he asked, understanding that this is what she wanted.

Another island.

Not Sicily?

It is like Sicily but much older. And much smaller. On my island it is flat, and hot, and dry.

Palermo must seem strange to you.

I live in Rome now. Palermo is not strange.

Ah.

I am an actress, she said. I am here for a picture.

He was quiet then, studying her, wondering if he had seen her someplace before. He did not think so. He was not a person who knew the world of the cinema well.

You are wondering if you know me, she said.

I am sure I have seen you in something, he said politely. What is the movie about?

You must promise not to laugh.

Why would I laugh?

It is an artistic picture.

Oh.

He could hear the creak of the swing as she shifted in the gloom. She said, I will tell you how Paolo described it to me. He is the director. He said to me: Imagine an island. It has slept in an empty sea for thousands of years. For a time no people lived upon it, for it was without fresh water, and sailors feared its cliffs. A monster lived in its waters, it was said. Ships were wrecked on its shores.

What kind of a monster?

She waved an impatient hand. The monster is not important.

Do I know this island?

No. It does not exist. It is just a movie.

Giuseppe watched a couple glide along the paths in the garden, disappear into the blackness. Please, he said. Go on.

I am not the lead actress, you understand.

I understand.

That is a French actress. You would know her, she is famous. Her character has come south to the island to be alone. Her husband has cheated on her and she is trying to decide what to do.

Giuseppe did not know what to say to that. He made a small gesture with his hands, turning them at the wrists, as if in resignation.

I read for her part, but I was not right for it. That is what Paolo said. The producers wanted a name, you understand. Not a face. That is how it is, in the business.

But you were right for a different character, he said.

She looked at him a long moment before continuing. The doomed friend, she said. That is who I play. I live with my father in a little dammuso of stone and mud. He is very old. My brother is dead, my mother is dead. There is a town on the island but we have little to do with it. Sometimes it seems, to myself and to my father, that there is in all the world only the two of us. Each evening when my father goes out to fish, I take bread down to him at his boat. Then one night the French woman comes to live near us, and everything changes. The war is on by then. In the night we can see the warships pass and the sea glows as if it is on fire. Just as it did in real life.

You cannot have been very old then. I mean, in life.

I remember the war. I remember how it was.

Yes.

But this is not a picture about the war.

No.

My character's father, who is slowly going blind, stops going out in his boat. The French woman sits with him at his bedside. We all grow very hungry. Some days I walk across the island through the myrtle and cactus and clamber down the cliffs near the Baia della Madonnina, and swim out into the shallows, diving for the sea urchins and oysters with a wooden crate. There are groupers in the crevices. They are dangerous. You must imagine how it will look on the screen, with the sunlight filtering in, lighting the seaweed and boulders. It will all be very beautiful, Paolo says. It is under the water there, one morning, that my character sees the cave.

Giuseppe lit a cigarette and smoked, listening. A light went out in the trellis behind them and the night grew colder. He could no longer hear the musicians or the guests.

Paolo has talked to me about this cave, the actress said. He could have built it on a sound stage but he wants it to be real. It will be very, very dark, in the finished film. Like an eyelid that is closed, he says. My character will be amazed never to have noticed it before. It is not deep under the water and so, by swimming to the surface and holding my breath, I will find I can dive down to it and explore. My character knows this is dangerous. She knows that if something goes wrong, she will run out of air and drown. But she is hungry and when we are hungry we are not always wise.

No one is always wise.

That is her motivation.

Hunger.

Yes. Of all kinds.

Giuseppe nodded. What happens at the cave?

Close your eyes. You must imagine it on the screen. The fisherman's daughter is floating at the mouth of the cave, peering in. Her hair is adrift all around her. The camera is inside the cave, as if the cave itself is watching her. She is in green water, sunlit, all around her is warmth, light. Then the shot changes, the camera is beside her. You can see that just in front of her face is a coldness, a blackness utterly absolute. It is as if she has found an entrance into some other sea. The cave itself is perfectly round, and smooth. She reaches out a hand into the coldness and sees it vanish before her and she pulls it back out, like she has been burned. She has a small knife for prying shell-fish from the rocks and this she grips in one fist, for safety. And it is then she sees the darkness move. It just sort of uncurls inside itself, slides sideways. Of course she is afraid, and lets out her breath, and then she has to swim back up through the bubbles to the surface.

What is it? What did she see?

Her mind tells her it was an octopus. But it was not an octopus. It poured across the darkness like its own kind of water. That is not like any octopus she has ever seen. She leaves that place, forgetting her crate of shellfish in her panic. And when she returns to her little house she finds her father has died, and the French woman has taken their only treasure.

Their treasure?

A painting. Of her dead mother. It was painted by a famous painter on a trip to their island long before the daughter was born.

Giuseppe could not see the actress's face for the shadows. He heard the slow creaking of her swing on its chains, the hiss of her feet in the grass. He felt very old.

It is a strange picture, she said. But I begged to be a part of it. My own grandfather rowed out one night with a shuttered lantern and an empty boat. He did not return. I was eight years old. In the dawn the sun on the sea was red. That is when I understood. In the film it is an island without beginning or end, and the crossing towards it is all. That is what Paolo says. It is like my childhood, I told him, like where I am from. Where we are going for the shooting can be reached only with difficulty. There is one ferry and one ferry only. Its passengers are few. The waters we must cross are wide.

You are going to Lampedusa, he said softly.

A rustle of cloth, like a wind withdrawing.

I was happy there, she murmured.

Who was she? asked Alessandra, later, in the night's cold gloom of their palazzo. A click; and then the lightbulbs in their stairwell buzzed and glowed into a steady brightness. His wife crossed to the little mirror in her heels, slipped out of her fur coat.

He knew at once who she meant. A fisherman's daughter, he said.

Licy paused, her hands lifted to one earring. He was standing on the second step with his hand on the railing and he could see her reflection clearly.

She was from the island, he continued. From Lampedusa.

I see, she said.

What?

So she is one of your subjects.

I have no subject but myself.

Mm.

You cannot be jealous, he said. Not truly.

Mm.

Licy came to him then and wrapped a strong arm around his waist and together they made their heavy way up the stairs to the second floor. They did not turn on any other lights.

There was so much sadness in her, my love, he said, breathing heavily from the climb. I could see she did not belong there.

He considered telling his wife the story of the cave, of the girl floating at the edge of that darkness, but some part of him did not want it told, some part of him wanted to hold it close for a while and keep it to himself.

Mirella was perfect tonight, he said instead.

Perfect. Yes.

It was not late for his wife though he himself felt the exhaustion of his years and at last they turned on a light in the historical library and sat. Giuseppe saw, to his disgust, the letter from Mondadori in its yellow envelope on the sidetable.

Look at this, he said. It is still here.

I will dispose of it for you, Licy said softly.

He took up the envelope and studied it, as if reading the address in interest.

We shall send the novel out again, she went on. We shall try Einaudi. They are a respectable publisher. You told me Flaccovio is friendly with Vittorini there. Flaccovio will send it.

He was quiet. He felt a great embarrassment when he thought of his novel directly and so he tried not to do so.

It only takes one publisher to say yes, she said. Just one.

He did not point out that if Mondadori did not find his manuscript publishable, there was no reason to think Einaudi would feel differently.

Giuseppe?

You always imagine a thing will get better, he said now.

She looked up in surprise. Because it will, she replied.

You are an optimist. I would never have married you had I known.

You are filled with hope, my love, she said. And that is why you are sad.

Crab was scratching at the ballroom doors. Licy half turned in her chair, she raised her face, but she did not go to him. And there, in the winter darkness of their library, alone with her, he reached across and took her hand in his. Her fingers were cold. He rubbed his thumb across the back of her hand to warm it and as he did so it seemed the years fell away; soon he felt as he had again at thirty, when he had held her hand in his own, before they had known regret, exhaustion, and all the rest. They sat like that a long time, neither speaking, and for a brief moment death seemed to him again a thing that happened only to others.

In the morning he walked down through the old quarter and stood outside the ruins of Casa Lampedusa. The party in the hills was fading in him, like a strange dream. You are a father now, he thought.

He did not feel any different. It was not raining but the cold was in him and he could not get warm. He had not returned to this street in ten years, and it was, perhaps, the visit to the notary's offices on Via Valverde which had stirred something in him. He pinched his eyes closed, remembering his mother on that first afternoon, how she had picked her way through the rubble, her flat leather handbag gripped whitely in her fingers. Giuseppe had wept. She had not.

In that year she was already dying, and he understood now that she had known it. He thought of this as he slowly walked the outer perimeter of the cracked stone walls, fifteen feet high, pale and abandoned, still in cold shadow. Something did not feel right inside him but it was not the emphysema, or not only. He stood in the middle of Via di Lampedusa, his walking stick scraping the flagstones, and he studied the depressed stillness of the narrow street. It might have been a world abandoned. At the corner of Via Bara all'Olivella he found the small locked door which had once been the porter's gate and which he remembered from his childhood.

The sky was grey, forbidding. It felt strange to him to go out into the city without his small bag, his familiar books. He leaned heavily on his walking stick, took off one glove with his teeth, fumbled deep in his pocket for the key.

That key he had taken from where he kept it on his desk, under the porous rock from the isle of Lampedusa, and he held its familiar weight now in the flat white light of the winter morning. What was it that girl had said, the fisherman's daughter who remembered Lampedusa?

He stepped forward and unlocked the door and when it did not open he pressed his weight against the groaning hinges and forced his way inside.

His breath plumed out before him. There were low trees, hardwoods and palms, growing crookedly up out of the rubble, still young but strange. Bushes with their leaves still green and yellow grasses grown to the height of a child's waist and puddles from the rain in the night.

He had loved this house as he had loved nothing else in his life. He remembered the rooms where he had slept until two months before the Allied bomb obliterated the palazzo. He had been born on a table five yards from that bed and he had believed his entire life that he would die staring at the plaster of that ceiling. No other house had been a home to him. Only here did he sense how belonging and time and space were one, how a life entered the world in a place fraught with pain and love. He had walked the halls of that love for most of his life.

The wing where his grandparents had lived had vanished in the bombing, its long white stone facade and sulphur-yellow windows gone, utterly. The eastern wing belonging to his own family had been torn open like a box, its ceiling frescoes and stone fireplaces exposed to the rain and the wind. Where his mother's delicate dressing room had stood he could still see half the floor, now unreachable, and the peeling walls that had once been so delicately rendered. There had been a window and balcony overlooking the narrow gardens of the Oratorio di Santa Cita. His earliest memory was of that room, of his mother dropping her hairbrush as his father stood in the doorway reading out the news of the death of the king. All had been sunlight and silver and softness, the ceiling scattered with coloured stucco branches and flowers of soft pinks and blues. He stared solemnly about as he wandered through the rubble. There were letters and photographs mouldering in the ruined library but he could not bring himself to collect them. He paused at a rusting tin-roofed structure, hastily erected in the outer court-yard, its brick-making machinery long since abandoned. Here he had seen his grandfather curse his father, shaking a fist at the sky while the servants stared from the windows, and two weeks later his grandfather was dead. That was almost the last memory he retained of the old patriarch. He reached a glove out and brushed the leaves of a palm tree twisting its way up out of the rubble. A web of rainwater came away, shivering with light. He lowered his face. How tired he was. How long the winters were now.

Something came back to him then, unbidden. It was a memory of those hollow years during the war. He had returned from Capo d'Orlando to check on his house and was trudging up the centre of Via Bara all'Olivella under the flat hot sunlight of late September when a very old man detached himself from the shadows of the palazzo's gate and approached. How long had he waited? Giuseppe did not know the man. He might have been a beggar, he might have been one of the war's recent victims. He shuffled slowly, ominously, towards Giuseppe, a bent figure dressed all in black, the pale dust of the street standing out clearly on his outsized clothes, his crumpled hat. He was very thin. His lips were bloodless, his skin leeched and grey. His left eyelid drooped as if from an old injury. He took off his hat and turned it trembling in his fingers. His hair was very white.

He called Giuseppe by his dead father's name and said he had been released from prison in the spring. He said he had made the difficult journey south to Sicily in order to make amends.

There was something wrong with his tongue; he could not speak clearly.

You must understand, I did always love her, Don Giulio, he said. I know it cannot be undone. I know it. But I have dreamed about her for thirty years. I loved her, I loved her, I should have died in Rome with her—

It was then Giuseppe, stunned, understood.

This was the baron who had murdered his aunt.

The sun was in Paternò del Cugno's eyes, illuminating the strange blue clarity of them. Giuseppe said nothing, could think of nothing to say, only stared hard into the baron's face. He felt a horror rising in him but he did not know what to do with the feeling. The sunlit street was empty.

Cugno was trembling, his eyes moist. He worked his lips as if to say something more but instead mopped at his forehead and then set his hat back on his head, one of the living, and free. He held out his hand.

Don Giulio, said the baron. Please.

Giuseppe looked at the outstretched hand, liverspotted, pale, like a thing left too long in the water. He looked at the man's face.

Don Giulio, Cugno repeated.

And Giuseppe reached out, though he could not have said why, and he took the man's hand in his own.

He did not tell his mother. For a long time he knew he had failed her and this knowledge had grieved him. Nor did he speak of it to Licy, fearing her own bitterness towards his mother might be used to lighten his guilt, to excuse what he had done, and so help him to let go of a pain he wanted to hold close. But it seemed to him now as he drifted through the ruins of his palazzo that it was not so appalling a betrayal, even perhaps a forgivable thing, that courtesy he had extended his aunt's killer.

The ruins of the house seemed now to go on forever. He looked up, then climbed a clinking mound of broken masonry, passed under a standing arch of stone that had once held a terrace, and carefully descended deeper into the ruins.

Here the light came in broken shafts. He could see what appeared to be half of the entrance hall, still standing, with a staircase leading up and stopping abruptly in the sky. But he felt confused, as if he had lost his bearings, for to one side of the entry hall he thought he saw the stables, and the tack room, but he knew that could not be right.

He shook his head. He set his walking stick uneasily for balance and shuffled forward, into the shadows, to find his way. The plaster crunched under his shoes like dead leaves.

The cold air went dark. And then darker still.

DEATH OF
A PRINCE

$$\equiv$$

JULY 1957

In the dream he was thin again, youthful. He had received a telegram instructing him to report to a barracks in order to be shot by firing squad. The wooden shutters in the long rooms of the barracks stood half-open, oblong squares of sunlight cast across herringbone floors, the clacking of a typewriter just audible at some distant desk. But he could not find the appointment, and there was no one to ask the way.

Why could he not wake from this? In the dream he was anxious, apprehensive. Sometimes he would glimpse a figure just turning a corner ahead but when he rushed forward he found himself still, again, alone. Finally he sat on a bench outside an office and dabbed at his forehead and upper lip with the back of his wrist. He sat a long time. A small window looked out onto a courtyard and he could hear the barking of a soldier below, the rattle of chains and a soft moaning. Slowly it occurred to him—always like a new thought—that he could just stand and walk out of those offices and elude his own execution; and so he rose, and walked the wide hall, down a curving staircase, outside into the summer heat of a Palermo fifty years gone. No one stopped him. He went to a patisserie on the corner of a small piazza and there he found his father, nursing a glass of ice water, and he leaned down and whispered into the old man's ear: Tell Mommy I've gotten away.

What had his mother to do with it? It did not seem a strange thing to say in the dream. For his father then would reach up and press a cool hand to his cheek, as if in approval, and he would feel the weight of it, staring at his father in wonder.

Then he would cross through the empty streets until he had reached the gates of the Villa Giulia, that vast city park off Via Marina where he had played as a child, and he would stand with his hat in his hands, staring upward, for the gates were locked to him, and though he called out and shook the bars no one would come to unlock them.

Only then would he wake, feeling as if he had come near to some essential truth, some understanding, and he would fold a damp elbow over his eyes in the darkness and breathe.

He was thinking of that dream as he lay awake in the unmoving heat listening to the roar of Rome's afternoon traffic far below. The red sun was in the west. His body was riddled with sickness, was rotting from within. He understood that he was dying but was surprised at how distant it all seemed, as if it were happening to some other's body, some other's flesh. He missed Palermo, missed the slow hiss of waves in the languid early-summer stillness. Even the sunlight here was different, cooler in its white gradations, lacking the steady stifling unpleasantness of Sicily. He licked at his dry lips. He could hear Licy's voice through the wall, could hear her sister Lolette say something sharp in reply. He closed his eyes.

Sometimes it seemed to him the world had been built on patterns, that there were messages being given to him, if only he could hear them clearly and make sense of them. He supposed some might mistake this sense for a kind of faith. Like that dream of the firing squad. It would return to him at unexpected moments, on nights when he had been sleeping fitfully, and he would try to make sense of it as if it were a novel of mysterious proportions.

As he lay in that bed he felt again a sensation that he had known for years. It was the feeling of paper ripping, someplace deep inside his lungs. Licy thought he had fallen ill only in these last years and that his sudden decline had begun in April but that was not the truth of it. For many years now, he knew, since before the death of his mother, he had suffered a sense of vertigo, as if he were standing at the edge of a precipice, the deep vast air below him, and as if he might be sucked out over the edge at any moment. It was a kind of diminishing of his self; but it was this very sensation which at first had reminded him that he lived, that he had not finished living, that he wanted something more. All that was now long past. He thought of his novel, of his fading astronomer prince who had believed in nothing but longed desperately to find something greater than himself. He crushed his eyes shut. To believe in nothing. That had never been his own failing. Literature had been a good and consoling guide since his boyhood and he had heeded it all his life though he had failed, he knew now, to comprehend its singular truth: to live. He had brought his novel north with him to the hospital for something to do and had reworked a late chapter about Don Fabrizio and the dying splendour of a ball but his heart was not in it and he had set the pages aside and not touched them again. It saddened him to think the novel might not be published and so immense was his sorrow that he could not look at it directly, only sidelong, like a man regarding a letter he did not wish to open. And that is how, he understood, he had looked at life for almost his entire duration on this earth. Could he have lived differently? It did not matter now. He had been waiting a long time for what he knew was soon to come, and he had cleared a space in the rooms of his mind for it, pushing most everything up against the walls, as if his death were a new piece of furniture to be delivered.

Perhaps only Giò had understood for a moment, when he said in a soft voice, at Capo d'Orlando: Father, you are making a space for death.

But his new son had not been smiling at the time, and there had been such a quiet bitterness in his gaze, that Giuseppe knew the youth did not in fact understand: how peaceful and consoling a deep melancholy could be.

It was a windy sunlit morning at Capo d'Orlando in the last days of April when the sickness made itself known. The zinc-white clouds were scumbled, moving high and fast in the sky. He had been walking with Giò and Lucio in the Piccolos' lemon groves, his mind adrift as his cousin talked poetry, when he had felt a catch in his chest and had started to cough. His handkerchief came away hot with blood. That blood was scarlet and vibrant on the white silk, theatrically so, and he stared at it, fascinated. It looked like a dollop of Casimiro's oil paint.

Then, because his cousin had caught a glimpse of the blood, he had lifted his eyebrows in a mild amusement.

I am like an English poet, he said.

But later in Palermo he had sought out Professor Aldo Turchetti for an examination, had climbed the old doctor's steep stairs and sat undressed in the ancient mahogany-panelled consulting room while the drapes drifted in the heat and a modern electric fan turned in its cage. All of it felt faintly ridiculous. Turchetti was a sallow man with a sunken chest and he huffed and cleared his throat and wrote long silent disapproving notes in a medical notebook. At the end of May Giuseppe did not return to collect his results but sent Giò in his place and so it was that his adopted son stood in the historical library at Via Butera in the early afternoon with his hands clasped uncomfortably before him and explained to Giuseppe and his wife the professor's diagnosis. Turchetti advised consulting an expert in thoracic surgery in Rome but Giuseppe, who had heard nothing after the quiet word "cancer," sat staring at his large soft hands, suddenly amazed, for he could not feel them, they seemed to him the hands of a ghost.

For two days he did not discuss the results. His cough worsened. He avoided Licy's aching presence, he walked the windy sunlit harbour, he did not call on his friends. On the third day he awoke feeling the weight that had settled on his heart and he understood he would die. It was the twenty-eighth of May. He sat down that afternoon in his study and drew up his will. He wished for no announcement of his death. His funeral, he instructed, ought to be held at an inconvenient hour, and kept simple, flowerless, without eulogy or hymn. Above all he wished for no one to accompany his coffin except Licy, Giò, and Mirella. It was his hope that the novel might find a publisher and that inscribed copies could be sent to a number of his friends and relations, but under no circumstances was its publication to be paid for by his own estate. He sat a long time in the late-afternoon light with his pen raised and his gaze drifting out the window and then he came to himself again and continued to write. He begged the forgiveness of all those whom he had wronged. Last of all he declared that in his time on this earth the only people he had loved were Licy, Giò, and Mirella, and his wishes were that all he possessed, including his name, find its way into their hands.

That night he and Alessandra packed their suitcases and old steamer trunks and took their black spaniel Crab to their old friend Flaccovio for keeping, and the following morning they set out for Rome. His depression had shifted inside him, had altered into a passivity. Even after they had disembarked from the train he could not shake the feeling of being seated, watching the fields and new concrete apartment blocks scroll past, the world in its passing unceasing and infinite. His life seemed to him like this also, and he knew the calmness that was in him was a sign of his deep resignation. But when he looked at his wife's drawn and grey face, the way her eyes had aged, he saw the sharp immediacy of her pain and knew she was already grieving. We are all of us counted among the dead, he thought with a faint stirring of his old irony. Only some of us more so.

Rome felt hot, the air clotted and thick with fumes. He could breathe only with some difficulty. He stared in disgust at the dense automobile traffic in the ancient roads, at the motor scooters threading aggressively between grilles and bumpers in the shadow of stone viaducts. This world, he understood, was no longer his world, if ever it had been. The clinic in Via di Trasone was modern, and ugly, and the white walls and steel gurneys and gleaming tile floors felt antiseptic, transient, like the efficient furnishings of a morgue. A nun greeted him at reception and he filled out many pages of documents, signing each with a tired hand, and then he was brought to a nurse in a stiff grey dress who led him silently down the corridors to his ward. He was granted a private room to his relief and unpacked his small suitcase and sat, quietly, at the edge of his bed, where the railing had been lowered. There were hospital machines on castors with looping tubes and wires pushed up in one corner, as if irrelevant, and he tried not to think of them. Alessandra was to stay with her sister Lolette, and Giuseppe had insisted on her settling in first, only coming to him when she was ready. He had worried for the anguish he could see in her, had wanted her to rest. He did not admit to himself the heaviness of her company, and how he wished to face this clinic alone, first, without having to hide his unhappiness.

The following afternoon he faced his first radiograph and then a battering of x-ray examinations and in the evening a specialist visited him to confirm Professor Turchetti's diagnosis. His cough was due to bronchitis and it was necessary, he was told, to treat this with antibiotics before the right lung could be seen clearly, and the nature of the tumour determined.

And how long will that take? he had asked, as if he had some other appointment to keep.

He did not believe they would operate. It seemed more likely the doctors would attempt a cure of cobalt bombs, which would take many weeks and leave him gasping. At the end of June he was transferred to a smaller clinic, the Villa Angela on the banks of the Tiber. He was forbidden cigarettes and had little appetite. Licy would come to him twice a day, with her sister, and his ancient uncle Pietro visited wearing a straw boater and carrying a knotted cane like a comedian from the revue stages of his youth.

Giò arrived from Palermo for three days with the sunlight in his skin and his easy silences and the two of them walked the corridors of the clinic, companionable, amused. In the evenings Giuseppe would slide his arms into a blue and red silk dressing gown, a gift from Licy, and make his slow way to the cobalt treatments. He worked and tinkered and adjusted some pages in his novel. He was thinking of Capo d'Orlando and the months of his recuperation. His tumour's progress was not much discussed and though he had lost weight he felt, somehow, that a future lay before him. In early July he moved into Lolette's apartment on the Piazza dell'Indipendenza, its white and red cushions, its sleek modern furniture.

Then on the morning of the eighth he received the new rejection, this time from Einaudi. They would not be publishing the novel, it said, though there were fine passages within the book, for they could see no market for such an old-fashioned story. This he read out loud in its entirety at the dinner table on the balcony, in a calm steady voice, despite his disappointment, and then he smiled and set the letter to one side of his plate and met Licy's angry expression directly. Lolette reached across, picked up the letter.

As a review it is not bad, he said dryly into the silence. But publication, no.

Four days later his cobalt treatments were suspended due to a sudden dizziness and an increased pressure on his heart, and then the cancer in his lung spread and started to eat away at him like fire.

Something changed in him after that. He had been weakening for some time, he knew, and had stopped writing entirely, but now he found he had relinquished even the desire for it. He would shuffle out to the balcony in the mornings and sit with a blanket on his knees and watch the skies above the red rooftops of Rome. The sun on the clay rooftiles was flat and hot and still. The Biancheris' was a long, pale, high-ceilinged apartment overlooking the piazza and light poured in through the tall windows and across the parquet floor.

Lolette was the slighter, milder sister. Her face was angular and Slavic and he could see in it the shadow of his wife's. Licy kept close, her hair pinned back, her eyes creased. Some days his thoughts drifted, confused, and he would find himself resting on the chaise longue in the sitting room and suddenly peer up in surprise to find Licy or Lolette beside him, speaking, as if they had been with him for some time. And he would close his eyes again, wearied, increasingly uncertain what was dream, what was waking. He had been given medicine for the pain but the cancer could not be stopped. He thought of his mother in her last days, defiant, angry, and marvelled at how far she was from him now. He felt none of her defiance. He was fifteen when he had journeyed with her to Rome in that terrible year of his aunt's murder. He remembered the grave stillness in the drawing rooms, the late king's portrait still on display, he remembered his mother weeping softly before her mirror and her soft hair plaited and wrapped three times around her head. He had not thought any other woman could ever be as beautiful. He remembered too the way she would curl a hand at the back of his neck, cool, soft, and guide him through a gilt archway and into rooms covered in yellow silk. He adored her differently now, feared her differently, for though she was dead he had lived a decade longer with the memory of her and he himself had changed. As long as we are remembered, we continue to change, he thought, unconsoled.

Giò and Mirella would carry their own memories of him into the second half of the century. A fat old man, eccentric, tired, filled with sadness and foolishness. That is what they would remember, he imagined. But they had been late sources of light and joy in his life. When he thought of his adopted son, he could not now separate the boy from the character in his novel, his Tancredi, though he had tried to take only Gioitto's joy and wit and energy, and none of the youth's moral core. He had written a careful letter emphasizing that Tancredi's opportunism was not based on Giò, as if some reader somewhere might someday wonder at it, and he wondered now at the audacity of it, at the hopefulness in it. *You are filled with hope*, Licy had said, *and that is why you are sad*. He was not so certain. She liked to say there were two kinds of unhappiness, the unhappiness of those who look for the sun to set, and the unhappiness of those who look for the sun to rise. The lived life, she would tell her patients, is experienced in the moment. Whether you expect darkness or light to come does not matter.

And what of his unhappiness? Did he expect the darkness or the light? He did not know if a life must always be reduced to fragments. But it did not surprise him, how little he had lived. When he weighed his life in the balance, it seemed little more than a few intensities of experience, a few great sorrows, perhaps two or three overwhelming moments of joy. It saddened him to think that the Lampedusa line would be extinguished so completely. His great-grandfather had produced nine children. Now he would be the last. He had been born into its casual decline amid the waste and drift of an age in decline and soon a new kind of aristocrat would take over, a bloodline of wealth and privilege whose eye was trained on the status of the new. There would be no historical memory, and therefore no grave understanding. What had held worth for its particular survival across centuries would cease to hold worth. There would be only the future, only what was to come. Perhaps, he thought sadly, that was no loss to any but himself. Perhaps nostalgia was its own kind of sickness. He turned his tired face to the wall, shut his eyes.

On Tuesday, Uncle Pietro came to visit. He had travelled from his house in Via Brenta by public bus and arrived hot, tired. He was to leave for Genoa soon. They sat in the sunroom of the Biancheris' apartment, two aged men, one ancient, the other dying, and spoke of the past that was still alive in them. Licy did not sit with them and Giuseppe listened to her in the kitchen, turning the grinder for the coffee, and wondered at this. His uncle was dressed in a white suit and hat like an American gang-ster and he wore a pink-collared shirt from Paris and a matching handkerchief folded square in the breast pocket and Giuseppe felt peculiarly grateful, seeing the care his uncle had taken. It seemed to him somehow that such attention stood on the side of life, and the living, though he himself had never given it such consideration before he fell ill.

You have gained weight, his uncle said approvingly.

Giuseppe struggled to smile.

The tall doors onto the balcony stood open; a faint breeze stirred the muslin drapes. They could hear the traffic in the street beyond, the rattle of the diesel autobuses every ten minutes. Giuseppe had shaved and dressed carefully in a white shirt and red vest. It was the first time in days he had changed out of his dressing gown, and though Licy had hoped it might diminish his sadness, it had not.

Pietro was nodding slowly. I have been thinking much of my years in London, of late.

It is the fate of the old to live in their memories, said Giuseppe.

Pietro smiled. You are not old. You do not get to say.

I think of London, too, sometimes, Giuseppe added. After you were married to Aunt Alice. I remember how beautifully she sang in the evenings. I remember walking the Thames in the spring, and the bridges, and the wonderful cabs. Umbrellas in the rain.

Yes.

We saw *Hamlet* in modern dress, at St. James's. The ghost in a gas mask.

And the king in pyjamas, Pietro said with a smile. I remember.

Aunt Alice did not like it though.

Alice always knew her mind, his uncle said. It is a Baltic trait. Your Alessandra is the same. The first time I met Alessandra she told me she did not approve of an Italian stepfather. She believed our climate made us too emotional, too unpredictable. We do not know our minds, she said.

And then she married me.

And then she married you. Yes.

Licy appeared in the doorway, a silver tray heavy with coffee and gleaming cups and saucers held low at her hips.

We are speaking of you, Giuseppe called to her.

She nodded. Of course you are.

She set the tray carefully down on the long dining table and poured and stirred the small coffees and brought one to old Pietro and another to Giuseppe. Pietro held the saucer and the little silver spoon clattered softly in his trembling hands and he set it carefully down in his lap.

You must have your medicine, she said to Giuseppe.

He took the pills and a glass of water from his wife, and he gave an apologetic smile to his uncle, as if to say, what foolishness is all this fuss. But he sat a long moment with his eyes closed after drinking and one hand splayed at his chest, and he breathed slowly, feeling the pain ebb.

The English, he said tightly, opening his eyes. The English always delighted me. They were so stern, so stubborn with themselves, so fond of paradox. A gentleman is one who does not care a bit whether he is or not. Sir Herbert said that. They kept so much back, the English did. I thought it was discipline when I first visited you in the embassy, and then I thought it was coldness, but it isn't either. They are a wonderful people, because they will bear up under any hardship. Do you know what it is? It is hopefulness. That is how they live. In hope.

Licy stood smoothing out her skirt and adjusting a curl of hair at her forehead. Giuseppe looked from her to his uncle and then let his gaze drift to the glowing curtains where they stirred in the air.

They are a remarkable people, yes, said Pietro.

We worried for you, my mother and I, said Licy to her step-father. All those years ago. You should not have opposed the Fascists like you did.

Giuseppe looked at his uncle. Licy has always thought it an act of some courage, he said.

Pietro blushed, old and frail and pleased. No, he said. Not that. Of course, the English did not like Mussolini.

No one liked Mussolini, said Licy. Except Mussolini.

That is not so, said Pietro.

Giuseppe was thinking of his mother, and her sister, both of whom had admired the dictator in their sharp way. He said nothing.

But the English did like Hitler, Licy said. I remember that.

At first, said Pietro. At first they did. Yes.

Mussolini did not recall you for a long time, said Giuseppe. Despite your views. I remember my father thought he would.

Your father, said Pietro. But he did not finish the thought. He stirred his coffee and said, I do not think Mussolini even knew my name. It was his ministry that I reported to.

They brought such destruction down upon us, said Licy softly.

We brought it upon ourselves, Pietro replied.

And the three of them sat a long moment in the sunlit room, the drift of the city beyond peaceful and alien and gentle, as if the horrors of the recent past were all long distant, as if the dead had been dead for decades.

When it was time for Pietro to go, he stood shakily, a small man, his old throat corded and loose and grey. Giuseppe saw the blotches in his forehead, in his hands.

We shall see each other again, his uncle said with a peculiar intensity. Gripping Giuseppe's hand with both of his own, clawlike, leaning forward, the smell of sausage and spices in his clothes.

Licy slipped a hand under the old man's elbow to steady him.

And something in Pietro's expression, something in the white of his lips, some flicker of the ancient eyelids, made Giuseppe understand that they would not.

He grew sicker by the day. More disconsolate. He ceased eating, drank sparingly of the water brought to his bedside. Hardly spoke. The hours slipped past, day turned into night, turned into day, and gradually he felt himself lifting, lightly, singingly, out of his riddled flesh.

The sheets were twisted at his feet. The sheets were pulled gently to his shoulders. His hands fumbled at his side. His hands were gripped in Licy's, firm, warm. Licy. Alessandra Wolff Stomersee would be, he understood dimly, the last face he saw when he closed his eyes. He had loved her with a cool passion for almost thirty years. Then his mind was drifting again, slippery, unable to find purchase. He did not think of the plum-stained flagstones at Stomersee, the sky grey and folding upon itself like a sea. He did not think of tasting the cool Marsala barrels in the wine cellar with Licy after her first arrival in Sicily, the smell of her throat as she came to him. Nor did he think of the weight of her, the slow violent desire as she climbed atop him in his small bed in the embassy in London, and how she leaned down and gripped his face with both hands and kissed him hungrily. Nor did he think of the clatter and sway of his carriage as he journeyed alone away from her castle in Riga. All this was in him but moved through him and did not pause. He was not remembering his mother's bony knuckles at the end, the way she had gripped his chin and tilted his face upward as if he were still a child. His thoughts did not stop on the light in the drawing rooms of his childhood house, the way each opened onto each in an endless linkage of rooms and sifting light. He did not remember the ancient cafés in Vienna, gloomy already by the afternoon, their coffees with whipped cream. He did not think of Giò, his quick mercurial expressions and the sly humour in his voice, he did not think of Mirella staring at Giò with a darkness in her eyes. He did not think of the view from the terrace at Via Butera, the harbour in its brown stillness. Not a single page from a single book came to him, no line of Stendhal or Dickens, no echo of the vast chambers of thought and human complication that made up the inner life he had lived all those decades. Nor, too, did he think of the slaughter and muck and horror of the Isonzo, and his own bloodied innocence, nor of the hunger and decrepitude and the blistered feet as he trudged back to Italian soil.

What came to him, instead, was altogether older: a memory

of the shaded greenlit garden at Santa Margherita di Belice, the sun roping downward in heavy vines of light through the palm leaves. He was nine years old, soft-kneed, in breeches tailored in Holland and a tight sailor's outfit shipped from Vienna. The purple flowers were in bloom, the still air was sweet in the heat and the stillness. He was crouched in a hollow of long spear grass near a stained fountain, empty of water, its stone swans entwined. A leatherbound book from his grandfather's library was clutched in his hands. Why this memory, why did he think of this now? He remembered the sound of his French governess calling to him, remembered the sweet smouldering joy in him as he did not answer, as he lay very still and listened to her shoes crunch past. He had taken a book he had been told he must not read and he opened it and studied the words with a fascination. *What was that bitter moment they called life?* he read. *Life to us now seems a strange astonishment, as death, all unknown, seems mysterious to the living.* He lifted his slow eyes and blinked and there before him in the cup of a flower was a bee, furred and perfect, its thorny rear legs rubbing together. He felt then something come over him, a kind of intoxication, a silent companionship that was the language itself, he felt its rhythms move inside him. *Strange astonishment,* he murmured, over and over, until the words held no meaning and the syllables were pure sound. *Strange astonishment, strange astonishment.*

There were standing figures, shades, at his bedside. Uncle Pietro was there, in his dazzling white suit, a red bow tie at his throat like a knot of blood. He saw Lolette staring down at him, her face very grim, a pained expression on her lips. She was clutching a glass of water in both hands like a precious thing, a vessel of light. Then he felt Licy's fingers entwine with his own, felt her squeeze his grip and whisper something. What she said was in German and he knew the words but could not make sense of them. He liked hearing her voice. He turned his face towards it but could not seem to find her. A shadow crawled across the ceiling like a monstrous spider.

He must have slept. For he opened his eyes, his breathing tight, a sharp pain in his chest, and found he was alone now in the great quiet. He studied the red glow of the horizon through the open window, the crack of red light over the rooftops apocalyptic and terrifying. Was it morning again? He shifted his head on his pillow and saw his wife, asleep in a chair to one side of the window. It surprised him that he had not heard her breathing. Her chin was pressed to her chest, her hair in a waterfall around her, her beautiful deep black eyes closed to him. All at once he wished she would wake and look at him and he waited but she did not. He blinked and worked his mouth and tried to raise his hand but it would not obey him. He could see a book turned face down on her knee but he did not recognize it. It was black and the lettering on the spine was white and yet he could not make sense of it, as if it were written in a strange script, in a language he had known as a child and since lost. He swallowed painfully. A glass of water beside his bed darkened. When he glanced up the red vein of light beyond the rooftops of the city was diminishing and he squinted and tried to speak and then the light was seeping back downward, as if the day were abandoning him. A dark morning was rising, very beautiful. His eyes were wet and he tried to keep them open, tried to see the world for as long as he could. He listened to his wife breathe. The black book on his wife's knee gleamed. How strange it was, he thought, that he did not know that book, what it contained.

RELICS

─────

AUGUST 2003

I had not known there was a letter, you see, Gioacchino explained gently. He ran a hand through his hair.

The interviewer, an American woman from a film company in New York, nodded. She seemed impossibly young to him, though she could not have been younger than thirty, and the easy confidence of her gestures might have been from another world. As, of course, it was. Not only a world an ocean away but also a world separated by time, which is the greater ocean. All this he thought in silence and did not say. He remembered his first wife Mirella and how they were in those early years together, and how she did not live to see such a world as this, a world of diminished distances and digital files and computers on every desk. Could not have even dreamed it.

They were walking slowly through a garden near the Teatro di San Carlo in Naples where he was superintendent. The heat was green in the leaves and he raised his face, closed his eyes, listening. He had become a composer and a music scholar and oversaw for a time the Italian Cultural Institute at New York University. Over the years he had spoken publicly about his memories of Giuseppe Tomasi di Lampedusa, and in the last decade had written prefaces for the novel when it was reissued in English, and French, and in the critical editions used in the

Italian universities. In this way he had come to be considered one of the last witnesses to its creation. He had resisted such a role while Mirella was alive, the two of them wishing not to contradict Alessandra's recollections, which were not his own. For a long time now there had been no one left to contradict. Now he was being asked to speak on the making of Luchino Visconti's monumental movie of *The Leopard*, which would be remastered and rereleased by this woman's company in New York, though he did not know what to say.

I was only a kind of translator, you see, he said.

A translator?

Of Lampedusa's novel, his writing. Of what he had intended. Visconti was very interested in finding the right houses, the right light for the film. It was 1961 and there was no infrastructure in place but he insisted on filming in Sicily all the same.

You admired him.

I admired him, yes. He was an artist.

She flashed him a dazzling smile, direct, American, unabashed, and reached out and touched his arm. I will want to ask you all about this on camera, again, if you don't mind.

Gioacchino lowered his slow head, unsurprised. He took a handkerchief from his pocket and wiped at his forehead. He did not mind. Though they had not begun, already he was tired. He gestured to a stone bench and when the young woman had smoothed out her skirt and sat, he sat also. He supposed the cameraman and lighting technician must be nearly ready. The enthusiasms of Americans had always astonished him. Across the sweltering courtyard, a small fountain stood in the sunlight and the falling water caught and flared and turned upon itself, all movement and light, like time itself.

Time is the one true clarity, he said softly, as if to himself.

The woman did not hear.

Tell me about the letter, she said instead. It was found three years ago, in his old library?

Three years ago, yes, he said.

Later, in his air-conditioned office, Gioacchino found himself shrugging, one elbow high up on the wall of an ancient green sofa, studying the interviewer where she sat beside the camera.

Many have asked me whether Lampedusa was betrayed by Visconti, he said. He paused, as if considering how to proceed. Which is a typically malicious question, he added. Why do I say that? When people pose that question, they think it will please me, meaning: Of course, what could Visconti know about Lampedusa? That's what people think. I've always disappointed them, inasmuch as I've made it—and I take the liberty of saying this—a question of class. Movies and other points of view regarding the Risorgimento are widely divergent. The Risorgimento is seen by Lampedusa through the eyes of those who lost, and by Luchino through the eyes of those who won. That's the truth. Luchino, in his heart, was one of the students willing to die at Curtatone and Montanara, and Lampedusa wasn't.

The interviewer was holding her notebook closed on one knee, nodding. Would they have liked each other, do you think?

Visconti and Lampedusa? Gioacchino smiled at that. I like to think so. They were both of a dying world, both of them could see the flaw in the glass, so to speak. They were critical of what had made them, of how it had destroyed itself.

They were both of them devoted to their art, she suggested.

Gioacchino nodded, crossed his legs, smoothed out his trousers. What was extraordinary about Visconti was his ability, while working with a script or an opera, to come onto the set knowing exactly what he wanted. Visconti would repeat something that he had envisioned perfectly, and he never made corrections.

The young woman flashed her smile. Whereas Lampedusa was more tentative?

Yes.

Perhaps it is the difference between the writer and the director.

Gioacchino thought about this, unsure. Then he said, cautiously: Luchino's contribution is tied to his idea that he was, as we would say today, a *virtual* student of Stanislavski. In other words, the starting point is always total authenticity. He used real objects, real situations, which were then reinterpreted. But authenticity was crucial. They were to use only real flowers, even when they were in the background and out of focus. There was a fresco artist who painted eighteenth-century decorations, little landscapes, those typical ceiling decorations with perspective. The mouldings were plaster, and the terrace was decorated with majolica made by De Simone and transported on site.

Such an exacting process, she said. But its effects can be felt in every frame.

The Americans did not think so.

No.

I remember when the movie was released there. It was not a success.

She gave him a quick sympathetic frown then, as if to say that her company intended to redress that. Would Lampedusa have recognized his novel in it, do you think?

Gioacchino hesitated, trying to clarify something, but not quite certain what. At last he shook his head, gave a brief exasperated smile. I've always considered the book a projection of the author's desire, he said. This man had had a gilded childhood, after which his life had all been downhill, until he reached a condition just short of misery, let's say. I'm talking about the years immediately following the war, 1944 to 1945. I can't say I understood him as a young man, but in later years, reading the lessons in *The Leopard*, the author's intentions are the same. He says, *My life as a Sicilian didn't go well. You youngsters try not to repeat my errors.* There's the need to know the world at large, to lose all traces of provincialism, and mostly this idea that the outside world is very different, and who knows who will ever bring it to Sicily. The desire not to die like a mouse in a hole, which was pretty much how he ended up.

But it is not an autobiographical novel. It is not about Lampedusa's own life.

No.

What I mean is, he was not the leopard.

That is correct.

And Tancredi was not you.

At this Gioacchino smiled. Tancredi was a rake and an opportunist.

Mm.

He glanced at the camera, then away. Lampedusa left a brief disclaimer on his views regarding the characters, he said. As for Tancredi, he clearly states that his features, his mannerisms, his appearance, a certain way of talking, *remind me of Gioitto*, as he used to call me. As for Tancredi's moral character?

A long pause; then Gioacchino gave a quick sharp ironic laugh.

That, he smiled, was modelled on other people entirely.

Lampedusa's farewell letter, discovered three years earlier by a literature scholar, had been folded into the endpapers of *The Voyages of Captain Cook* in the historical library at the Via Butera palazzo where Gioacchino and his second wife, Nicoletta, lived. The letter had gone unnoticed for forty years. There was nothing strange in this. The library's books were preserved rather than read. And both Lampedusa and Alessandra had often hidden papers away in their books. The letter had been addressed to him. *My dearest Gioitto, I am anxious that, even with the curtain down, my voice should reach you.* How moving it was, hearing that voice cross the threshold again. Gioacchino sat now at his desk and brushed at his lips with an open handkerchief as the shadows deepened in his office. The American woman was gone, the summer sky over Naples hazy and nearly brown. He thought of those days before Giuseppe Tomasi di Lampedusa's death, how the old man had suffered as he made his weary slow way through the world. The yellow gravel in the path below shimmered in the heat and a great silence overtook him. *I am anxious that my voice should reach you, to tell you how grateful I am for the comfort your presence has brought me.* He folded the handkerchief into a clean diamond, folded it again, a tiny white square of light, his fingers busy. *These last two or three years of my life, which have been so painful and sombre but which, had it not been for you and darling Mirella, would have been an utter tragedy.*

In the end the novel had been a success. It had outsold every other Italian novel in the twentieth century, had been debated and attacked and celebrated for forty years. Gioacchino had lived alongside it his entire life, had been a part of it. He remembered in those first months after Lampedusa's death, when Bassani had come to Palermo and spoken with Alessandra in her grief, determined to hunt down the lost chapters. How fateful that seemed now. *Our lives, Licy's and mine, were on the point of running into the sands, what with worries and age, but your affection, your constant presence, the gracious way in which you lived shed a little light in our darkness.* Bassani's imprint at Feltrinelli had wanted the book, and the man would not be put off.

After Lampedusa's death, Alessandra had aged overnight. He recalled how she had not liked to get up from her chair by the window, would rub at her aching wrists, her back bent, a small pillow laid out across her knees. Her grief had surprised Gioacchino, the intensity of it, and he had felt at times as he sat with her that they were creeping down an unlighted staircase, very steep, fumbling with their toes for each step. Her psycho-analysis had been too stark to bring her any comfort and he and Mirella had watched her with fear in their hearts. Gradually she sharpened in her solitude, into a woman too intelligent to bear her infirmities, and too lonely to be patient with anyone else's.

She would speak to journalists and critics with a savage tongue, then complain of their portraits of her. He remembered how she would lace her red fingers together at her belly, and stand with her feet apart, her head jutting forward, like a wrestler sizing up an opponent. In those early years she had gone through Lampedusa's private papers and removed any passage that she feared indelicate and had published the edited works as complete. Gioacchino knew this was an effort on her part to preserve his reputation but he did not think, now, forty years later, that it was the right thing to have done.

How long ago all that seemed. He had not thought much of it in recent years, except when it could not be avoided. Mostly his life had been his own. He had been invited to speak in Iceland at a conference on opera in the new year but he did not know if he would attend. There were several unanswered letters needing his attention. He owed a telephone call to a publisher in New York, a man he had come to respect, about an essay on melody and meaning in Puccini. And Nicoletta was expecting him back in Palermo in a fortnight.

He put one arm through his sleeve, turned at the door, walked back to his desk with the linen jacket trailing and sat again. He opened the drawers one by one until he found the cigarettes he had been seeking and then he paused and picked up a twisted white rock, a paperweight, which he had taken from Lampedusa's desk in the months after the poor man's death. This he held a moment in his hand, then slipped into his coat pocket.

Failure, he thought to himself, suddenly realizing. That is what the American woman had been interested in. He smoothed the papers on his desk, turned off the light, but did not get up immediately. He had dedicated his own life to music, to echoes of the infinite that were forever vanishing. What has failure to do with that? But in his heart he knew the answer. In the glass, the afternoon was darkening. He had been so young when he had known Giuseppe Tomasi di Lampedusa, too young. He had understood almost nothing of the older man's moods. He thought of Lampedusa's sad eyes, the way his craggy face used to fall into an ironic smile, the heaviness and disappointment in his thin dry lips. Every sound we make travels, he had read once, is in constant motion, is forever leaving us behind. And, too, forever arriving. There are sounds, millions of years old, only just reaching us now from the edges of the universe, and these also are a kind of music. The last time he had seen Lampedusa was in Rome three weeks before he died and the old man had looked thin, defeated. What was that line in the letter? *I have been enormously fond of you, Gioitto; I have never had a son, but I do think I could never have loved one more than I have loved you.*

The silence of that, its stillness. He had stood at the ballroom window in Palermo, in a familiar slant of light, among the heavy draperies and furnishings that Nicoletta had preserved, and read and read again that letter, the music reaching him as if from a long way off.

At the harbour, he walked a long time alone thinking about those days. His life had come and passed and come again and Lampedusa had known none of it. How strange, he thought, that our lives should overlap, and some of us go on after others have ceased. He felt the twist of rock from his desk, the weight and rough scrape of it in his pocket, tugging heavily at the side of his jacket. Alessandra had said once, years after Giuseppe's death, that it had come from the sharp white cliffs of Lampedusa, that Giuseppe had kept it as a bitter reminder. When a thing is taken from a place, some part of that place goes with it, she had said.

And she had raised her hand to Gioacchino's cheek and held it there, dry and light as paper.

He did not know if that was so. The sea now was black and charred and the hot sky above the horizon was a very deep rich blue. He stood with his hands in the pockets of his suit jacket, feeling the late sunlight on his face. He was older now than Lampedusa had been when he died. He watched a boy carrying a red ball pull away from his mother, run to the seawall. He wondered what that child would see, peering in his direction, man or ghost. Gulls were wheeling out over the black water, flashing white, cutting sharply in the summer air. He was tired and was not thinking clearly. Time is the one true clarity, Gioacchino. Lampedusa had said that to him, fifty years ago, under the garden trellis at Capo d'Orlando. Lampedusa had felt close to a world long vanished, distant from the one before him. Had he been more alive for the past that moved within him, or less so? He had grown old without noticing. The boy with the red ball turned away from the seawall, stepping through the body of his self to who he would become. Gioacchino Lanza Tomasi felt the warm air on his face like a lingering hand. Our bodies are all doors, he thought to himself, and whether they are opening or closing is not for us to say.

ACKNOWLEDGEMENTS

I am indebted, firstly, to Gioacchino Lanza Tomasi and his wife Nicoletta Polo, for their generosity and kindness during my time in Palermo.

I would like to thank also Francesca Lombardo and Cataldo Failla, patient guides around Sicily; Francesca Gugliotta, for her help at the Piccolo Villa in Capo d'Orlando; and Salvatore Tannorella, deputy mayor of Palma di Montechiaro.

There would be no novel without the tireless efforts of Ellen Levine, my agent, fierce supporter, and friend. I owe her everything. Jonathan Galassi has been a guiding light in the imagining of this book, as in others; no thanks can properly suffice. The brilliant Ravi Mirchandani at Picador UK offered suggestions and encouragement at a critical point. Above all, Martha Kanya-Forstner steered this novel with a gentle hand, helping it to become what it wanted to be. She is a wonder; this novel is lucky to have found her, as am I.

I wish also to thank: Jared Bland, Sharon Klein, Kelly Hill, Shaun Oakey, Joe Lee, and everyone at M&S; Lottchen Shivers,

ACKNOWLEDGEMENTS

Jeff Seroy, Alex Merto, and everyone at FSG; Ami Smithson and everyone at Picador UK; Claire Roberts, Martha Wydysh, and everyone at Trident Media. Also Ivan Strausz, whose face lit up as he murmured the name "Tancredi!" to me across a dinner table in Toronto one night, and the delight in it stayed with me throughout the writing.

Finally, the lives that make mine possible and worthwhile: Jeff Mireau, gentle giant; my parents, Bob & Peggy; my brothers; my beautiful children, Cleo & Maddox.

And forever, always, my beloved: Esi. Word by word we build this life.